My Mother's Son

JOSEPHINE C. M. FAAL

ISBN: 978-1-3999-6063-2

DEDICATION

In loving memory of my father, George Stephen Mukuka Chilangwa.

From when I was a little girl, you saw my potential, the glimmer of my unique voice and gift for writing. Your words of love and encouragement have continued to resonate with me and shape my path.

MY MOTHER'S SON, my debut novel, is dedicated to you—a tribute to your wisdom, guidance and fatherly love that shaped me into who I am today. You left this world seventeen years ago, but your legacy endures through the stories I tell and the knowledge I seek to impart.

With eternal love and gratitude,

THANK YOU

To you, the loves of my life:
Sasha Sefuke and **Tiffany Sefuke**
Everything in my life begins and ends with you.

Ebrima Faal
Thank you for your love and for being the
wind beneath my wings

To My Family & Friends
There are too many of you to mention, but you know
who you are. Thank you for every moment in the past or
present that I have had the honour to share with you.
You all have inspired me in ways I will forever
be grateful for.

My
Mother's
Son

Chapter One

ANDREW MULENGA MICHELO
KABULONGA, LUSAKA, ZAMBIA

We all have wahala in our lives. I get it. But have you ever had it so bad that it feels like your mind is on a hamster wheel for days?

Two weeks ago, I went to bed as usual, with my life intact and a bright future ahead of me. The following day, I woke up to a young man's *mother of all horrors*. As it is, I now have girlfriend issues that I didn't know existed, and they've come to haunt me—*twenty-four-seven*.

Beyond that complexity, *I am my mother's son*. My mother's expectations of me as a devoted, upright, and ambitious son come above all else. I'm about to lose my marbles between the two opposing forces, my mother and girlfriend. I can't catch a break. Eish!

As if that's not enough—have you ever been to Zambia in October? It's 06:30, for example, and the hot season's oppressive grip has already taken over my life. In this kind of weather, I haven't had a wink of sleep since my life went belly up. If you live in Zambia, you already know what I mean.

At this time of the year, the temperature is not only intense. Brace yourself! It also comes with a wicked agenda that wreaks mayhem on unsuspecting citizens, residents, and tourists. Picture a relentless heatwave where the sun wages war with every living being. It covers the entire country and leaves no escape from its scorching rays. It's hard to win!

When you dare step outside, there's an immediate attack on your senses, and your first instinct is to rush back indoors. The air is thick and heavy, almost suffocating. At the same time, it feels like an invisible woollen blanket has enveloped your skin. Oh my, I yearn for the tiniest breeze or a few moments under a large, leafy, umbrella-like Acacia tree on such days.

The nights are perhaps the cruellest of all. Sleep, which should be a sanctuary from ruthless weather, becomes an elusive and precious commodity. The whirr of pedestal fans, usually comforting, becomes a constant reminder of the futile attempt to find rest. It's no wonder insomnia ranks number one as a collective problem and is on almost everyone's lips.

During the day, the vicious cycle of sleep deprivation takes its toll on everyone, especially those in the workplace. Office environments transform into scenes of sluggishness as employees struggle to concentrate and keep their energy levels. The once-patient bosses must, without success, deal with a workforce that can only muster half-hearted efforts—much to their chagrin.

In extreme cases, some employees—typical repeat offenders in the art of attending fake funerals, take their *skills* to the next level. Their *big and small* mothers and fathers, long gone from this world, suddenly, one by one, start to die again.

Such elusive funeral hoppers, in a bid to escape the heat, master the art of deception. They are so creative that they always hoodwink their employers with fabricated tales of profound grief.

On the home front, the searing heat burns a hole in household pockets. The nightmare of dysfunctional fridges and frequent expensive fresh food shopping sends marriages into turmoil. Tempers fly as husbands and wives squabble over out-of-control monthly budgets. They nitpick through shopping lists in a shameless witch hunt of who spent the most money and on what.

At the bottom of the pyramid, the domestic staff gets the short end of the stick. It's not uncommon to find the madam of the house in highly contested debates over perishables. *Had the food gone off, or did the housekeeper steal it?* Everyone is looking for someone to blame to keep expenses in check. I'd skip the month altogether if it weren't for our beloved country's Independence Day on October 24th.

D**n! My phone vibrates again. It shows a *million* missed calls from my girlfriend, Dailess. I have been dating Dailess for three months. Two weeks ago, she shocked me with the sudden announcement of her eight-week pregnancy. I can't begin to tell you what that news has done to my life.

It's not hard to imagine that I've been ghosting her since she and I had the most intense discussion ever. My phone is usually abuzz with calls from clients, friends, colleagues, family, and everyone. But I now keep it in silent mode or completely switched off, lest Dailess catches me off guard.

I'm not proud of dodging calls and sending faux text messages. Who am I? I don't recognise myself anymore. I'm a poor version of the young gentleman my mother raised me to be.

But at twenty-one, I've found myself in the worst possible dilemma—lost for words and confused. I don't know what to believe and, most of all, what to do. I have a million questions, starting with why Dailess waited so long to tell me she was expecting. Not that I could have changed anything. But didn't I have a right to know, seeing where we are now?

As I lay between my sweaty beddings, my head pounds like hell. I stare at the ceiling and search for answers—no luck. Between the weatherman's punishment and my futile wishes to turn back time, it's a baffling conspiracy that fate has dumped on my doorstep. Dailess' news has completely robbed me of my peace of mind.

When I was a little boy and couldn't fall asleep, my mother made hot cinnamon milk. She would then read a story to me until my eyelids gave in. Last night, I made my mother's magic drink at 02.00 hrs and tried to soothe myself into oblivion.

Unfortunately, the trick is one that only works for little children. Young men my age with unsavoury girl issues and secrets must find more solid and mature solutions. Yet, I'm still far from figuring out what that is.

All logic tells me I should inform my mother about my impending fatherhood. But my prayers for strength to do so remain unanswered. The question is, how will I keep this sort of thing hidden from her? My mother trusts me—there aren't any secrets between us.

Besides, I know from experience that lies and deception don't *go down* well with her. They are a trigger of a painful past she would rather forget.

Wakey, wakey, my seven o'clock alarm sounds, and not that I need it. The sun is high in the sky; I would think it was already midday if I didn't know any better. I long for the Rainy Season, which is still a few weeks away. For now, even a light shower would make a massive difference in these searing October days and nights.

As I reminisce, a wave of nostalgia washes over me and, with it, a sense of calm. Rainfall in Zambia is extraordinary in a way that's best experienced and not described. I think of the enchanting aroma of petrichor—a sign of the imminent arrival of rain.

No other scent in nature lingers in my memory with such clarity and depth as petrichor. And that moment when the clouds give in is everything. Big and velvety raindrops fall from the sky and gently nourish the ground.

The once-dusty earth, usually in September and October, reveals a lush mosaic of fresh green grass and trees with vibrant and glistening leaves. It's a sight to behold—a reminder of nature's inherent beauty. Indeed, this is one of the reasons why Climate Change matters so much to me.

Aaah, what a dream—a luxury I can't afford in the middle of my life storm. It's time I got out of bed and hit the shower. Besides, life around me is in full charge. How can anyone ignore the pesky noise of the neighbourhood mukolwes (roosters)?

The mukolwes in my country have egos the size of China. From about 04:00 hrs, they prance around with arrogance and belt out their proud *kokoliko* (cock-a-doodle-do). As if they have somewhere urgent to be, the mukolwes are relentless and overzealous as they announce a brand-new dawn. They boss everyone to wake up on their watch. Unless you have dropped into the blackness of a comatose, you have no choice but to obey the call of these unwavering birds.

The neighbourhood dogs also have their own conspiracy going. It's a plot that has me both worried and confused. Or perhaps I should be grateful. The dog's early morning anxious and borderline aggressive barking is unsettling. It's as if a new day's quiet and gradual yet resilient appearance threatens their existence.

But in solidarity with such dogs, I think they mean well because they worry about their owners as they slumber. Unlike the indoor pups that get a front-row seat to their *parents'* night activities, an outdoor dog spends the whole time guessing—*will my dog-mummy or dog-daddy wake up today?* It's a weird kind of love. But love, nonetheless.

And then there are the cunning, in-your-face stray dogs you can't miss. Their bark signals everyone that they are alive and will look for food everywhere and by any means possible. These adrenaline-charged canines roam the streets in the early hours and knock over bins as they ravenously scavenge through garbage.

The naughty hounds, without a care in the world, leave behind a colourful and terrifying mess strewn across front yards and the street. The unsightly carnage reveals things you never want to see or know about your neighbours. Alas, these animals *do not know what they are doing.* Lol.

Outside my bedroom window, I can see Ba (Mr) Bwezani, our seventy-year-old garden worker, who has already begun his day. Don't let his age, bald head, and toothless smile fool you. The gentleman is stronger and more alert than most young people I know.

Ba Bwezani has a robust, stocky frame with powerful muscular arms and legs sculpted through years of toiling under the Zambian sun. His veins pop underneath and strain against his dark and shiny skin—a hint at the countless hours spent in the garden. They carry the stories of a lifetime of nurturing and tending to my mother's flowers.

Year after year, Ba Bwezani meticulously attends to the needs of our garden. Arguably, we have the best flowers and yard on our street—in the whole suburb town of Kabulonga, if I may say so myself.

Nothing is ever out of place, starting with the rose garden. Our green and white striped silver streak plants beautifully border our cobbled driveway. And you can't miss the red hibiscus flower plants that neatly line our yard's high walls.

This morning is like any other day. Ba Bwezani hums away in high spirits as his lawn mower blades through the thick and hot air outdoors. Intermittently, his melodious hum intertwines with the gentle resonance of a soft bass. He fills the air with songs in Tumbuka—his ancestral language from the Eastern Province of Zambia.

The meaning of the lyrics eludes me, yet an inexplicable comfort emanates from each joyful note. Ba Bwezani, a guardian of tradition, has carried these tunes since I was a little boy. Their familiarity etches into the core of my being, much like a cherished childhood toy that forever holds a place in your heart.

I glance at my phone; time is running. A delicious cold shower is all the therapy I need this morning. As I dash into the bathroom, my reflection in the mirror greets me.

Hmmnn, the dark circles around my eyes look better than they did yesterday. I grin at the young hunk in the mirror—d**n, am I a *catch* or what? I lift my chest, flex my muscles, and let out a low whistle. I'm glad my Dailess troubles haven't run off with my good looks.

Thank God I have my mother's *fine* features and my father's flawless chocolate skin, except for this crazy *facial foliage* of mine! I've been trying to grow it out for a while now. It has a mind of its own when it does grow. But, in between growth episodes are the notorious razor bumps that swamp my jawline each time I shave. No matter what soothing balm I use, nothing seems to work. Give me a break already!

Today, however, I must keep the *swagger* going to appear normal and throw off my mother's scent. I can't afford to tip the apple cart before I figure out my next step. It wouldn't be wise to do so. My mother doesn't miss a thing.

I must admit, though, the struggle to accept the idea of becoming a father is *real.* It wasn't supposed to happen. Where will I get the courage to tell my mother the worst news ever? My body shudders each time my mind goes there. Besides, I'm not trying to give her a heart attack. I need time.

Fifteen minutes later, my grooming sorted, I exit my bedroom—a strong whiff of my favourite cologne trails behind me as I walk to the dining room. I look dapper in my new navy-blue Ralph Lauren sports jacket, which flatters my broad American footballer shoulders. A short, white-sleeved V-neck t-shirt underneath the jacket clings to my torso and shows off my budding six-pack. It's getting there—well-deserved dividends from my investment at the gym.

My long legs, clad in Hugo Boss slim-fit jeans and a pair of Air Jordan trainers on my feet, carry me swiftly along the corridor. The trainers were a birthday gift from Auntie Francine, my mother's young sister. She's cool, like that.

As I bounce along the hallway, I hear Ba (Ms) Esther Konkola, our housekeeper, chef, and my mother's fierce ally, bustle away in the kitchen. Like a satellite navigation system, the delicious smell of bacon and sausages lures me to the dining room, my morning sanctuary.

The room boasts excellent style and elegance. It has French doors and oversized windows on the east side. I love its high and intricately decorated ceiling from which a massive chandelier dangles.

The gorgeous natural sunlight streams through the windows. It softly hits the chandelier's crystal accents and sparks a mesmerising kaleidoscope of colours that dance across the room. The interplay creates a breathtaking *ambience* that lifts my spirits every morning. Thank God for the beauty of life.

Ba Esther elbows her way through the French doors. An elaborate white head tie delicately frames her round and brown dimpled face. Bright and sunny, as always, her natural exuberance precedes her. She flashes a wide smile with pride, her large eyes bobbing in their sockets—*is she ever in a bad mood?*

Ba Esther stops before the head of the table and twirls at a forty-five-degree angle to her left as if to say, *how do I look?* The tray in her hands wobbles. I try not to laugh. To her credit, the new purple and white gingham uniform, teamed with a large purple apron, is becoming on her. It flatters her short frame better than the last uniform, which wasn't the right fit.

The tenacity with which Ba Esther gets things done never ceases to amaze me. She makes magic happen in all kinds of ways. The mango season has just begun, but surprisingly, Ba Esther has a tray of juicy, ripe mangoes this morning. I gaze at the arrangement of the complementary yellow, orange, red, and purple fruits. It's enough to summon my appetite, which scampered for the woods together with my peace of mind. Who would have thought I'd be dealing with baby daddy issues?

Besides the mangoes, the dining table displays an assortment of food, literally a *banquet* for the Chipolopolo Zambia national football team. Food and feeding are Ba Esther's *language of love*. My mother has long given up on explaining how wasteful and costly it is to keep preparing large quantities of food.

Ba Esther greets me with a cheerful tone. "Good morning, Bwana (Master) Andrew. Breakfast is ready."

"Good morning, Ba Esther. Thank you for this delightful feast." My voice is pleasant in response as I tease her. "What would we do without you?"

Ba Esther giggles like a girl and continues to examine her handiwork as she briskly walks around the table. Despite being heavier than the doctor would like her to be, she is very light and swift on her feet. Speaking of her feet, I notice that she has them neatly tucked away in white plimsolls—which are also new. Hmmnn, it explains the bright twinkle in her eyes. Bless her.

At forty-five, Ba Esther has never been married and has had no children. Over time, she has poured all her love into her work and my well-being—a coping mechanism that helps her forget what could have been and might never be in her life. But then again, she is clever and understands that taking good care of and loving me is my mother's *language of love.*

My mother, April Michelo (née Mulenga), is a Bemba *Princess.* She comes from a line of strong and intelligent women in a matrilineal society. They are quick thinkers, articulate, and believe in taking charge of their lives and upholding the Bemba tradition.

Some might find Bemba women like my mother very strong and self-assured. But why is that a bad thing? I always remind my mother that there's nothing wrong with a woman knowing her worth. And that she must be quick to remind those who forget. Men walk around daily with the same strength of character, ready to conquer the world. No one disapproves of that. Society admires men for it—so much for gender equality and women's empowerment.

My mother's beauty is breathtaking. She is tall and slim—a statuesque figure that embodies grace and elegance. She has stunning facial features, with luminous brown skin that captivates all who behold her. But what I love the most about my mother is her personality. She exudes a magnetic charm that hypnotises those around her and draws them into her glorious orbit.

A keen lover of all-things-fashion, my mother believes in looking fabulous. Like her sister, Auntie Francine, she keeps up with the fashion trends, where some of her friends have long given up. More importantly, my mother has taught me the value of investing in a good image and behaviour. She stresses that both are powerful tools of self-expression.

With a knack for business in the world of Interior Design, my mother has run her own company for years. It's clever of her to use part of our house as a perfect showroom and a testimony of her passion and talent. This arrangement has helped her acquire a strong portfolio of companies and individual private clients.

My mother delights all of them with an array of rare and exquisite soft furnishings sourced from far-flung corners of the globe. She aims to transform their spaces into culturally dynamic places of wonder. But her most prized items are the Persian rugs she imports from Dubai. You should see how excited she becomes when a new order comes in—she is literally in heaven.

Ah! There she is. My mother finally arrives in the dining room. She glides through the French doors with ease. I love to spend time with her—mealtimes are always enjoyable, with great conversations between us. But lately, it has been difficult for me to relax in her company. Guilt has taken over my whole being; I can't look her in the eye.

As she approaches the dining table, I rush to my feet and step in her direction to greet her.

"Good morning, darling mummy," I kiss her on either cheek with exaggerated enthusiasm. She hugs me, and I take in the delicate fragrance of her perfume—*Un Jardin Sur Le Nil* by Hermès. It has been her signature perfume for years.

My mother's face lights up. "Good morning, Sonny," she laughs. "The whole neighbourhood can smell your cologne from a mile away."

I pull her chair out. And then, with suave confidence and a flair of showmanship, I bow like a garçon in a fine-dining Parisienne restaurant.

"Asseyez-vous madam."

"You are such a charmer; what are you hiding?" She laughs, but something is not quite right.

Firstly, my mother held onto me a bit longer than usual when she hugged me. Secondly, her eyes are red and slightly puffy. She looks like she's been crying.

My mother's mood and energy aren't complex to read when something's on her mind. I would ask her about it in normal circumstances, but not today. In the depth of my psyche, I know that whatever is *eating* my mother has something to do with me.

At last, my father, Roger Michelo, shuffles into the dining room with an expression of disinterest. Increasingly, he resembles a mysterious figure bound by the weight of an unknown enigma. He walks with a perpetual stoop that thrusts his head forward. His feet, as though made of lead, barely lift off the floor with each step.

My father is a tall, dark, handsome man capable of holding his own in the looks department. I've seen how women look at him when my mother isn't with him. He has deceptively smooth, youthful skin that keeps people guessing his age.

Yet, something has shifted in his life because he has let go of his appearance. My father insists on being old-fashioned—the *eighties* are tired of asking for their suits and hairstyles back. And lately, he's at war with every Barbershop in Lusaka.

OMG, my old man has been *rocking* an unevenly grown-out and sun-bleached afro. I am amazed at how jagged it looks. It resembles pockets of tiny bird nests made from old hair and split ends.

It's hard to say why there's no life in my old man's wardrobe because money isn't an issue. He is a wealthy-*ish* man who runs a successful car dealership called Michelo Cars Ltd.

The showroom is on Cairo Road, close to the Kafue roundabout. It occupies a perfect spot, easily accessible to everyone, with lots of parking space. Even after the COVID-19 pandemic, the business is still flourishing, unlike other companies that succumbed to the disease's unforgiving wrath.

Oh well, successful business or not, as in the case of Ba Esther and her bountiful cooking, my mother has made peace with my father's declining dress sense and general appearance.

My father has become grumpier as he ages and makes mountains from molehills. This morning, he has his usual severe and officious expression as he stares at me. His scary mask is to remind my mother and me how hard it is to build and run a business like his.

The only time I see him *chilled* is when he watches football. He has been an avid Arsenal football team fan for years. But as one might learn to manage a rottweiler, my mother and I know how to handle my father's *grumpy old man* nature to keep our sanity.

"Good morning, Dad," I say from my chair.

I don't give him a hug or fist pump, not because I couldn't care less. But the dude hates any public display of affection—even in the confines of his home. That's still public for him. I wonder, what's he afraid of?

But then again, his mother—my Grandma Selina is a weird, cold old woman. She looks the type that would let her little boy cry himself to sleep every night. My Grandpa, Dominic Michelo, a remarkable man, sadly died when I was seven years old. He should see what's become of his wife. Eish!

"Good morning, son," my father responds formally and glares at my mother, who continues to fuss over me. In addition to PDA, he hates how my mother gives me so much attention.

"April, this boy is not a baby anymore. You're the main reason he wakes up so late and sits at the table like the man of the house."

My mother lifts her brow and throws him an eye. "Roger, for God's sake, it's only seven-thirty."

My queen is very protective of me against my father and will always choose me over him. He knows to his bones that he can never win this battle. But still, my father tries.

Irritated, I *butcher* through my cinnamon roll and dare to stand up against my father.

"Dad, I don't start work till 09:00. I work for you, remember, or did the start time change?"

My father looks at me with a severe face, not saying anything for a few seconds. His skin tightens around his mouth, and he pushes out his jaw.

"On that note, it's about time you found another job; no more handouts from me."

Wait, is he serious? My father's words leave a bitter taste in my mouth. Did he fire me, or am I reading too much into it? Unbelievable! What about all the long hours that I put in month after month? Don't I deserve a salary?

I can't wait to go to England and leave this ungrateful man and his business behind. Thanks to dear Uncle Michael, Auntie Francine's husband, I recently secured a scholarship for a master's degree in Climate Change in the UK.

The university sent me the confirmation email last Friday—something I have yet to reveal to my mother. So, with everything I have going on, I have little patience for my father's mood or whatever is stealing his joy.

"Dad, with all due respect, I'm the reason why your car sales have increased. I bring in the younger demographics whose hard-earned Kwachas have fattened your bank account."

My father stops a forkful of scrambled eggs halfway to his mouth.

"So, you think you can run my company?" He creases his forehead. "Do you know how long my business has taken me to build?"

My mother looks like she is about to explode.

"Roger, what has my son not done for you?" She sighs heavily. "Please tell me what you have against your own flesh and blood?"

My father pushes his plate of food away.

"April, who do you think will inherit everything I have worked so hard for?"

My mother rolls her eyes. "You don't want me to answer that question, Roger."

An awkward silence descends upon the table like a thick fog. Unspoken words over *forgiven but not forgotten sins* between my parents hang in the air. It's not surprising that breakfast is over sooner than planned.

When people live together for a long time, they communicate intuitively. My father glances at his watch, my mother at the wall clock, and I at my phone. It is precisely 08.00 hrs, and we all rise from the table in tandem—three slices of bread out of a toaster.

My father grabs his briefcase and heads towards the door. He zooms past my mother and then makes an abrupt stop. As an afterthought, my old man turns around to give my queen what might look like a quick kiss to the untrained eye. But his lips barely touch her cheek, in what I have come to call a *non-kiss* kiss.

My mother cringes as my father's warm breath fogs on her skin. She turns away ever so slightly.

"Have a nice day," my mother says.

"See you later, April. Don't forget to call my mother," my father mumbles.

A frown highjacks my mother's brow, a sign of a deeper turmoil beneath the surface. You must know my mother very well to catch this expression, let alone understand its nuance.

The beef between Grandma Selina and my mother has a history that stretches beyond my twenty-one years. And so, my mother dismisses my father's instruction to call Grandma Selina. Instead, she addresses me.

"Sonny, please wait; I must talk to you before you leave."

The word *talk* is enough to send my heart racing. Oh my God, my mother must know I have something to hide. My brain screams, and my thoughts jangle. I swear, this woman is a mind reader.

Determined to avoid a tête-à-tête with her, I try to dive in for a quick peck before I dash out. But my mother grabs my arm tightly. Her bright red gel nails dig into my forearm. They look and feel like a dangerous weapon.

Fear takes hold of me, and my heart leaps with rampant intensity as it threatens to escape through my mouth. Dailess and her nonsense news have got me in such a twist that I can't control myself. It will soon be too difficult to cover my tracks if I don't find a way out of this trap.

My mother leans forwards and looks at me. Her eyes are dark with a *thousand* questions.

"Andrew, you seem on edge these days. Is everything okay with you?"

My face feels hot and itchy as I search for a suitable response. What can I say? I am not ready to share my issues regarding Dailess. So, I try to make light of my mother's question, but my mouth, too dry to produce any sound, doesn't cooperate. Lord, please do not let me pass out.

Breathe, Andrew, breathe; I try to calm myself. Just as my mother is about to ask me another question, I suddenly find my tongue. What comes out of my mouth is alien, even to me.

"Mummy, we must visit Grandma Bertha and Grandpa Simon this weekend. It has been a while," I say, trying not to sound desperate. "I must show them how to use the television we bought for them last week. You know how they love to watch Judge Judy."

My words tumble out of my mouth so hastily that they knock my mother's next question to the back of her mind. The speed and context of my words distract her and disrupt her train of thought.

Years of practice have perfected my art of manipulating my mother. Sold and sinking into the thick honey of my words, my mother drowns in its sweetness. Her eyes glisten with pride within her response.

"Aww, that's so sweet and thoughtful of you; your grandparents would love that."

This split-second of distraction is everything I need to escape all kinds of questions. The front door and key to my freedom are about four metres from where my mother and I are. With a few quick and long strides to the door, if only I could get past her, I'd be outside, away from the threats of a *Spanish Inquisition*.

Yes! There it is! The front door swings open without warning, and Ba Bwezani's bald, sweaty head extends around its frame. A burst of hot air charges into the foyer, but the weather does not bother me now. I can only see the opportunity to escape.

Ba Bwezani has a massive bouquet in his calloused hands. It partially obscures his face as he flashes my mother a big, gummy smile, proud to show her the *fruits* of his garden.

"Madam, *ma flaouwzi* (the flowers) are ready for your coffee table."

My mother's eyes twinkle at the sight of her gift.

"Aww, Ba Bwezani. How thoughtful of you."

It is now or never. I sneak past Ba Bwezani and my mother and shamelessly shoot outside. My mother tries to rush after me, her hand outstretched as she tries to catch me, but I'm too fast for her.

"Andrew, I'm not done with you!"

As my mother's words hit the back of my head, I race across the lawn and head straight to my father's car. I forcefully yank the front passenger door open, and as fast as a cunning snake, I slither into the leather seat—just in time. My odd behaviour creates an aura of apprehension and unease. D**n! My mother can see through me!

I know I'm in trouble when my mother wags her finger at me. "Iwe (you)!"

That *iwe* is enough language for me to know my mother will not give up until she gets me. The urgency in her voice echoes in my ears.

My father ignores my desperate rush to get into the car. He has long learnt not to ask what happens between my mother and me.

"Ready, son?"

I avoid my father's eyes and steer the conversation to business.

"Yes, Dad, I forgot I had an early appointment."

My father is surprised and wonders why I hadn't mentioned this before.

"Do you? Okay, that's great; is it with a potential buyer—who is it?"

Eish! I'm in a bind and can't think straight. I wish my father would let it go because I don't have an answer for him. What comes out of my mouth next is so shady that even I don't buy it.

"Uh uh. The *one you* said might be interested in one of our new cars."

My father throws me a confused glance and waits for me to add context to my story. But there's no such client—whatever his suspicions may be, my father must accept my rigamarole as it is.

I reach for the car radio, pump up the volume, and grab a piece of tissue. I blow my nose loudly to muddle our conversation. *Tsk, tsk.* A man of few words, my father makes a mental note not to put any more energy in the direction of our conversation. He shakes his head and rolls the car out of our yard.

The traffic into town is thick, bumper-to-bumper. A typical Monday morning picture unfolds before our eyes. The roads are a *battleground* of frayed nerves and short tempers amid the never-ending stream of vehicles.

It's easy to spot those guilty of ruthless weekend hangovers who shouldn't be behind the wheel. They flounder on the road as they try to shift their brains into Monday morning mode. It's time to catch up with the rest of the world. At the same time, teetotallers vent their impatience behind clenched fists and expletives. What a circus!

A great song suddenly bursts through the car speakers: *You to Me Are Everything* by The Real Thing. I reach for the volume knob, and my father gives me the *stop-it* look he used to give me as a little boy. I'm no longer a little man, so I ignore him.

"Come on, Dad, don't tell me you never crooned to Mummy when y'all were dating."

"I don't know about crooning, but the sixties' and seventies' greatest hits are still some of the best songs the world has ever heard," my father smiles.

"That's what I'm talking about! No matter one's age, these tracks are *serious heaters*," I chuckle.

The song cuts through the tension, and its rhythm takes hold of the car. My father has no choice but to join me in my love of music. He bops his head and sings along. Yeah! That's more like it! For a fleeting moment, Dailess does not exist.

As we pull into the Michelo Car Dealership's bustling parking lot, I see that the business day has already sprung to life. Even from a distance, the cars in the showroom look shiny and spotless, courtesy of Daliso, Ba Bwezani's oldest son. The apple does not fall too far from the tree. Daliso, a replica of his father, is a dedicated and hardworking employee.

Across from the showroom, the reception area, a shrine run by Belita, our office manager, is alive and kicking. The space hums with activity as she carries out the day's agenda with remarkable efficiency, a testament to the system she has meticulously crafted over the years.

Though too friendly at times, Belita is a blessing to our clients, whom she has looked after for a decade. She is cheerful and helpful—everyone loves the vibrant energy from every corner of her space.

My father cuts the engine and grabs my wrist firmly as I open the passenger door.

"Son, I don't know what you are up to. But don't forget; you can't hide anything from your mother. You can't outrun her."

Of course, my father should know. He is the King of Secrets and epitomises the words *still waters run deep*. It surprises me, though, how he figures that my issue, whatever it is, concerns my mother alone. I spend more time with my father than my mother—car rides to and from work and business hours.

How has he not noticed that things are not okay with me? My mother spots even the slightest changes in my mood. Her instincts are consistently exact.

But then again, what if my father is also onto me but has chosen not to say anything? The thought is enough to send me to dark places. I have never had a panic attack, but I am sure it feels like I do now.

I clutch my chest, jump out of the car, and rush past reception without saying hello to a puzzled Belita. I arrive in front of my office, air barely squeezing through my flared nostrils. It takes me ten minutes to find my key in my briefcase. Once inside, I lock the door behind me and, with a fluid motion, drop into a squat position—unable to move.

My rib cage feels compressed, and it hurts to breathe. Am I going to die? As the thought of my death sinks in my head, a chilling realisation sets in—how will anyone find my lifeless body if they can't get past the entrance? *Lord, please help me*. I try to pray, but the torrent of competing thoughts about my future does not allow me to pray meaningfully. Aaah!

Chapter Two

APRIL MULENGA MICHELO
KABULONGA, LUSAKA, ZAMBIA

A mother's intuition wields an extraordinary power. It's a mystical gift that allows her to see and hear things beyond the grasp of explanation. In this remarkable way, mothers protect their children, and only God, the benevolent benefactor of this divine connection, truly understands its depth and significance.

Trust your gut, April. I hear my inner whispers again, louder than the last few days. Andrew is my only child—my *Ibeli* (firstborn) and *Kasuli* (lastborn). He is my everything and Achilles heel.

Like any mother, it has not escaped me that my son hasn't been himself for the past week or two. He has skipped meals and avoided our traditional Friday soirées the last two weeks.

My son *lives* for those moments; something big has to be the matter for him not to show up. I might have looked the other way this morning without his nonsensical and dramatic *performance*. But how he shot out of the house like a slippery thief took things to a new level.

Andrew and I have always had an open line of communication, and he knows I'm his go-to person whenever he needs help or has exciting news. Nothing is off-limits between us—the *good, the bad, and the ugly*; we face it all together. So, what's with the distance and reluctance to talk to me—what has changed?

I pray that Andrew's stupid friend, David Likezo, did not get him into trouble. How the two have remained such good friends since the Sunday School years and against all odds beats my understanding. I swear that David lacks discipline—it's criminal!

Eish! I can't handle this—it's time to call in backup: Francine, my young sister, ride-or-die, and Andrew's godmother. She's the last born in our family of three boys and two girls.

Francine's beautiful, fashionable, and super bright. It didn't surprise the family when Francine graduated at the top of her Law class at the University of Zambia, *UNZA*. My parents couldn't have been prouder when she went on to take the BAR at the National Institute of Public Administration, *NIPA*. Francine aced that, too.

My sister's desire to become a Corporate Lawyer propelled her to do her MBA in England. As fate would have it, Francine achieved more than her MBA distinction. She gained a fiancé, Michael Thornton, a very kind British man who later became her husband.

Francine and Michael now have two children, seven-year-old Ryan and five-year-old Molly. My father fondly teases my sister about her motives for going to England in the first place! Lol!

I swear I'll come unglued if I don't speak to my sister today, this red hot minute. Please, Francine, pick up the phone, *pickup, pickup.* Where is she? My sister usually answers on the second ring.

"Hello, sis! How are you?" Francine sounds perky. I wish I were in a lively mood myself.

"Finally, you answer. What took you so long to answer?" I ask, slightly agitated.

She chuckles. "What do you mean? What's going on, that's got you so wound up?"

I dive right in. "It's your nephew; something is up, you know?"

Francine hesitates. "Aa-ah, what do you mean?"

"It's hard to say what, but he has been avoiding me for almost two weeks," I quietly reply.

"Have you spoken to him about it?"

"Sis, I tried this morning. The silly boy almost knocked me over as he bolted for his father's car—a convenient *getaway ride*. Has he mentioned anything to you that I must know?"

Francine clears her throat. "No, nothing at all. But, April, has Andrew told you that his scholarship came through last week?"

Another red flag—I'm confused.

"No way, what, whaaat? Roger and I have been anxious about the outcome of Andrew's scholarship application. Why would he keep such great news under wraps."

"Well, I only just found out this morning when Michael called. Could Andrew have changed his mind about his master's degree?"

"No, I don't think so; there's more to the picture. I can't put it into words."

"April, do you think Andrew is unwell?"

There's silence between us as I desperately try to hold back the floodgates of emotion. *Please, God, let my son be okay*. I blink back the tears that quickly fill my eyes and try to find my tongue, but I have lost control. My sister picks up on that.

"Listen, Michael and the kids do not return from London for another two weeks. Why don't I come over on Saturday, and we can think things through together?

Hallelujah. Francine knows me so well.

A croak escapes my lips. "Thank you, sis; I'll see you on Saturday."

"Oh, and by the way, April, don't nag Andrew over the next few days. I know it's difficult, but we must find the right moment to corner him."

"I hear you; bye."

The uncertainty and worry gnaw at my heart as an uneasy feeling settles in my bones. I sink to the floor, draw my knees to my chin, and let the ugly cry out. Today is only Monday; how will I get through so many days till the weekend? I need strength, Lord.

The possibility of a hidden illness crosses my mind again. I pray that whatever is the matter with my son isn't some incurable disease. After all the trouble it took for me to have Andrew, I would die if life took him away from me.

No one who knows me well can blame me for my state of mind over my son. I still recall how miraculous his arrival into this world was. The journey to that point is one of the most harrowing experiences I have ever been through. It left indelible lessons imprinted into the depths of my heart—ones that I will carry to my final resting place.

I first met Roger, who would become my husband and our cherished son's father, at UNZA. We were both first-year students in the School of Social Sciences. We had a beautiful courtship, and when we graduated, it only made sense to shift gears in our relationship to the next level—marriage.

If only someone had given me a crystal ball back then, I would have saved myself a lot of heartache, for what followed was worse than a heart-wrenching story in a fiction novel. Roger and I, our heads in the cloud, didn't know that in the eyes of our parents, our relationship was not the most ideal.

Despite our profound love, the *tired* tribal barriers set in very quickly and cast a dark shadow on our plans. What was supposed to have been a happy time for both families instantly became a senseless power struggle. In the minds of our parents, nothing good could come from a union between what they saw as two opposing tribal groups, Tonga and Bemba.

Often, we deceive ourselves into believing we genuinely know people merely because they offer a smile and a warm greeting. It isn't always true—I learnt the hard way.

When Roger initially mentioned to his mother that he wanted to marry me, she showed a side of her personality that I couldn't have imagined. A Bemba girl was not the *moye* (bride) she had in mind nor ready to accept for her son.

My mother-in-law was livid—she thought I was too talkative, proud, thin, and not submissive enough. Mrs Michelo wondered if I could cook, clean the house, and keep it together. She believed back then and still does that Roger could and can do better. Whenever she saw me with her son, Mrs Michelo asked why Roger couldn't find a girl from Mazabuka, where he was born and raised.

My parents, Mrs Bertha Mulenga (née Chishimba) and Mr Simon Mulenga, weren't innocent bystanders in the infamous *North-South* tug of war. My father, especially, had some questionable, unfounded views.

Stubbornly rooted in the past, my father's Bemba and Roman Catholic superiority complex further threatened our marriage agenda. He unreasonably vowed not to surrender his firstborn daughter to what he called a *joke of holy matrimony*. In his unfair judgement, he believed a Tonga marriage had a high chance of becoming polygamous one day.

Our cultural differences weren't the only barrier Roger and I had to overcome. Religion was another thorn in the side my parents couldn't get over. They were worried that I would switch from the Catholic church to the Seventh-Day Adventist denomination. Not that I thought it would be wrong if I chose to.

My mother couldn't stop worrying about the baptism of our future children. All these questions were a non-issue because Roger wasn't a big church-goer. He preferred to read the bible quietly at home and follow different religious sermons on TV. Roger wasn't in a hurry to convert me to anything. But my parents surprised me as they continued to poke around at everything. They clutched at straws to dissuade me from marrying a Tonga boy.

Roger and I realised there wouldn't be any wedding if the exchange of harsh words and hostile tribal mudslinging continued. It made sense to up the ante and move to plan B after an infamous impasse. Support from both churches is what it took to help the two families pursue a more peaceful approach to our planned nuptials.

Father Franco at the Catholic Church was relentless. He preached the oneness of everyone in God's eyes, calling on congregants to get past the superficial barriers like tribe.

The holy man further had one-on-one meetings with our parents, questioning why, in God's name, Roger and I couldn't marry. He impressed upon them that as children of the Kingdom, all human beings are equal in God's eyes. Where was Christ in our parents' divisive motives? Father Franco queried.

Over time, the hearts of the *Doubting Thomases* softened, and in the end, love won. Roger and I married in the Catholic Church in February 1997, followed by a lavish wedding reception at the Pamodzi Hotel.

Sadly, for me, our honeymoon phase was short-lived. In hindsight, my marriage never stood a chance—it was dead straight out of the gate. Within the first six months of our new life together, it became plain that pregnancy would be an uphill climb—a young bride's nightmare.

I had difficulties conceiving, and the pregnancy ended in a miscarriage each time I did. My days snowballed into hopeless months and eventually five devastating years of shattered dreams of having a baby. The aching emptiness that engulfed me in those horrible years was like a piece of my soul was missing.

Looking back now, it is frightening how the mental health of young brides is secondary to everything. Is it enough that Bana Chimbusa's (Traditional Marriage Counsellors) teachings focus solely on how to pleasure a man?

My case was no different—Bana Chimbusa kept me indoors for days, cooped under layers of chitenge wraps (traditional fabric). Eager, to achieve their goal, Bana Chimbusa were on a *fast-track* mission to teach me how to feed Roger, keep him sexually happy, and produce lots of babies. Nothing else mattered, least of all my mental and emotional well-being.

Amidst the thunderous drumbeat and electrifying ululations, they forgot I existed—I had vanished into the pulsating energy of *amasha yabukulu kuboko* (traditional Bemba dance). None of the so-called wise women prepared me for survival when my marriage crumbled under the strain of childlessness.

Why didn't Bana Chimbusa rescue me when everyone considered me an outcast and a fraudulent letdown to my husband? They all buried their heads in the sand when I became fair game for friends, relatives, and strangers.

I still feel the pain of how our community sent me on a lonely, thorny path of ridicule, shame, gossip, and betrayal. I had to fend for myself—putting out fires in all directions became the order of the day. I was losing my mind.

My mother-in-law, who never hid her disappointment that Roger married me against her wishes, gave me a run for my money. It was payback time. She finally had the ammunition to tear me down and push my husband to divorce me. My mother-in-law was at the forefront of inciting Roger to find a new wife since I was a useless disgrace of a woman—her words.

Across town, the news spread fast; society wrote me off and cruelly crowned me *Miss Infertility Lusaka.* With that news bulletin, the shameless and *thirsty* ratchets of Lusaka started to posture as wife replacement material. When the cheetahs smell a childless marriage, they all get out on the prowl, voracious wild animals, claws sharpened and ready to stage a coup d'etat. They pounce on your husband and trap him in a grip so tight no amount of wriggling will set him free. How difficult can it be to snatch him? Right?

The calculated vultures know the math—it's simple. Your wife cannot give you children, but I can—a whole football team is yours for the asking. In the worst-case scenario, even your housekeeper joins the bandwagon. The *boss* is free for all, so why not give it a go? Eish!

To survive, I avoided social events and Church gatherings for fear of what nasty surprise the day might bring. Family and friends asked cruel and inappropriate questions. It did not matter that I was only twenty-four, a young newlywed girl trying to navigate marriage as best I could—oh no, the gloves were off.

Mean questions, such as when would I have a child or what was I waiting for, were on everyone's nasty tongues. The lack of tact and callousness was horrific as it cruelly implied my situation was a matter of choice rather than a difficult challenge. Lord knows if I could have had things my way, any day would have been a good day for me to conceive and have a child.

In sickness and health—do Brides and Grooms ever really mean these words as they stand before God in their marriage ceremonies? Or do the words just have a nice ring to them? In my grief of childlessness, I asked myself the same question over and over again. The question was critical to me because the heartbreak and pinnacle of my fertility frustrations was my husband's disregard and lack of genuine support.

Roger never put it in so many words, but not once did he stand up for me against his mother—that spoke volumes. Instead, he defended her, claiming to be powerless in the situation. Roger also reminded me that it was his mother's right to want grandchildren and that I was denying her the opportunity.

What a blow to me that was. It's sad how often people become myopic when not *in the shoes of others*—separating themselves from the pain. How quickly my husband abandoned our wedding vows was alarming. He did not see the difference between a grandparent who yearns for grandchildren and a malicious mother-in-law who demonised me at every chance she got. Was Roger married to me or his mother?

As much as they were unwelcome, grief and loneliness in my heart became my constant companions. After four miscarriages, I was certain Roger blamed me for our hardships. He was aloof and quiet and didn't speak to me unless I did. My husband no longer *saw* me— how could anyone when my *stock value* as a wife had hurtled down a dark, bottomless pit?

To Roger, I was a *blurred* version of the woman he married, who deserved the blame. With my self-esteem in tatters, my head told me it was *okay* for my husband to treat me like he did—if only I could give him children, he would love me better. If only I could stop his pain, if only, if only, if only. How I wish someone had told me, that was not the answer. They would have spared me so much heartache.

Eventually, my God, who never sleeps, answered my prayers. The winds of change swept through my life. They brought the most improbable and wondrous surprises I could ever have imagined. My son Andrew was born on 4th May 2002—what a moment!

Finally, I was a mother and could exhale the air of barrenness that held me captive for years. I broke free of the chains that held me prisoner of my circumstances. The birth of my *Prince* took away the weight of shame I carried on my shoulders.

With Andrew's arrival in our lives, I left the shackles of silence and found my voice. I could walk with my head held high, knowing I had overcome my deepest fears. My beautiful boy replenished my fountain of joy, which had long dried up from years of low self-worth as a wife, a woman, and a human being.

As I tearfully reflect on the past, it's not unreasonable to second-guess my husband and his loyalty. I didn't just wake up on the wrong side of the bed and lose confidence in my partner out of the blue—I have my reasons. Can Roger stand by his son and me, his wife, protect us, and put us first?

I have come to believe that the measure of one's strength lies not in the absence of pressure but in response to it. Under the weight of life's trials and tribulations, the superficial layers slip off, revealing the raw core of one's true nature. Good or bad, the heart of one's spouse will unveil itself as the couple confronts their fears, limitations, and vulnerabilities. How did Roger fare when luck wasn't on my side?

As it turns out, some secrets can never stay hidden in life. Five years ago, I discovered that my husband of thirty years had been sitting on an explosive secret. It was a landmine with the might to break the strength of the most self-assured woman and shake the trust and love of the most loyal wife a man could have.

Long before Andrew was born, I was lost in the *labyrinth of baby wahala,* constantly worried about what lay ahead. Meanwhile, Roger had *options.* Sure, I could see that he had his fair share of pain, nightmares, and feelings of hopelessness. But sadly, I was not the person my husband bore his soul to. Roger found solace in the arms of another woman from Mazabuka, long enough to father two sons with her—older half-siblings to Andrew.

With my history of tortured days of mental and emotional anguish, Roger's deception was more than I could bear. My world collapsed, and I lost the meaning of life. My joie de vivre drained out of me, accompanied by the light in my eyes—something in the depth of my soul died.

On most days, I was too exhausted to care about anything. All I could do was mourn the loss of what I thought Roger and I had built and continued to build. The heartache reduced me to a hollow shell of myself, and my beauty became a dull and rough imposter of what it once was. I was unrecognisable to anyone who knew me before the bombshell.

Trust me, no married woman or one in a committed relationship who has loved and sacrificed would have wanted to be in my shoes five years ago. Roger's secret cannibalised the bedrock of anything we could ever hope to share now or in the future.

Once more, I was a broken woman, left destitute in what should have been a *happily ever after* situation. What kind of a man lies for that long? I'll never heal from that trauma—it's the kind that breaks one's bank account in therapy.

This morning, as I sit here on the floor and pray that nothing life-threatening is bothering my son, I worry if Roger will see things as I do and stand by my side. Or will history repeat itself?

Chapter Three

DAILESS BANDA

KAMWALA, LUSAKA, ZAMBIA

I t's happened to most of us—that moment when desperation got the better of you, and like life depended on it, you did something without thinking. That one time you convinced yourself that you had everything on lock. And the false comfort of the classic adage rang in your ears—*I'll cross that bridge when I come to it.*

The crazy thing is that reality always sneaks up on you, no matter how long it takes. Like a merciless whirlwind making its course on an open field of dry land, it hurls your life together with dust and debris into chaos. It's too late to break the momentum at that point—the s**t has officially hit the fan.

One day, you wake up in shock and shame to your life's dreadful, unintended shambles. And at that point, you think, holy s**t, what have I done? Your once bright future, poof—gone right before your eyes. You can't think, eat, drink, or sleep. Sadly, this is my clichéd story; *the shoe fits, and I must wear it.*

It was pure coincidence when Andrew came into my life through his cousin Lombe Mulenga, my fellow Media and Communications student at Evelyn Hone College. I had just broken up with my first boyfriend, Charles Muyunda, a possessive and emotionally abusive hater of a man.

In contrast, Andrew was a kind, funny, exciting, and intelligent gentleman. He checked all the boxes—qualities that drew me closer to him. Our friendship blossomed into a meaningful relationship built on shared values. We especially agreed to commit to safe sex until marriage. But somehow, I don't know what possessed me—I fell off the wagon.

We relied on condoms and contraceptive pills to prevent unwanted pregnancies and diseases. But money is always tight for people like me. I live in Kamwala with my parents, with little or no luxuries. It's a hand-to-mouth way of life.

So, one day, I thought, what the heck, I must make a few budget cuts. I analysed my monthly expenses and foolishly decided contraceptive pills had to go. They were chopping a significant share of my already skint bank account.

Besides, it was easy to get rid of the contraceptives because, for some reason, they were making me sick. I was feeling nauseous all the time. The thing is, I didn't tell Andrew about this *new* plan. It wasn't that *deep*, I told myself—besides, one form of protection was all we needed.

One month into the relationship, on a sneaky afternoon during passionate sex, luck was not on my side—the condom unexpectedly broke and changed the rhythm of our intimacy. My mind went into a frenzy: *hide the condom, Dailess*, a little voice in me whispered. I swiftly and discreetly disposed of the condom, careful not to alarm Andrew. It wasn't my proudest moment.

I couldn't tell if I was protecting him or myself, but I prayed that nothing would come of it. Yet here I am, a nine-week expectant young woman with no husband, money, or security to offer my baby once it gets here. As I stare into the uncertainty of my future, I have no clue how I'll make things work; where do I begin?

Ouch! I wince as my bloodshot and puffy eyes sting from bawling myself to sleep. My knees, which are no better, crack as I stretch and unwrap my body out of the fetal position—it's time to get out of my old and tiny bed.

But I don't feel like it or look like someone fit to go anywhere. I know I should show up and keep going, but my part-time job at the City Council Library and my boss, Mrs Siame, will have to wait.

My mind is also a mess; it torments me with random thoughts and a million unanswered questions. I struggle to keep track of anything daily as my sanity competes with my fear of what lies ahead.

Caught up in an emotional torrent, I have cried myself to sleep every night for the past two months. It's a draining pattern that has taken hold of my life. If it comes, the sweet solace of sleep is the only time I am at peace—somewhere to rest my mind for a moment.

The mornings are just as unkind. Fear claws me into a cruel bondage with the first lift of my eyelids. My demons eagerly jump on my case and greet me in haunting whispers—*hello, Dailess, welcome to the world of unwed mothers.* They quickly remind me that the road ahead is one of hardship and societal judgment.

I heave a sigh of regret and nervously reach under my pillow to retrieve the slender plastic gadget—AKA my pregnancy test. For some reason, I can't explain to anyone or myself why I haven't thrown it away.

There are days when I can't think straight. I imagine that I might have misread the result or something. Is there a chance that a negative reading might magically show up?

But I see that the two stubborn pink lines are still there. They stare back at me like an unyielding adversary. The positive reading presents a life-changing and non-negotiable deal—*face it, Dailess, you're still pregnant*. I would give anything to reset my life and return to everyday life with my darling Andrew.

Shame and regret wash over me as I think of my Bae in despair. I wonder whether he's still mine—could he have dumped me? Andrew has been *MIA* since I told him I was carrying his child.

Call me needy if you like, but I wish he would let me in on what's on his mind. He might need time to wrap his head around his new reality. But who thinks that long? What's there to mull over that Andrew should *ghost* me like this?

I guess I grossly miscalculated; why did I get the impression that Andrew was committed to our relationship? Was I wrong to trust him? I tried to call him on WhatsApp several times last night. I feel insulted that he had the cheek to ignore my calls. All I got back from him was the impersonal automated response—*can I call you back later?*

Dude, later? What does that even mean? How do two people go from seeing each other daily to annoying and empty responses? In other words, I'll call you back *never*!

My woes are endless. I can't tell you how much it kills me to think I might be a single mum. Sadly, Andrew and his ostrich-head-in-the-sand antics pale in comparison to my mother's wrath, which I'll soon face.

I can tell you, without a doubt, that before my future *single-parent* profile can kill me, my mother, Quietness Banda (née Chirwa), a feisty and uncompromising woman, will have had a go at me. My stomach turns as I imagine her fury.

My mother has a deceiving appearance that masks the cunning nature of her character. With her sweet and demure face, many residents of Kamwala easily mistake her for an innocent and kind-hearted soul. My mother's good looks add to the confusion about what to make of her.

Thanks to her ancestral Zulu genes, she has an alluring beauty—a voluptuous figure, beautiful, smooth brown skin, and tightly wound black hair that she wears in tiny cornrows.

You'll be surprised that beneath this captivating presence, my mother masterfully conceals her assertiveness that sometimes mirrors cruelty. It makes me sad and fearful that she won't spare me even though I am her only child.

My mother navigates through life with a one-track mind and a firm resolve to get her way. Her ability to bend others to her will is a skill she uses unsparingly in peace and war. Once my pregnancy comes to light, she will take that as bait to create a new *battlefront*—Kamwala will be ablaze with the dragon fire from her nostrils.

As for the Michelo family, I shudder to imagine the rage and vengeance my mother will unleash upon them. She will scorch their *bougie* lives and the streets of Kabulonga, dragging anyone on her path as collateral damage.

Nothing, not even my father, will be able to stop her. If anything, my father's intervention will stoke the flames of her relentless pursuit of retribution for my pre-pregnant days. *Lord, help us all.*

Luckily, I have a bit of breathing space now. My mother, who typically has the eyes of a hawk, is busy with preparations for a huge annual event at the United Church of Zambia (UCZ) in Kamwala. As one can imagine, my baby bump has gone unnoticed—my mother is fiercely involved in the flurry of activities on that agenda.

The adrenalin rush my mother gets from being the boss lady is everything to her. Nothing can separate this woman from the UCZ congregation—she's like an elephant and its calf.

Within the confines of the walls of her church, my mother has the platform to show off her good looks and flex her muscles. I have no clue how a woman of medium height can wield so much power among women twice her size.

When not at her place of worship, my mother runs a Kamwala market stall. Post-pandemic, her informal business has struggled to stay afloat amid the erratic fresh produce supply and shifting supplier prices. In such uncertain times, it's hard for my mother to keep up with the shifting cycle of products—*anything goes.*

My mother sells whatever she must. Her mishmash products range from beans, *kapenta* (dried anchovies), dried fish, fresh fish, rape, mushroom, tomatoes, and onions to *salaula* (second-hand clothing) and back again. She must constantly spin desperate stories about her products to retain loyal customers.

My dear father, Radio Banda, an unassuming and quiet observer of life, will be the last to notice any physical changes in my appearance. To begin with, he has a demanding clerical job at ShopRite in the Manda Hill Shopping Mall.

For this reason, my father is usually gone before daybreak to ensure he gets to work on time on the other side of town. Coupled with the distance between kamwala and Manda Hill, my father doesn't return home until after dark.

At the risk of sounding ungrateful, it devastates me to see how the cost of transport to and from my father's job grazes through his meagre salary. It's even more distressing to hear my mother callously admonish him over the same. *Radio Banda, that expensive bus fare can buy us nyama (meat). Stop wasting money!*

My mother would rather see my father walk hours to Manda Hill in worn-out shoes as long as the salary remained intact. She is very selective in how she views life. Often, she overlooks the small blessings, like how lucky we are that my father has a job in the first place.

Many men and husbands in our township are still unemployed and struggle to feed their families. If given half a chance, the distance would be the last thing on their minds. They would take anything, anywhere, just to put bread on their table and look after their families.

My parents never run out of things to bicker about, with my mother always as the *prosecutor* and my father as the *defendant*. But there is one matter that I know they have never been able to resolve. The problem, like an amoeba, is in constant flux—changing its shape and size depending on the day's stakes. The root cause, however, stays the same.

The most dangerous place any married man can be is between a no-nonsense, testy wife and a possessive mother who treats him like a husband. My parents' acrimonious financial troubles carry the added pressure of my father's ailing and widowed mother, my Grandma Khetiwe Banda.

My grandmother has been my father's *dependant* for as long as I can remember. And it doesn't matter how you look at it; the situation isn't about to lighten or change. It's not a mystery how this less-than-ideal arrangement is a fertile source of the theatrical spectacle on the home front—between the two women, it's more drama than my poor father can take. Run for cover!

As I lie in bed, I find myself lost in thought about money. How can I disentangle the fibre of our household money dynamics from my destiny as a young, unwed mother? A new mouth to feed is bound to give my father a heart attack—his paycheck won't *cut it*, hard as he might try.

Luckily, I hope to graduate in another year and a half. Bae promised to help me get a job through some of his father's dealership clients. The rich and famous of Lusaka all patronise Mr Michelo's business, and Andrew has most of them on speed dial. I'm amazed how many influential people, including government officials, recognise and greet him at restaurants and cafés.

But a quick reality check tells me Andrew's silence is a red flag. Given the odds stacked against me, I don't see how any such job opportunities will come my way. Unless Andrew reconsiders in my favour, it will take a miracle to see a turn of the tide in my circumstances.

I have always dreamt of an upgrade out of Kamwala. But that ambition, once a bright light in my future, has become an elusive flicker of wishful thinking. Still, the optimist I am, I can see the *silver lining* in this overbearing dark cloud.

I have hope that, given Andrew's mother's story about his birth, he will not turn his back on our baby. I'm sure Mrs Michelo will see that her son does the right thing, including marrying me. But how will Andrew see things my way when he won't even talk to me?

Bae's silence is one of the main reasons I've found it challenging to open up to anyone about my pregnancy. Afraid to blow my cover, I have avoided everyone who mattered, even though it has been as lonely and scary as hell.

But for how long can I go on like this? It means, apart from Andrew, no one knows about my condition. I have bottled everything inside me for so long—seriously, I'm about to explode.

Thank God for the silver lining in my dark cloud. As much as today is a rubbish Monday, and I'd prefer to continue hibernating, my girlfriends have convinced me to have lunch with them. The invitation and acceptance came after fourteen days of silence and no-shows on my part. We plan to meet at Rio for lunch at 13:00 hrs, so I must hit the road fast.

But I'm nervous and insecure about everything. Do I have something to wear that does not show my growing tummy? Come to think of it, my tummy looks bumpier than I would expect at nine weeks. A wide, flowy dress might be my best bet to help conceal the obvious. I'm not ready for the world to gawk at me and make their narrative of what is.

I take after my mother both in her good looks and medium height. The latter doesn't work in my favour. If I were taller, my tummy might show less. The front view doesn't give me away when I look in the mirror. But the side view looks suspect, though not too prominent. Just as well, it's only my girls— I'll come clean. They're my support system. But that's where it ends. Until I hear from Andrew, I won't tell anyone else.

I glance over at my tiny wardrobe and imagine what to wear. My so-called wardrobe, planted against the wall in the corner of my bedroom, was once a broom cupboard in a house where my mother worked as a cleaner. The tour of duty of her employers, a White South African family, had ended, and they were due to return to Cape Town. The family generously let my mother have some furniture and kitchenware—*we hit the jackpot.* It was more than we could have asked for; our first decent set of pots, cutlery, plates, a narrow broom cupboard, and my father's little prized portable radio. We all wept with joy.

The broom cupboard is now a valuable multi-purpose possession in my bedroom. Besides my old, tired, and creaky single bed, it's the most significant item. My scanty collection of cosmetics and hair products neatly occupies the upper section of the closet. The elongated and more spacious lower area houses my clothes.

For a young lady like me, it's hard to keep up with the fashion trends, let alone compete with the rich kids. I usually spend arduous hours rifling through asphyxiating bales of my mother's salaula in the market. It's the only way I can afford decent and fashionable outfits.

Sigh! The day will come—maybe when I have a ring on my finger. As Mrs Andrew Michelo, I can freely walk into a fancy boutique, select a beautiful brand-new dress, and pay for it at a formal checkout counter. Leaving such a boutique with a store-branded bag in my elegantly manicured hands would be exciting.

I swallow hard and flutter my eyelids to trap the tears that threaten to spill. If only I could control that narrative. My daydreaming will not change my circumstances nor get me dressed and out of the house on time for my lunch date with my girlfriends.

I steer my mind to what's before me and reach for something to wear. My Kamwala *Haut Couture* lies in little squares stacked together systematically in a neat pile. It resembles a tower of multi-coloured books in a nursery school library. I must be careful not to knock anything over, or my mother will throw a fit. She's such a neat freak.

The time on my phone shows 12:30; I must hurry or be late. Who knows how long it will take to find a taxi by the dusty roadside and in this unbearable heat? If I bail on my girlfriends today, they will lynch me. Besides, I have used every excuse in the book and know they have run out of patience.

The last thing I want is to have the three ladies show up unannounced at my parent's house and set my mother off. She will question why I haven't seen any of the girls for two weeks. The inevitable will then follow; my mother won't rest till she's had a satisfactory answer from me. So, as lousy as I feel, the better evil is for me to meet with my girls and face their music than my mother's probing.

Time to go—eish! The front door lock is such a nuisance. It has slowed me down, but I can hardly leave the house unsecured. Thieves from the neighbourhood had tampered with the lock in an attempted burglary last month.

My father has since ordered a new lock and a grill door to go with it from Mr Sujay Patel's hardware store on Cha-cha-cha Road. Mr Patel is my father's old boss and was kind enough to offer him an instalment plan. Otherwise, the scumbags will return to finish what they started.

Phew! There we go; finally, the door locks and I can get on with my plans. It's tough out by the roadside as I flag down every car, taxi or not. I figure it's best to have options in this weather from hell. But fifteen minutes later, I still have no paid or free ride. What is going on?

My dress feels like second skin as my pores give way to floods of sweat. Let's not go to the transformation of my shoes—they are unrecognisable under the thick film of grit.

Pregnancy nausea isn't giving me a break either. My hand flies to my face and clamps my mouth. The hot season is the worst time of the year to be pregnant. I struggle to control the tsunami of morning sickness brewing in my system.

OMG! *Lord, please do not let me vomit on the street.* I rifle through my little handbag, desperate for some chewing gum—it should help to quieten the storm in my belly.

Where are all the taxis today? My eyes dart in all directions as I silently pray for one to show up. Before despair can set in, a ray of hope appears on the horizon. Thank heavens, here comes one—it's my lucky day. As soon as it stops, I snatch the door handle and throw myself inside the car with such vigour that it rattles the driver.

"Eeee sista, take it eazeeh! Why do you want to break my door? Anyway, where to?"

"Hello, sorry. Levy Junction Shopping Mall, town centre, please."

The driver doesn't respond but studies me in his rearview mirror. How inappropriate—it makes me uncomfortable. I slide across closer to the door and out of his direct view. Gosh! It feels like a death trap inside the car. I vigorously fan my chest to let air down my dress.

"Do you have air conditioning?" I ask.

"Aa-ah, sista, you will pay a high price for air conditioning. It's not free of charge."

This idiot. "Not free of charge? What do you mean? Isn't it important to make your clients comfortable in your space?"

The driver is unmoved by my words.

"Sista, don't waste time. Where to, please?"

"I already told you, Levy Junction Shopping Mall; how much?"

The driver switches off the engine and extends his hand out to me. "Okay, my sista, 100 Kwacha, pay now before we go."

This dude. "What's going on?"

"Sista, I don't like to talk. Pay before I drive, olo (or) you can walk—it's a free country!" He rudely replies.

I swear this clown would treat me with more respect if I were a man. But I'm not about to argue with him, not in my condition.

"There's your 100 Kwacha, and please don't call me sista again; I am not your sister."

I wipe the sweat from my forehead with a piece of tissue. It leaves powder skid marks on my face, but who cares?

Chapter Four

WHY NOT DAVID?

I can't remember a time when I felt this unproductive at work. Even though it's a Monday and almost lunchtime, I haven't had the energy to chat with my colleagues or reach out to potential clients. Honestly, I'm surprised my father didn't chase after me when I *houdinied* out of his car this morning at lightning speed.

I started my day early at the office with a plan to stay late, all to keep my mind occupied and preserve my sanity. Unfortunately, that genius plan has knocked me sideways, and I can't switch off my brain—flashes of my complicated life keep running in a loop inside my cluttered mind.

To make matters worse, being unable to talk to anyone has messed with my head. Typically, my mother is the one I turn to when I need to confide in someone. But in this case, it just hasn't happened. How can I possibly bring myself to share such disheartening news with her? It would crush her.

At one time, I thought Auntie Francine might be a good substitute, but I can't expect her to keep secrets from her sister. If only Uncle Michael had been around, he could've helped me figure out the best way to approach my mother and deal with this whole mess. What a dilemma!

Since Dailess broke her unexpected news, I've had moments to reflect positively on our situation. But other times, the human in me has wallowed in bouts of self-pity when I have wished my misfortune on someone else. *Dear God, why me?* It's a selfish question, and you'd be right to say *why not you?*

But aren't some men better *wired* to deal with dodgy relationship issues than others? My mother and Auntie Francine call such men *Nyelas* or *Ba Kandile,* and I call them *Playas.* Whatever name you want to give them, when it comes to women, such men operate agendas driven by selfishness.

Playas have a particular skill in the deception department that, thankfully, I don't have. I also have zero head space for games. It takes too much energy to keep up with all the lies—which chick did I tell what or didn't? And don't get me started on the courage and mental strength it takes to handle relationship shenanigans. It's all too intimidating for me.

My childhood friend David Likezo is a playa and the perfect candidate for this type of wahala. David can wiggle himself out of any situation. For him, getting into trouble with women is like a game. So, I have asked God several times, *why not David?*

Circumstances reversed; the handsome devil would not lose any sleep over Dailess. In the first place, no chick would have the courage to approach David with any shady conversation regarding anything. Needless to add, my friend has never been in a relationship that has lasted more than three months.

David loves to boast about his conquests. *Bruv, it's called a situationship for a reason.* It's unbelievable how he can treat women's feelings as if they don't matter. Lusaka is not an impossibly large city, so it's not hard to imagine how frequently David has run-ins with his conquests. His *situationships* always overlap, and in the past, I have witnessed lots of nasty and public breakups. But, of course, the cheeky fool comes out of his silly *situationships* unscathed.

David, a wild spirit through and through, is one of my closest childhood buddies. Our parents went to the same Church, and even though we were from different social backgrounds, destiny had other plans. Our lives intersected, and as they say, *the rest is history.*

My friend grew up in Kalinga Linga, where he rolled with older guys who taught him how to *work* the streets and hook up with vulnerable women. Eventually, his widowed mother got tired of the grief and shame brought on by her son's *sinful* behaviour. Convinced that her son had sold his soul to the devil, she threw David out of their home.

Like a cat with nine lives, David landed on his feet with eight lives intact. He found a job in town at one of the travel agencies, where he works as an Office Orderly while studying part-time for a diploma in Travel and Tourism. The lucky fool now has a small house in Nyumba Yanga, but unfortunately, more hookups continue to happen.

As you can imagine, David has also failed to get on my mother's good side. She has never liked his ways. We all have that one childhood friend our parents detested—*if eyes could kill,* who knows what might have happened? Lol!

My mother thinks David is a bad influence on me, and she has blamed him for everything I did wrong growing up. She always feared that I might become like David if I continued to keep his company.

When I was growing up, as a young boy, my mother never hit me. But David is the reason for the one time she ever put her hands on me. Like all children, sometimes I tried to push boundaries with my parents. One day, when my mother was out shopping, I went behind her back and invited David to come and play and watch movies at our house.

When my mother returned home sooner than expected, she found David and me goofing around in the TV room. Oh, I remember how livid she was. My mother ran David out of the house like a little common thief. *Get out of my house, you sinful little scoundrel. If I ever see you back here again, I will set the dog on you!* To date, my poor friend, David, is not allowed anywhere near our house.

The main takeaway from this back story is that you understand that, unlike David, I am good to women. Perhaps too good to even see when they take me for a fool. But I do not know any other way to be. How do guys like David get away with all the horrific things they do to women? While good guys like me get *played* by women? What am I doing wrong?

I'm indeed a novice in the area of women and romance. I've only had two serious relationships—something my friend finds incredibly amusing. *Bruv, the problem with you is that you take these girls too seriously. Chicks are like buses; there is always one on the way.*

My first girlfriend was Maria Sosala, and Dailess is my second one. Although the situations differ, I strongly suspect my current and past relationship *wahala* come from the same cloth. When I think about what I'm going through, I can't help but conclude that there's a *déjà vu* element in it.

Maria and Dailess might be two women who happened in my life at different times. But they've both pulled a fast one that has left me confused, hurt, and suspicious of women. How do other young men find honest women they can trust?

In 2019, I met my first love, Maria Sosala—the love of my life. Or so I thought. I was nineteen and a virgin when I met her. She was ten years older than me and more sexually experienced than I was.

Maria was beautiful and tall, a fashionista with the body of a goddess, a smooth brown complexion, and a captivating smile. Polished and well-spoken, Maria was ready to conquer the world, and my nineteen-year-old mind was ever so impressed with her.

David, being the wiser one, was less impressed than I was. He tried to raise red flags about Maria many times. *Bruv, this chick is a scam, trust me. I'm a scam, so I know one when I see one. Just look at all her window dressing.* Really? I couldn't believe this was my homie talking trash about my girl. *Window dressing?* That's just mean and disrespectful; I fumed at the time.

Back then, the slightest criticism of Maria was all it took to set me off. It led to many heated disagreements between David and me. How dare he? Maria could do no wrong in my eyes. I was a young man in love and would let nothing come between Maria and me.

Intoxicated with love, I was on a mission to plan a future with Maria. I convinced myself I would marry her one day when I had a good-paying job.

So, I wanted my mother to meet Maria and approve of her. I tried to plan the best time for the grand introduction every waking moment. A part of me was apprehensive that my mother would disapprove of the ten-year age gap between Maria and me.

I had run out of options when my mother told me she wanted to have a big fiftieth birthday celebration with family and friends. Bingo! There was my opening, and I grabbed it. Elated, I invited Maria to my mother's lavishly planned fiftieth birthday party amid David's protests.

Bruv, this is the biggest mistake of your life. How can you invite that chick to your mum's shindig? Trust me, that snake is a scandal on two legs! But I didn't heed David's words—I was eager for my parents to meet and accept Maria as my future wife.

With so many guests and everyone celebrating, I thought it would take the pressure off the introduction. It was a party; there'd be no time for prolonged conversations between my parents and Maria. Cunningly, it meant the age gap wouldn't come up. And if it did in the future, it would be after they had already accepted her.

On the night of the party, my parents' guests turned up dressed to the nines. The evening was a whole mood—with high energy as elegant ball gowns of all colours and designs floated around the room.

My mother's girlfriends had never looked so stunning. It was like witnessing a Haute Couture Fashion Show at Paris Fashion Week. Plumes of various fragrances filled the air! Lusaka had transformed into Tinsel town—simply magical.

As for the male guests, it was like *Mr James Bond* had undoubtedly come to town. The men complemented their partners perfectly, dressed in tailor-made dinner suits, crisp white shirts, and bow ties. Engulfed in the *on-top-of-the-world* vibe, everyone, a movie star in their world, took pictures on the red carpet.

As for the food, my mother outperformed herself. She hired the most talked about new chef in town, *Jean-Marc of Les Étangs*, a French outside catering company. His food was exquisite—creatively prepared in a mouth-watering five-course *degustation menu*. Jean-Marc tantalised the guests and teleported them to the fine dining restaurants on the streets of Champs-Elysées in Paris.

Outside in the garden, Jean-Marc's team had set up a luxurious and stylish outdoor bar stocked with every drink under the sun. My mother's favourite Veuve Clicquot champagne flowed non-stop and sent the party off with a bang!

What could go wrong, right?

Maria arrived late to the party. My father had just finished making an uncharacteristically sentimental toast to my mother. There was massive applause, the glasses clinked, and everyone shouted cheers!

My turn to give a speech was coming up next. Halfway to the front of the room, Ba Bwezani intercepted me and said someone was there to see me. Yes! Maria. I could not believe she had finally arrived. I enthusiastically thanked Ba Bwezani, punched the air, and gave him a friendly slap on his back.

At that moment, I forgot about my mother's toast. Anxious to find Maria, I squeezed past the guests, dodged their raised alcohol glasses, and bolted to the gate. I couldn't get there fast enough.

And there she was! What a beauty, and she was all mine. Sweet! Finally, the two women in my life would meet.

"Hey Maria, you are here! Thank God, I thought you had stood me up," I kissed her on the cheek, my mouth upturned into a big, welcome smile.

"Oh no, not a chance. I had to wait for the delivery of my new wig," Maria explained. "Then, I needed someone to install it for me. It took longer than usual,"

"Well, you look beautiful."

I proudly took Maria's hand and headed back to the party. The guests filled the house with laughter and good cheer—they moved and grooved to the DJay's exciting selection of eighties and nineties disco tracks.

Lionel Richie's *Dancing on the Ceiling* had everyone bopping away, all their troubles forgotten. As for me, there was no better feeling than having Maria by my side; *Dancing on the Ceiling* was an understatement.

I guided Maria through the merrymakers. "Let's find my mother."

We checked inside the house but couldn't find her. So, I figured she might be with other guests in the garden where ten round tables *polka dotted* the area. Perched on each table were Ba Bwezani's stunning flower arrangements as centrepieces.

A *bee colony* of Jean-Marc's catering team efficiently weaved in and out and served food and drinks. Everything was going according to my mother's plan.

I smiled at Maria and squeezed her hand. "Oh, look, there she is!" I waved at my mother and motioned her towards Maria and me.

"Mummy, Maria's here!"

Within a second, before I could understand what was happening, the whole garden spun on its head in a shocking revelation. Eish! My entire plan for the two women to meet went up into smoke.

As we walked towards my mother, a splash of liquid suddenly hit Maria's face, stinging her eyes. She screamed and frantically wiped her eyes. Her false eyelashes partially came unglued and hung from the corners of her eyes like giant poisonous black spiders. Angry tears and mascara ran down Maria's face.

"What the f**k just happened?" She screamed.

I protectively thrust my arm in the direction the liquid came from.

"Hey, watch it!" I yelled. But it was still not clear who the assailant was. The horror of what came next is something that, to date, I am still reeling from.

Out of the blue, Auntie Wendy, one of my mother's BFFs, suddenly appeared behind me. Her lips contorted into a vicious scowl, and her eyes bulged out of their sockets like broken car headlights; Auntie Wendy lunged forward. I had never seen this side of my mother's friend before—it was shocking and frightening.

Auntie Wendy threw another drink at Maria and hauled nasty insults at her in the most embarrassing fashion. Why would she attack my girlfriend? What's the connection between the two? It can only be a case of mistaken identity, I rationalised. I wormed myself between the two women to try and referee.

"Auntie, please calm down. You might regret acting in haste."

"Get out of the way, sonny; you do not know what you're talking about."

I could no longer recognise my sweet Auntie Wendy. She had become an unstoppable bull at the *Spanish Running of the Bulls* event in Pamplona. Eish! There was no time to think or talk. Auntie Wendy, now a wild animal in full attack mode, yanked Maria's new wig off her head.

"Who brought this prostitute here?" She fumed, nostrils flaring.

"I'm not a prostitute, you stupid woman!" Maria screamed.

Hands flew about, clawing at everything, and legs kicked out in all directions. The two women were entangled in a furious brawl and didn't give a toss about what anyone thought. I cringed when bare skin started to show as pieces of fabric scattered on the ground.

I panicked, trying to find ways to keep the two women apart. But breaking the momentum in this catastrophic feline fight was impossible, and help was nowhere in sight. The music was so loud that this undignified scuffle continued with little disruption to the party.

I looked for my mother again, hoping she could reason with Auntie Wendy. But strangely enough, my mother had mysteriously disappeared from the garden. Where did she go?

Desperate to get someone else, I tapped a few guests on the shoulders for help. But no one wanted to get involved. The men pretended not to hear me while the look in their wives' eyes said: *don't you dare!*

I spotted Uncle Justin, Honourable Kandolo, from the corner of my eye. Yes! Finally, I can get help. If anyone could stop the fight, it was him.

"Uncle Justin, please come quickly!" I yelled at the top of my lungs.

Much to my horror, Uncle Justin ignored me. He, instead, gingerly sauntered from the garden into the house. What was that about? Honourable Justin Kandolo is Auntie Wendy's husband; why would he leave his wife outside in a fight with a stranger? You can't imagine my confusion.

My mind switched gears and went into high speed as I quickly tried to work out the math. Oh no, could Maria have something to do with Uncle Justin? I thought as my heart threatened to stop.

Meanwhile, unwilling to back down, spit was flying out of Auntie Wendy's mouth.

"It's stupid prostitutes, *vimahule,* like you that are *finishing* people's marriages in Lusaka!"

Maria panted wildly. "Whose marriage have I *finished?* Yours? Are you the only one in Lusaka who doesn't know your marriage is over? You stupid old fat *has been!*"

Stung by those words, Auntie Wendy became unstoppable and went for Maria's jugular vein. She ferociously threw her onto the ground and pinned the poor girl down. The heavy blows that *rained* on my girlfriend's face were enough to rearrange her features.

I curiously watched the two women as they continued their mutual *attempted murder* boxing match. It heightened my quest for answers, and my whys and hows became more urgent. The penny never too far finally dropped, setting my mental *rewind button* in motion.

What the hell! The floodgates of my mind opened as flashes of my relationship with Maria gushed past my mind's eye. I clutched my chest as everything unravelled. My temples throbbed with panic and frustration. It hit me then; David had been right all along. *The designer handbags, the beautiful outfits, matching shoes, glue-less Brazilian hair wigs*—you name it. Maria had it all!

How could my girlfriend afford all this expensive stuff? I know that I didn't pay for it. I had only bought an iPad for Maria, which I paid for in twelve instalments. I recall how proud I felt then, happy to have bought her something special. Looking back now, she and her friends must have laughed at me for days. How stupidly naïve could I have been?

Maria, *Miss Sneaky of the Year*, had always defended her bougie lifestyle. She feigned hard work and determination, buying and selling clothes and perfumes. But Maria also travelled to expensive holiday resorts, places I could only dream of. Finally, the truth had come to light—Uncle Justin was the man behind everything material that I admired about Maria.

So, what did I do about it? I did what any *young man scorned* would do. I vengefully watched Auntie Wendy give Maria the whopping of her life. In my eyes, Maria had lost all the dignity she might have pretended to have had. How could she do this to me?

"Andrew, don't just stand there! Stop this ugly old woman from destroying my dress!" Maria screamed.

I did nothing to help. So, Auntie Wendy ripped Maria's shocking pink mini dress and reduced it to the size of a tank top. Luckily, Maria had black cycling shorts underneath the dress—her saving grace.

"If you ever dare go to my husband's office again, I'll kill you with my bare hands," Auntie Wendy panted.

Finally, Ba Bwezani, thoroughly confused, arrived in time to do what no one was willing to do—he *peeled* Auntie Wendy off of Maria.

"Bwana Andrew, what is happening?"

"Ah, boss, it is a long story. Please escort Maria out onto the street. I never want to see her here—never let her through the gates again."

That was the last time I had anything to do with Maria. Looking back, though, I had no business loving a woman like her. David was spot on.

Fast forward to today. I am in my second relationship with Dailess. Or perhaps I should say I'm in a dying relationship with Dailess. David warned me about her, too, and I don't know how to get past our issues.

I like Dailess—I might even love her. I thought our relationship had potential until she catapulted us into a whirlpool of problems—to which neither of us have answers. I don't know what she was thinking, but we are now in this mess, trying to stay afloat.

Dailess asked to meet me to talk about something important and couldn't do it over the phone. In my mind, I imagined she might be ill or something along those lines. I had a whole supportive speech prepared, only to get a rude awakening.

Dailess didn't have a life-threatening disease—she was eight weeks pregnant! The ground shifted the minute she told me the news. I didn't understand how Dailess could get pregnant when we used protection, and she was on the pill.

After a long time of coaxing, Dailess eventually told me that the condom had broken. I don't know about other guys, but shouldn't it be evident to a man when a condom breaks? But, also, to my horror, she confessed to not taking the pill, as agreed, which meant I was f**ked—period.

When I look back at that day, I feel cheated. How could Dailess arm-wrestle me into fatherhood? Even if the condom broke, as she explained, shouldn't I have been part of the problem-solving or otherwise? Women like to talk about the benefits of communication and forget that it goes two ways.

There's also the question of the scholarship. My mother has big plans for my future. I can't give it all up and play happy families with Dailess and an unplanned baby. Where would I take them? How could she not have thought things through? My mother will kill me.

I wish I could tell David what's happened, but I have not yet gotten my head around the news to begin sharing it with anyone. David would know what to do and how to get to the other side without trouble. He understands the ghosts from my past and what Maria's lies did to me. The insecurities, trust issues, and low self-esteem that came out of that situation are something I don't want to face again. *So, Lord, why not David? If not David, then give me his strength to face my troubles.*

Chapter Five

MY-RIDE-OR-DIE SISTAS

Flustered and sweaty, I arrive at Levy Junction Shopping Mall just in time, glad to have escaped the taxi and its ill-mannered driver. Outside the restaurant Rio, I try to imagine what I might eat. I've had no appetite except for cornflakes and peanut butter—I don't imagine Rio serves that. Sigh!

Why do I feel so nervous? Do I look the same or different? Thank God for the glass doors; I can check myself out before I enter. I quickly adjust my wig, apply a fresh coat of lip gloss and straighten my dress as chunks of fabric wiggle up to my thighs. I hate that I've gained a few pounds.

The air conditioning breeze in Rio is a lifesaver. I'm incredibly thankful for the coolness of the fresh air that softly caresses my face and arms. It leaves a trail of tiny goosebumps with the sudden temperature change and gives me a slight chill. I didn't think of it, but I should've brought a light scarf.

OMG, you've got to love Rio—it's the best restaurant & bar and the hottest new place in town. This afternoon, it's a whole mood! It has the best kind of feel-good music vibe.

As I step into the main reception area, Afro-Cuban jazz music greets me; I smile and relax—just for a moment, my growing belly and Andrew aren't the focus of my miserable thoughts. Seriously, what's there not to like about this place? After weeks of feeling rubbish, I needed this precise *pick-me-up* medicine.

The place is *lit!* I love the combination of music, friendly faces, laughter, long-time-no-sees, high fives, fist pumps, and celebratory toasts—this joint is good for my soul. The who's who of Lusaka and plenty of other young folks are all in on it. I recognise some chicks and wave at them as they chat and sip their delicious cocktails and mocktails.

The atmosphere seems right for young professionals as well. The city has taken *working from remote* to a whole new level post-pandemic. IPads and laptops are open on every other table as everyone tries to earn their bread. It's the new normal, I guess.

My girlfriends, tucked away in the far corner at our usual table, appear animated as they babble away with their heads close together. It could be my guilt that's got my mind out of control, but I wonder if all that chinwagging amongst them isn't about me.

My friendship with them is about to be tested—I wouldn't blame them if they chose to have nothing to do with me. I have played *hide and seek* with them for two weeks without a decent explanation.

We all have insecurities, even in the best of friendships. The fear of rejection has been my main concern. What if my friends thought less of me and chose to distance themselves because of my condition? I love these girls with all my heart—they are my *ride-or-die-till-the-wheels-fall-off* sisters.

But lately, my emotions have been all over the place. If my girls were to dump me like Andrew, I swear, I'd jump off the roof of one of the tallest office buildings in town—FINDECO house.

Finally, my girlfriends look up and see me approach. I wave at them with an enthusiastic smile on my face. But I crumble inside. "Hi there, wassup!"

All three of them smile and wave back. If they said anything in response, I didn't hear it. Perhaps I'm too far from their table. But they smiled; does that mean I'm off the hook for my disappearance? And here we are about to have lunch together; it must mean we're good. I'll take comfort from that and confidently walk over to them. What's the worst that can happen?

Hold on; something's up with the table situation. What's with the narrow spacing? Did the staff add extra chairs to the tables? Gliding through has always been easy, but now I must *shimmy sideways*. And, of course, my Zambian version of a Brazillian *derrière*, thanks to Eastern Province and Zulu blood, isn't helpful in such tight spaces.

An angry voice rings across the room. "Oh no, you didn't! Watch where you're going to, stupid cow!"

Oops! Did I squeeze past too snugly against someone's head? My bad—but d**n of all people! Did it have to be the head of Andrew's ex-girlfriend, the legendary Maria Sosala? Just my luck.

"I'm sorry, why so rude," I respond.

Maria turns around, rolls her eyes at me in disdain, and then throws me the dirtiest look she can muster.

"Next time, go to the gym before you show up at places like Rio with that fake butt of yours."

"Excuse me; I did not mean to brush against your head with my not-so-fake butt," I retort.

"I'm surprised people like you can afford Rio," Maria continues, trying to push my buttons.

"Yes, Maria, yet *people like me* got the guy."

"*Maria?* So, you know my name?" She cackles and turns to speak to her friends. "Guys, this *downgrade* is Andrew's new chick." There are shrieks of laughter from her table.

"Again, yet Andrew chose this *downgrade* over an old prostitute like you," I clap back. I then proudly shake what *my mama gave me* in Maria's face. Foolish woman!

Phew! Finally, I'm at our table. My usual mouth-watering Rebujito awaits, chilled and delicious. *Lord help me*; the thought of the lemon splash in it is enough to make me sin. This new baby mama life is a *killjoy*—alcohol is off the table for the next seven months. I'll have to drink my Rebujito with my eyes until after delivery.

I'm pleased to see the girls—I pray that my chirpy energy is contagious.

"Hey, ladies!" I force a wide smile.

"Hey, stranger," they respond, their voices low and detached.

"Ouch, I guess I deserve that."

The girls aren't impressed with me. Sally Katongo, a *dog with a bone,* is the first to attack.

"If it isn't her Majesty herself." Sally gives me a sardonic gaze.

"What's with the shoddy treatment?" I bite my tongue lest I fall into the trap of an equally condescending response.

My friend Sally got an A plus in the looks department, and she knows it. For that reason and more, Sally thinks the world revolves around her. She reminds me of my mother. Every agenda is about her, no matter what else is happening around her or who gets hurt. So, I'm not surprised by her attitude.

Sally and I grew up together in Kamwala. Her mother, Mrs Zondiwe Katongo, née Moyo, and my mother are best friends from their High School days. Joined at the hip, our mothers now have side-by-side market stalls and are members of the same Church.

Given our mothers' history, Sally and I became best friends. We went to the same primary and secondary schools, set on our mothers' paths, with one exception. We chose different careers—Sally is pursuing a Nursing course at Zambia University Teaching Hospital.

Carol Masaiti comes to my rescue before Sally can rip off my head.

"Sally, let the poor girl sit down before you show your claws."

"Thank you, Carol, for standing in my corner," I say, giving Sally the eye.

Carol gives me a big hug and kisses me on the cheek.

"Bonjour, Chérie. How are you? We've missed you, girl."

My heart melts in Carol's long embrace.

"Hi, sis; it's so good to see you," I respond, relieved to hear someone missed me.

Carol is the oldest in the sister group, with a six-year age gap. She is the level-headed, sweetest, and most diplomatic of my friends. In a good way, Carol doesn't pry unless you specifically seek her opinion. Steadfast and sincere, I am grateful for her friendship—she's the big sister I never had.

Although Carol is only twenty-five, she has endured the life experiences of a fifty-year-old woman. At sixteen and still a virgin, her mother and greedy stepfather *sold* her to a fifty-five-year-old maize and cassava trader, Kitenge Tshisekedi, from the Democratic Republic of Congo—DRC.

Kitenge took the sixteen-year-old Carol back to the DRC, where she discovered the oppressive life of being one of four wives. Unable to live a typical young adult's life or continue her education, Carol broke in ways that can take a lifetime to mend. She fell into a depression, which left deep scars that carry raw wounds underneath the scabs.

Four devastating years later, Carol, who fortunately did not have any children with Kitenge, managed to escape the DRC and return to Zambia with the help of her father's family. Fluent in French, she now works at the Alliance Française de Lusaka.

Bridget Monze, the fourth sister in our group, looks disinterested in my presence.

"Finally, you show up!" She forcefully tugs at the hem of my dress and almost knocks me over. "You must think very little of us.".

I open my mouth to respond, but Bridget cuts me short and shows me her hand.

"Oh please, sit down, Dailess—you aren't a Princess."

"You can at least say hello." I put my foot down. "Why the rush to *crucify* me?"

Bridget dismisses me with her hand.

"You'd better have a good excuse, my friend."

Bridget is my *bully* sister, who has meddled in my business for as long as I can remember. For the first time, I dared to lay boundaries and chose not to seek her support the last two weeks—she isn't a happy bunny.

Fate brought Bridget and me together at Evelyn Hone College, where she became my instant protector. When I could not stand up for myself, which was all the time, she fought my battles. One time, before I met Andrew, Bridget beat up my boyfriend, Charles, for the scumbag that he was.

College food being what it is, a good meal is the one thought that's always on students' minds. One evening, I bought some takeaway sausage rolls from town for Charles, which I thought was a loving and caring gesture. As one can expect, Bridget and I assumed Charles would appreciate the surprise. And a big surprise it was, but just not as pleasant.

My stomach dropped when Bridget and I entered Charles' dorm room. Romping away in bed was Charles and some random chick. A *hule*—whore, from the nearby streets of Addis Ababa Drive. The two lovers went into a frenzy of futile efforts to cover their naked bodies when they saw us. Their private moment was no longer a secret but a public spectacle.

Did Charles and his hule get more than sausage rolls that night? Let me tell you. The gangsta in Bridget was out of its cage, and there was no stopping her. She grabbed the *hule* by her *had-seen-better-days* braids and dragged her naked body out of the room into the hallway. A mob of college students soon gathered to jeer and poke fun at her—a punishment that might have been excessive when I look back and possibly against the law.

Satisfied with Part A of her mission, Bridget pounced onto Part B and ripped into Charles like a wild cat. The idiot was no match for her, too disadvantaged by his guilt and birth suit to fight back. I shudder at the memory of that crazy night. Eish!

The atmosphere is tense at our table. I'm unsure how to open up to the girls, but the only *currency* for my olive branch is to *lay my cards* on the table, however imperfect they may be. I take my sweet time settling down while I give the impression of calm and control. But inside my head, I'm a scared little girl. When does the torture end?

"Wassup, ladies! I've missed you."

"Dailess, stop it; no more games." Bridget can't hold her tongue. "S*pill the tea*—what's with your new *shady* behaviour?"

I ignore Bridget's rant and address the waiting staff, Kennedy. "One Fanta, please, with lots of ice."

The ladies exchange puzzled looks. "Fanta?"

"Dailess, is the Rebujito I ordered for you going to drink itself? Sally is quick to issue an ultimatum. "Don't you dare waste my money, or you'll have to pay me back!

"There goes *Shylock;* she never disappoints," Carols says, tongue in cheek.

Sally isn't amused, while Bridget's in hysterics.

Kennedy takes our food order—as I hand the menu card back to him, my hand trembles. The girls stare at me, their eyes full of questions. I am grateful that none of them says anything. Yet, at the back of my mind, I know their silence is a sign of unease—they can't figure out what has come over me.

The desperation to get the weight of my issues off my chest is mounting—the fetus inside me, Andrew's *stonewalling*, my mother's impending wrath, and my bleak future, I can't bear it anymore. It's all too heavy to carry on my own. I squeeze my eyes and prepare my thoughts for what I'll say. In the end, I blurt it out without warning.

"Guys, Andrew is *ghosting* me!"

"Fancy a pot calling a kettle black." Sally raises her hand. "What do you call your behaviour? Girl, please!"

"Enough, Sally, give it a rest!" I raise my voice. "Why is any of this about you?"

"Is he cheating on you?" Bridget, on the far end of the spectrum, thumps her left palm with her right fist.

I rush to set the record straight. "No, Bridget, it's not like that."

"I'd happily chat with Andrew or *rearrange* his face for you." Bridget is relentless.

"Please, Bridget, let's not have history repeat itself here, no violence," I caution her.

"Chérie, you and Andrew are so tight." Carol looks me in the eyes. "What do you mean *ghosting* you?"

A wave of emotion washes over me. How did I get here? There's no way to explain where life has got me without anyone questioning my judgment. Sally and Bridget are two crazy *ninjas;* I must ride on Carol's empathy and take the plunge.

"I'm pregnant."

Silence, no reaction—*wonders never cease.* I didn't know these women had it in them to be quiet. I'm confused. I lean forward and whisper.

"Ladies, didn't you hear me?" I raise my voice. "I said I'm pregnant."

There's a loud gasp from all three of them. Without warning, like in an exorcism session gone rogue, tongues become loose, and demons are out on the prowl. The pandemonium of questions that follows is enough to stop the restaurant for a few seconds. Other diners, including Maria Sosala, stare at us and wonder about the kefuffle.

"Please keep your voices down!" I hiss at the girls. "I don't want the whole of Lusaka in my business."

"Dailess, what the f**k is this?" Sally is incredulous. "You cut me off to play happy families with Andrew?" She boomerangs my problem and misses my point entirely.

"Is that what you heard me say?" I'm tired of Sally's self-centred theatrics. "Nothing in this equation is about you!"

"How did you get pregnant? You've only known Andrew for three months," Bridget sounds suspicious. "Besides, aren't you supposed to be on the pill?"

"Give Dailess a chance to explain!" Carol shuts her up.

"I don't know." I close my eyes and shake my head. It was just once that I forgot to take the pill."

"Chérie, don't tell me you've been having unprotected sex?" There's dread in Carol's eyes. "Look at me, at twenty-five; I've been living with HIV since I was sixteen. It's a prison sentence."

"No, the condom broke." I cast my eyes down, ashamed of myself.

"Hold up, Dailess, that's bulls**t. Bridget confirms her suspicions. "How does a condom break, and neither you nor Andrew realised it?"

"That's because ever since she met her *Prince Charming*, Dailess has had her eyes set on Kabulonga!" The loathing is now crystal clear in Sally's voice. "Why don't you just stick to our kind in Kamwala like the rest of us?"

"Oh, I know you, Sally; if Andrew were to *cough* in your direction for a second, you'd *fill the earth* with a million offspring." The gloves are off. "Face it; you've always been arrogant enough to think every man will choose you over me. You, the so-called beautiful one!"

Carol reaches for my hand. "Chérie, calm down; let's return to what's important."

I hyperventilate. "This is why I've kept this news to myself!"

"*Whatever*—is loverboy ready for a forced baby daddy role?" There's no way to stop Sally now that her knife in my back has found a weak spot. "There goes your future down the toilet—bam, gone, poof!"

Sally might as well flush me down the toilet together with my future. In times like this, the true colours of the company you keep start to show. Sally's words have pushed me so far into the corner I don't have the strength for a *comeback*.

Luckily, Kennedy soon returns with two trays of our food order. He saves me from Sally's smug face just in time.

"Ladies, here's everything—one plate of..."

"Does it look like we want to eat?" Bridget bulges her eyes and rudely cuts Kennedy off midsentence. "Go away!"

Kennedy jumps backwards and almost drops the trays. "Ah-ah, madam, is this not your order?"

"Tone your voice down, Bridget." Carol reigns her in. "How's it the man's fault that we find ourselves in this situation?"

"It's not our fault either." Sally folds her arms. "I didn't sign up for this baby mama and forced baby daddy wahala."

"I am sorry, sir." Carol takes a deep breath before she speaks. "Please pack everything for *takeaway*— I'll sort out the bill shortly."

Frustrated, Kennedy shakes his head and walks away without saying another word.

Meanwhile, I've lost the battle to turn off the waterworks. Hot tears run down my face into the collar of my balloon dress. Not a pretty sight at all. But at this point, I couldn't care less. Maria Sosala can help herself to a picture and post it on social media.

"Dailess, ma Chérie, how far along are you?" Carol gently asks.

"About nine weeks now," I whimper as I wallow in self-pity and shame.

"I still don't get the sneaky part in all this—Dailess, you must think we are stupid?" Sally complains.

I can't believe *Miss Thang*. One minute, she's not interested or sympathetic; the next, she wants a *front-row seat* in my life.

"Sally, I haven't even told my mother—you, if anyone, should know why not."

"Tell me something, does Andrew know about any of this and is ghosting you?" Bridget brings up questions I buried back to the surface. "Or he doesn't know but has dumped you?"

"It's complicated—I don't know the answer myself; what can I say?" I respond in between tearful sniffles.

"It's a simple question, Dailess." Sally stokes the fire. "What's the story?"

"Ladies, show some kindness," Carol takes control. "Andrew has been incommunicado. What's there not to understand?"

"Give me his number now." Bridget hisses and clenches her jaw. "I am going to kill someone today!" Without warning, she reaches out and grabs my phone.

Too exhausted to resist, I let her have it. Bridget craftily unlocks my phone. Of course, she has the passcode. *Note to self*: Change the passcode and set some boundaries from now on. Before anyone could stop her, Bridget punches Andrew's number into her phone keypad.

"Andrew will pick up my call with an unknown caller ID," Bridget says, pleased with her strategy. "He'll think I am a client."

Carol tries to stop her. "*Hold your horses*; we've just found out Dailess is pregnant. Let's think this through—we need to strategise."

"Dailess has no game plan." Bridget glares at Carol. "And frankly, neither do you."

"Yes, Dailess, what's the plan?" Sally jumps on the bandwagon. "Will you keep the baby or have an abortion?"

Harsh—way below the belt, it can't get any lower. When such wicked words come out of the mouth of your childhood friend, your heart shatters into a thousand pieces. Time might allow it to mend, but you never forget it.

Ever since I met Andrew, Sally and I have had a weird undercurrent between us. The friendship hasn't been the same. I've had suspicions, but judging by her snide remarks and general unkindness, I now know my friendship with Sally will never be the same again.

"Don't listen to her, Chérie." Carol comforts me, appalled. "Whatever you want to do, we shall all support you."

"Sally, I know you think you are better than me," I respond and look her in her eyes. "But I'll keep my baby, whether you approve or you don't."

"It sounds like I must whip your baby daddy into shape," Bridget says, her menacing eyes widening.

"I agree; Andrew can't distance himself from this." Carol jumps on board Bridget's idea. "It takes two to tangle. Why isn't he looking for answers together with you?"

"That part!" Bridget claps and rubs her hands together. "Bruv must fess up to his mess."

"Chérie, too much time has passed with no word from Andrew." Carol's expression is pensive, though not with judgement. "If you don't hear from him by midday tomorrow, we must devise an intervention plan." She looks at each of us intently to ensure we are all on the same page.

"In the meantime, here's *plan A*. Bridget, call Andrew and ask him to meet us on Friday at 18:30," Carol suggests.

"If Andrew fails to show up on Friday, we must move on to *plan B*, which may or may not be for the faint-hearted," Bridget threatens.

I love my friend, but sometimes, I wonder whether we know everything about her past. As usual, it is no use arguing with her once she disappears into the wild corners of her mind. Thankfully, Carol wisely steers the discussion in a safer direction.

"Chérie, whether Andrew is on board or not, you must tell your parents. They have the right to know what is happening with their daughter."

"My mother needs to know, too." Sally tries to guilt-trip me. "Remember, she's like your second mother, Dailess."

I choose not to validate Sally's point. "Okay, Bridget, I'll call you by midday tomorrow to let you know what's up."

"I could also just show up at Andrew's office and wring his loser neck," Bridget goes off on a tangent, contrary to what we'd just agreed upon.

"That's not the plan." Carol is frustrated with Bridget's lack of focus. "Are you listening to yourself?"

"Please, I appreciate your support, but let's keep Mr Michelo's offices off-limit." I can't have Bridget jeopardise my future. "That's not Andrew's property."

"Okay, I hear you," Bridget grudgingly responds.

"And Chérie, don't contact Andrew at all. Wait to meet him here on Friday, understood?"

Sally starts to say something.

"No, you've said enough." Carol puts a stop to Sally's whiney nonsense. "Let's sort out the bill and return to work now."

Not entirely convinced about the plan, Bridget says bye and leaves the restaurant.

"Would you like to share a taxi?" Sally asks quietly.

"Why not?" I'll bet this is a part of her plot to dig deeper. But I let it go. "Thanks, Sally; I'm happy to save some money."

The ride back to Kamwala is weird and mostly quiet. Sally makes a few attempts to get me to talk about Andrew. But I refuse to give her more information; I pretend that nausea has gotten the better of me and prefer not to talk.

I lean back into the dusty back seat of the taxi. My heart is heavy from the lunch date with all three sisters—their spoken and unspoken words linger in a way I've never felt before. All of it combined unveils the hidden truths beneath the surface that can strengthen or weaken my bond with each of them.

Bridget's unwavering loyalty is undeniable, yet I can't ignore that her support might not align with what I need. The last thing I want is to bring physical harm to Andrew.

Carol brings me comfort—she has seen more life than I can describe. The looming prospect of my sudden motherhood doesn't faze her. She has the heart and strength to stand by me through whatever lies ahead.

Sadly, Sally worries me the most, even after many years of friendship. Tucked away behind the façade of closeness lies a fierce competitiveness in which she'll do anything to ensure that she emerges the winner—all the time. Something in my gut tells me to watch my step with Sally. What future betrayal does she have up her sleeve?

Chapter Six

IT'S NOT A SOCIAL CALL

Oh my! I can't believe it's Wednesday already. It has been super busy with clients at the office—we closed two deals in forty-eight hours. A miracle that seldom happens. Typically, our clients take their time—they run back and forth with queries before we can *nail* the deal. I can say with relief that work has given me respite from my Dailess issues, which I have failed to erase. Between customers test-driving cars and crunching numbers to suit their budgets, my mind has been too busy to wander off to anything else.

Fortunately, for some reason, Dailess hasn't called me in the last couple of days; she might have realised that her phone calls were one step away from sending me over the edge. I need time—I hope she now gets that I'm not ready to talk, knock on wood.

I'm mad that Dailess didn't consult me in her sneaky *family planning plot*. Did she plan the pregnancy? I'm confused; if the condom broke and Dailess knew it, why didn't she say anything? I can't get past this story; it just doesn't track.

What's uncanny is that my mother has also backed off and hasn't said a word since Monday morning. It's unlike her to give up on me without beating an answer out of me. My mother lives for me; our relationship comes first in everything she does.

When I was a little boy, she protected me from real or perceived harm—wicked teachers, bullies, nasty family members, etc. My mother once threatened my seventh-grade Teacher for making me cry. *I will take you and the entire Ministry of Education down!* Hmmnn, should I worry or be grateful that her questions have stopped?

The morning has gone by quickly; I've had to review our numbers to ensure we meet our target for this year. It's a good outlook. My old man will be chuffed, and I'm super excited.

I've locked in my Christmas bonus! It will help fatten my savings for my January trip to London now that I have my formal scholarship offer. Although I have the financial backing of my parents for the first academic year, I must arrive with enough cash to minimise the pressure of desperate part-time job hunting.

The scholarship offer is another thing I have hidden from my mother, even though I got the good news last Friday. I'm surprised Auntie Francine hasn't called to inform her sister or me. I wish I didn't have to lie to my parents, but what must I do, with everything tangled up in stressful, tight little knots in my head? Honestly, what news gets to go first? The Scholarship or Dailess?

Imagine this scenario: *Hi, Mummy, you and Dad will be grandparents soon.* And then I'd add: *by the way, I also have great news. I got the scholarship! But guess what? You two will be parents to my baby while I am in England getting an education.* D**n, even I don't want to be my parents in this s**t storm; it's a messed-up situation that can do one's head in.

There's a knock at the door; Jordan Kaonde's voice yanks me back to earth.

"Hey, bruv."

I snap into a relaxed pose. "Hey, wassup man?".

Jordan is a hardworking recent addition to my team, the *first to arrive and the last to leave the office* kind of employee. I like him, but he's too much of an apple polisher for comfort. You should hear my father speak of Jordan—he'd adopt the guy if he had his way.

Jordan walks over to my desk. "We missed you on Monday night for the chess game as planned." He considers me for a few minutes. "Everything okay with you, bruv?"

I scramble for a lie. "Ha, ha, my bad, bruv. I had to help my queen check on Grandma, who hasn't been well the past few days."

"I hear you, sorry, man. Keeping your priorities straight is good—we can always play chess another night."

"That's my queen's mother." I worry that Jordan's *goody-goody* nature might lead him to say something to my father, so I try to get in front of the problem. "By the way, my old man isn't in the loop of this information...his blood pressure, etc., you know the drill. We want to protect him."

My long-winded explanation sounds suspect; Jordan raises his brow but doesn't get into it.

"Again, I am sorry to hear, bruv, and of course, protecting our parents is important."

"Thanks, bruv; it's time to grab a bite. I'll catch you later."

I usher Jordan out of my office. That's another person I've just lied to; the list is growing. I can't keep track of this web of senseless tales—*what I said to whom, where, when, and why* is a game I prefer not to play; it's not who I am. I never like it when people lie to me; it kills me that I've done just that. This *new Andrew* I have become is not the one my mother raised. She would be ashamed of me if she knew.

***

After my lunch break, I head straight to my office, mindful to keep my head low. Unless it is business, I have minimised small talk with my colleagues. Luckily, they know nothing about my private life, and I keep out of their business.

My mother has taught me that respect and a healthy distance are essential to maintaining a good working relationship with my team. But I'm friendly enough with some of them to ensure an open communication line between us.

I'm back in my office; the heat is about to bake and suffocate the misery out of me. I have an air conditioner if one counts the useless giant off-white machine on the wall. But the stupid machine ridiculously blows warm air, no matter what temperature one selects on the control panel.

Coupled with the horrendous noise it makes, it doesn't function the way the manufacturer intended. Left up to me, I would uproot it from the wall and dump it in the recycling centre, where it might be of use.

I have had maintenance guys come in to assess the repair required. But my old man, the *tightwad*, won't pay for it. My father is stingy beyond reason; I don't understand how he expects me to take money out of my paycheck to complete the repairs of his office building. But honestly, why would I finance my father's office repairs? Crazy!

My mobile phone, which has not rung since morning, suddenly comes to life. It interrupts my thoughts about my useless air conditioner. The caller ID is withheld, which isn't unusual. Most prospective buyers withhold their numbers to avoid unwarranted sales pitches should they take their business elsewhere or put off the purchase. I take a deep breath, put on a sales agent's smile, and enthusiastically answer the call.

"Hello, this is Andrew." My voice sounds smooth and inviting. "Can I help you?"

"Hello, hello, Andrew. Can you hear me?"

The caller sounds like a young woman. It's common for young women in this town to buy brand-new cars. How they can afford to do so is a million-dollar question. But this burg is full of *Maria Sosalas*—I reflect bitterly.

"Hello, Andrew, it is Bridget!" The caller shouts impatiently.

"Who's calling?" Between the whirring racquet of the air conditioner behind me and a bad phone connection, I can't hear a thing.

"Can you please speak slowly?

The woman sounds angry. "It's Bridget. Don't play games; I know you can hear me!"

Oh no, it's Dailess' hench girl on the phone. My heart drops, but I try to sound cheerful.

"Hey Bridget, what a surprise. How're you?"

"Andrew, this is not a social call."

Her tone irritates me. "Of course not; I am at work."

"Don't be cheeky with me; I'm not Dailess!"

"Bridget, unless you want to buy a car, you have no reason to call me."

"In that case, I'll keep it simple. You'll meet Dailess and her sisters at Rio restaurant on Friday at 18:30."

I cup my mouth to control my tongue. "For what? Why would I do that?"

"I'm not asking you, Andrew. I'm telling you to be there."

I raise my voice. "Bridget, you can't just..."

She cuts me off. "Can't just what, Andrew?"

I take a deep breath. "You can't..."

"Shush, you'll either meet us at Rio. Or I'll bundle Dailess in a taxi and send her to your parents' house." Bridget lets out a sinister chuckle. "You'll find her in your precious mother's living room."

My breath quickens. This *Jezebel* and poor excuse of a woman has got me. I must play nice.

"Okay, Bridget, wait, please calm down." I shut my eyes and speak through a clenched jaw.

"I hear you. I'll be at Rio Friday at 18:30."

"That's what I thought, anyway; your call!"

The phone goes dead.

Stupid woman! I raise my trembling hand to wipe my brow. How does any man get himself into such deep trouble? Better yet, how does one get out of it? I should have listened to David and avoided Dailess and her friends. Much as I hate to admit, they have pulled the rug from under my feet and shifted the gears in our *cat-and-mouse* game. I must think fast.

My mind races through possible *escape* scenarios, but there are glitches everywhere. Why did I pick up that call? The claws of another panic attack start to tighten around me. Wild and frantic, I stagger across the room and fling open the windows. I can't breathe. How will I get out of this silly ultimatum? I'm not ready to meet Dailess; what am I to say?

A thought crosses my mind. A delivery trip out of town might do the trick and buy me some time till I figure things out. Dailess knows that I sometimes get clients from other parts of the country. This idea is my perfect ticket out of this jam for now.

Determined not to waste time, I punch the keypad ferociously on my office phone extension. "Jordan, hey, it's me, man." I clench my fist. "Do we have any out-of-town deliveries scheduled for Friday?"

"Oh hey, bruv; the last one went out this afternoon with Mr Kabwe. He'll be back tomorrow."

I hesitate. "Bruv..."

"Did you need something?" Jordan asks.

"Nah, thanks, bruv." My knees rattle, weak from disappointment. "Let me know as soon as there's a change in the schedule."

Bridget wins, for now. It's hard to think straight about anything. I might as well *call it a day* and head back home. I feel and look like s**t—not good for business. Our clients would be horrified if they saw me right now. Harassed and sweaty beyond imagination.

I phone my father on his extension line. "Hi, Dad. Do you mind if I take the rest of the afternoon off?"

My father sounds alarmed as he picks up on my sombre mood. "Why, are you okay? You know COVID is still with us—I hope you are being careful."

"Of course, Dad, it's nothing to worry about." I feign extreme fatigue and steer my father's thoughts away from COVID-19. "I just need to recharge; it's been quite hectic."

"Ok, son, let Jordan know you're leaving now."

"Yes, Dad, I'll do that."

A window opens for me to introduce the subject of car delivery, and I go for it. "By the way, I spoke to Jordan earlier; I might travel outside of Lusaka to deliver a car on Friday."

"Okay then, let me know when you are sure. In the meantime, ask Mr Phiri to drop you off at home."

What a relief; I can't get behind the wheel in my messed-up state.

***

Half an hour later, with minimal traffic on the road, Mr Phiri drops me off. As soon as Ba Bwezani sees me, he runs to get my briefcase.

He looks worried. "Bwana Andrew, you are back early."

"I just need some rest, boss."

"Don't work too hard; even young people need to rest."

"Tru dat, boss!" Ba Bwezani always looks out for me. After my conversation with Bridget, anything is possible. I must put him on alert.

"By the way, boss, please don't open the gate for any visitors."

Ba Bwezani nods thoughtfully. "Yes, Bwana Andrew. I understand your instructions."

"Thank you, boss. I'll see you tomorrow morning."

I slip through the front door but suddenly stop in the entry hall. My heart jumps at the ring of chatty voices from the main living room. My mother sounds animated—there are visitors in the house, after all. Why didn't ba Bwezani warn me? Who could it be? I try to hold still, but the door behind me bangs shut.

My mother calls for assistance. "Ba Esther, please check who's at the front door; I'm busy with some people here."

Relax, relax, relax, Andrew. Caught in a frantic dilemma, I wonder if I should dart back outside or sprint down the hallway to my bedroom. Alas, my legs betray me. I can't move. My ears are on high alert as I struggle to hear and understand what my mother and her guests are discussing.

"Ladies, I appreciate your position, but can we come to a fair agreement?" I hear my mother say.

"Mrs Michelo, we understand, but it's a tough decision for us to make."

I loosen my tie and unbutton my collar. What *position* is my mother referring to? And what tough *decision* is there to make? My fear heightens. Could that crazy Bridget have brought Dailess here? Those women will put me in an early grave if I'm not careful.

Ba Esther soon finds me lost and confused in the hallway. "Oh, Bwana Andrew, it's you—madam wants to know who's at the door. She's in the living room with some guests."

I motion Ba Esther to come closer to me as I whisper. "Who is it?" I gesticulate wildly. "What do the visitors look like?"

Surprised by my questions, Ba Esther steps back, arms akimbo, and cocks her head to one side. "Why, Bwana Andrew? It's two women; I've never seen them before."

"Young or old?"

Ba Esther laughs. "Bwana Andrew! Are you looking for a wife?"

"No, no, no! Forget I asked." I've managed to thoroughly confuse the poor lady.

"The women have wigs to sell; does that help you?"

"Ba Esther, why didn't you say that in the first place." Elated, I throw my arms around her. "Thank you. Now, I must say hello to my mother."

I rush to the living room and feign innocence. "Hello, Mummy. It's only me; I've just walked in and run into Ba Esther. Were you expecting someone else?"

"Oh, Andrew, you're back so early? My mother drops the packet of wigs in her lap. "Is everything okay?"

"Everything's fine, Mummy." With a subtle yet calculated flourish, I let out an exaggerated yawn. "I 'm just a little exhausted; I asked Dad for the afternoon off."

"Okay then. These lovely ladies are here to show me some wigs for sale." My mother turns her attention back to the two businesswomen.

I tease the two women. "Good afternoon, ladies. Do you have a nice wig for me?"

We all burst out laughing. My mother tries on one wig, looks in the hand mirror, and turns her head from side to side. She smiles broadly, pleased with her look.

"Wendy sent these two nice ladies to me with what she swears are the best wigs in town, but I want to negotiate the price down."

"Ah, Auntie Wendy and her wigs; they look good on her." My mother gives me an expression full of jest. "And you, mummy, of course."

"Okay, run along and take a nap. I'll come and check on you before dinner."

"Thanks, mummy; bye, ladies."

Chapter Seven

A ROCK AND A HARD PLACE

Smartphones are our modern-day BFF. As I stare at the neon flash on my phone screen and listen to the melodic ringtone, it hits me just how attached we are to these little gadgets.

We reach for them first thing every morning when our eyes flip open—an essential part of our daily routine. We all love to share stories of their reliability and impressive features, a common icebreaker in awkward conversations.

We trust smartphones to manage our lives and proudly demonstrate their genius capabilities to friends and families. Goodness knows how we survived before their grand arrival!

This morning, I have mixed emotions about my electronic BFF for the first time. It reminds me that today is Friday, and I have an 18:30 appointment with Dailess and her sisters.

F**k! My immediate impulse is to throw it away or smash it against the wall. But that won't change anything; I can only pray that by sheer luck, the situation might have changed from when I last spoke to Bridget.

Fingers crossed, Jordan might report new cars we must deliver and allow me to take a rain check on today's plan. Later, I can meet with Dailess alone, as it should be. I don't understand the *committee's* involvement in something that's supposed to be private between two people.

***

I arrive at my office earlier than usual, having crept out of the house before my parents could notice anything. Anxious to find wiggle room in the silly plan, I burst through the entrance door to the reception area with more force than necessary. The urgency to find a solution to my unwelcome agenda propels my actions as I swiftly make my way through.

Belita looks at me with a quizzical eye and gives me a slight smile. Like my mother, she doesn't miss a thing. Her little smile tells me she has a sneaking suspicion that something's wrong.

"*Hurricane Andrew*, you're early and in a mighty rush today. What's going on?"

I stop briefly and smile wryly. "Hi, Belita; excuse my lack of manners. Is Jordan in yet?"

"Yep, in the showroom—you know your guy. He came in thirty minutes ago." Belita deliberately flags a timesheet in the air. "By the way, I'll send over my overtime request shortly."

I'm too distracted to listen to Belita. "Yeah, send it to the Accounts Department—I'll approve it later."

Yes! I punch the air and dash off in search of Jordan, with my personal crisis at the top of my agenda for this morning. Belita's overtime can wait.

Jordan is in the showroom with one of the clients from yesterday evening. It's a good sign for business. But it also means my little mission to escape Dailess and her mean friends have to go on the back burner.

I swagger forward and shake the gentleman's hand. "Good morning, sir. Andrew Michelo."

"Rodney Meleki, nice to meet you." The man nods his head slowly as he checks me out.

"Are you the owner?"

I smile to myself. Luckily, my father's not part of this conversation, especially after his Monday *tantrum* to get rid of me. "Oh, no, sir. I'm flattered, but it's my father's business."

Mr Meleki gives me a proud pat on my shoulder. "Good show! Jordan has convinced me to give all my money to your business."

I grasp Mr Meleki's hand in a firm handshake. "Well, thank you very much, sir."

Jordan and I wink at each other. How exciting! I can't wait to get away to draw up the paperwork immediately.

"I'll leave you in Jordan's capable hands."

Mr Meleki flashes a broad smile. "Thank you, young man."

"Jordan, I'll see you later when you finish with Mr Meleki."

Three deals in one week make an excellent start to the weekend. I pray that my father will be in a happier mood and that he'll get on better with my mother. Nothing can ever go wrong when my mother is happy. If only my old man would learn this simple lesson—a happy wife equals a peaceful home.

As I walk away from the showroom, I reflect on how, without warning, my life has changed; so much has gone pear-shaped overnight, and it's hard to put one foot in front of the other. Will I ever find my way?

But after my encounter with Mr Meleki, I can't dismiss the exhilaration that has punctuated my darkness to let in a glimmer of light. If only for a few minutes—I need all the respite I can get.

I let out a long sigh. It's time to regroup and get back to my purpose for today. Jordan might have given Mr Phiri and the other drivers instructions on delivery schedules. I feel renewed hope and quickly approach the three drivers' shared office.

After a sharp rap, I yank the door open without an invitation to enter the room. Breathless and unable to contain myself, I get right into it. "Good morning, gentlemen."

Mr Phiri and his two colleagues abruptly stand up to greet me. "Bwana Andrew, are you better today, sir?

I crack my knuckles. "Ah yes, we haven't seen each other since Wednesday afternoon, when you dropped me off at home. It was just a migraine." I clear my throat and look around the room. "Mr Phiri, has Jordan mentioned anything about clients from outside Lusaka?"

There's an awkward pause.

"Bwana Andrew, Mr Jordan didn't give us that information."

"Are you sure Jordan didn't say anything?"

Mr Phiri, surprised by my question, stutters as he tries to wrap his head around the point of the discussion. "I think everything is under control. Did you check the system, Bwa, bwana Andrew?"

My face flushes, hot with embarrassment. "Oh yes, I should do that—you're right."

My desperation is plain—everyone, including these three humble gentlemen, can *smell a rat*. My questions couldn't have sounded more random. I should have waited for Jordan to fill me in. I must try to control myself going forward.

Bridget's call on Wednesday sealed my fate. What's more unsettling is that I don't have answers to anything I imagine Dailess would like to know. It might come across as selfish, but I can't see past what all this will do to my mother as hard as I try.

I could call David and ask him to go with me. But that would start *World War III* with Bridget and David in the same room—both are capable of the worst trouble without help from the other.

My phone rings; it startles me, and I draw a sharp breath. Who could it be this time? Should I answer it? I pick it up and brace myself for the worst. Phew! It's my old man, thank heavens.

"Hello, Dad? Sorry, I left the house early this morning. I had a client to meet."

My father coughs. "I'm proud of you, son."

I exhale softly. "Did you want something, Dad?"

"I've got a meeting at the Rotary Club at 18:30. Will you drop me off?"

I squeeze my eyes shut in disbelief and skip a beat before I can speak. I then reluctantly push the words out of my mouth and nearly choke on them. "Yes, sir, no problem, Dad," I reply.

"Thank you, son."

OMG! What just happened? How's this possible? Of all the days and times my father could schedule an appointment, must it be today at 18:30? It's impossible to do both with Dailess on one end and my father on the other. This mother of all calendar clashes is about to ruin my life! It has jammed me between *a rock and a hard place.*

What must I do? I stare at my phone and wonder if I should call Bridget to reason with her. I could cancel the meeting. But that wouldn't be a wise move. No excuse in the entire world would be enough to get me off the hook with that quiver of female *Ngoshes* (cobras).

A no-show would encourage *Spitting Bridget* to carry out her attack and plant Dailess in my mother's living room. But perhaps if I called to request more time—a delay of 30 minutes, it would help me honour both obligations.

Hmmnn, what if the Ngoshes don't *buy* it? There's a real risk that Bridget especially doesn't believe me. Who knows what her next mad move would be? I'll just have to give it my best. It's all I can do.

***

At exactly 17:30, my father's on the line and tells me to hurry to the parking lot. I wouldn't have initiated the call had he not done so.

I make the sign of the cross and get in the car behind the wheel. With a slight tremor in my hands, I pull the car out of the parking lot and reluctantly head out to the road Show Grounds. I'm about to walk into the wrath of four women, and I don't know if I'll come out alive.

On the road, exhaust fumes choke up the air and seep through the car vents. My father starts to fidget with the air conditioning knob.

"Andrew, what's going on? Are you sure this thing is on? Why is it so hot in here?"

"We just started driving, Dad—it will cool down in a few minutes," I reply with a smile.

But inside my head, I only want to remind my father of his double standards. Why can't he show the same concern for my office air conditioning as the one in the car? But I am wiser than that. I decide to bite my tongue and focus on my driving.

Friday evening rush hour in Lusaka is a hell-raising experience. It's a mess that requires superpower driving skills. The traffic, a sea of metal and rubber chaos in every direction, becomes a battle of egos. Every driver is confident they have the right of way.

Worse still, Lusaka residents love Fridays. Nobody works late; everyone is out on the road racing to get their hands on their first ice-cold Mosi beer. This beverage's demand and stock value triples this time of the year. *It's everything.*

In a bumper-to-bumper caterpillar crawl, we approach the Kafue roundabout. It's a mess—drivers angrily tangle and detangle their vehicles. Together, they look like a giant multi-coloured and shiny metallic knot of a monster.

My father furrows his forehead. "Look at this confusion. The Traffic Police aren't competent—too many dangerously overloaded minibuses get away without a fine."

"You're right, Dad; almost everyone is guilty of not observing road safety laws."

Traffic offenders in Lusaka come in all shapes and sizes. Pedestrians randomly dart in and out of the road between moving vehicles, and today is no exception.

I jump and swerve the car as a street vendor knocks on my window.

"Boss, please open the window," the young man yells, dangling a bag of carrots.

"Hey, son, watch it; these people think they're invincible," my father cautions.

My knuckles tighten around the steering wheel. "Don't worry, Dad, I'm alert."

Lusaka town centre street vendors cause more trouble than anyone. One can't blame them, though. It's a brutal economy after COVID-19, and folks who have fallen on hard times risk their lives daily to earn a living.

During rush hour, vendors can test your last nerve. *High* on the laws of self-preservation—a primal survival instinct, they dangerously weave in and out of traffic. They knock on car windows, desperate to sell their last batch of vegetables, fruits, nuts, or maize.

It's annoying but not hard to understand. Most of the vendors have little hungry mouths to feed. It's also a double whammy for them as the failure to sell their produce in this unforgiving heat of the hot season can be catastrophic.

Ten minutes later, there's still no way to escape the traffic madness. My father cranes his neck as if there's a chance to take a side street that doesn't exist.

"Are we going to sit in this senseless trap all evening?"

"Dad, call the people you are meeting and tell them you are running late."

"You are right, son. I'll send a text message."

I wish I could take my advice. But the last thing I want to do is call Bridget when in my father's company. So, instead, I slide a Barry White CD into the player to take my mind off things.

"Let's enjoy some more oldies music in the meantime, Dad. We might be in this traffic jam for a while."

"Good idea. By the way, son, I forgot to mention your mother called,"

A tremor of anxiety rips through my heart. "Oh, she did? What did she say?" I try to sound casual.

"Just that Auntie Francine will come for a visit on Saturday."

"That's wonderful!" I lie.

Don't get me wrong, I love my Auntie Francine, but mummy couldn't have picked a worse time to invite her sister. There'll be no room to escape the two if they get onto my case.

"Have you heard from Uncle Michael about your scholarship application?"

I hesitate and swallow hard as I think about what to say. "Ahem, I wa...was.."

As my words struggle to form a sentence, my father's phone thankfully rings, and my getaway window beckons me through.

"Take care of your call, Dad, while I focus on the road," I hastily advise.

"Hello, April; Andrew and I are trying to beat the traffic on the way to the Show Grounds."

My father speaks louder than necessary to amplify the extent of our *suffering*. I can't hear what my mother is saying on her end. But whatever it is, I hope she keeps my father on the line long enough for me to drop him off. I doubt he'll return to the scholarship conversation once we approach his meeting destination.

At exactly 18:30, we enter the Show Grounds and park in front of the Club House. My father is still on the phone. He slides his handset between his shoulder and ear as he tries to open the door.

"Hold on, April; we're here—let me get out of the car," my father says to my mother.

I'm already late and worried about my next stop. I can't let my father dilly-dally my time away.

"Here, Dad, don't forget your briefcase."

"Thank you, son. By the way, your mother will pick me up later at 21:00 hrs."

What a relief!

"Okay, Dad, enjoy your evening."

Before I can drive out of the Show Grounds, my phone rings. It's Bridget calling to yell at me—I'm already ten minutes late. I reluctantly answer the call.

"Bridget, I am on my way. I had to drop off my father at the Show Grounds."

"Whatever, Andrew, that's none of my business. You're late, and please don't try me!"

"Bridget, this is way too much pressure," I respond, but she's already hung up on me.

Determined to get to Rio quickly, I reverse and skid out of the Show Grounds and cruise back towards town. With any luck, I should get there in the next fifteen minutes.

Of all places to meet, why couldn't Bridget have chosen a less busy venue? The parking lot at Levy Mwanawasa Shopping Mall gets bloated with endless *wheels*. It's Friday evening, and many people of all ages will have choked up the place: moviegoers, those on romantic dinner dates, supermarket shoppers, etc. My evening doesn't look promising.

***

Ten minutes go by, and my frantic search yields nothing; I'm out of luck. There must be a way the girls and I can come to a reasonable compromise.

"Hello, Bridget. I'm outside in the parking area, but I can't find any vacant space for my car."

"Liar! I knew it. Andrew, if you are serious, you'll figure that s**t out!"

I can't believe she called me a liar and hung up on me. The plan was dead in the water from the outset. Why can't she see that there's a problem with this venue? There's no way I can afford to park illegally; that would just invite Police trouble and vandalism—possibly theft. Besides, it's not like the ladies plan a five-minute conversation. I'll be lucky to come out alive if I don't have the answers they want. What if I called Dailess?

I should've known there was no way around this mess because Bridget's harsh voice intercepts the call.

"Bridget, this isn't your phone. Let me talk to Dailess. Put her on the phone."

"So now you want to talk to Dailess? That's not going to happen, bougie boy. Park your car and come and meet all four of us."

"You know my problem. Why can't you guys meet me in the parking lot? We can all sit and talk in my car."

There's a slight pause, and the tension rises as the four ladies consult in sharp whispers in the background. It's like Jurors trying to reach a verdict in a murder trial. I'm afraid this Jury would sooner send me to the gallows than find merit in my suggestion.

"Andrew, the answer is no. You have another ten minutes to find parking, or the deal is off!" Bridget hangs up the phone abruptly before I can argue otherwise.

As well-intended as I am, I've run out of options. I'm defeated, and I know this meeting won't happen tonight. But I can buy time. As I recall, my mother won't be home until after 21:00 hrs, so I'll go home and take my chances. I've claimed back some of the control—the *Ngoshes* can't hurt me, at least not tonight.

I pull out of the Levy Junction Shopping Mall premises onto the streets and drive off with my music on full blast. My phone rings and momentarily distracts me as I approach the Longacres roundabout. S**t; it's Bridget; *Chief Ngoshe,* she's back!

Dailess and her *committee* must have realised by now that the tables had turned. They weren't going to see me tonight. As it is, I won't allow Bridget to bully me into anything—her call will go unanswered. They can hiss and strike all they want.

In front of my house, **Ba Bwezani** rushes to open the gate when he sees the car headlights.

"Welcome back, Bwana Andrew."

"Yes, boss, thank you. Is my mother in?"

"Madam has gone to East Park Mall and will pick up the boss later."

I'm so pleased that I could dance. "Listen, boss, don't open the gate for anyone other than my parents. If anyone else shows up here, please call the Police. Don't waste time."

"Yes, sir, Bwana Andrew, I understand the instructions very well."

I dip into my wallet and hand Ba Bwezani 1000 Kwacha. Hush money, I guess.

"Here's some money for the weekend, boss."

And as for Bridget, girl, bye!

Chapter Eight

Last night was an exception, a gift from above. I fell asleep quickly, and this morning, for the first time, I feel rested after weeks of counting the stars all night long. My body, however, is stiff and sore; my whole left side feels *dead* from poor circulation.

I push myself into a sitting position and reach for my phone. It's been vibrating non-stop from under my sweaty pillow. Oh wow, ten missed calls from Bridget? What could have gone wrong? Something very exciting or tragic must have happened while I slept.

I'm disappointed to see no missed calls or text messages from Andrew. Shouldn't he have tried to reach out to me after the way things ended yesterday evening? Did he ever intend to meet me or what?

Andrew's parking shenanigans, *now we see him, now we don't,* have got me on edge more than ever. It worries me that even Bridget's threats did not get him to meet with us. Should I have gone to meet him outside? But it wouldn't have been easy to do so with Bridget *in charge* of my life. Sadly, I'm back to square one—how can I face my parents without a position from Andrew?

I pick up my phone to return Bridget's call. Fingers crossed, Andrew might have rescheduled our meeting. It had better be good news. I dial Bridget's number three times, but she doesn't pick up.

Bridget didn't like that Andrew escaped her wrath yesterday. If anything, she'll want him to *burn* for this more than ever. Sometimes, I wonder which dog of a man wronged Bridget so much that the menfolk must always suffer at her hands. It explains why she has no boyfriend.

As I'm about to make my fourth attempt to reach Bridget, the metal handle to my bedroom door crashes into the concrete wall. It frightens me.

I slowly look up to find *Hurricane Quietness Banda*, my mother, in my doorway. She has a crooked smile, and her narrowed eyes sharply focus on me as she stands inside my room, arms akimbo. I don't know why she's here, but my mother looks ready to tear down everyone and anything in her way.

My eyes dart around the room; I'm unsure where to look. I finally settle on the little mound of white, chalky paint particles, damage caused by my mother. I look up and run my eyes along the wall to the source of the flaky bits—a rugged dent in the cheap cladding. My mother snaps her fingers to draw my attention to her.

"Dailess, what kind of a woman sleeps through the morning until 11:00 hrs?"

"I... I'm sorry, mummy." If only she knew what little sleep I've had lately.

My mother tugs at my thin bedspread. "Get up now, you lazy girl!"

I clutch my chest in fear. "Mummy, what's going on? Tell me?"

She locks her eyes with mine. "What's this rubbish I am hearing from *Amake Sally* (mother of Sally)?"

OMG, this can't be what I think it is. "Mummy, I don't know what you mean."

My mother points her index finger at me.

"Dailess, what are those big useless ears of yours for? Didn't you hear me?"

"I'm sorry, Mummy."

"Sorry? What're you sorry for?"

I open my mouth to ask my mother to elaborate, but my pregnancy hormones stop me. The force of nausea explodes in me, and the thick saliva and bitter taste in my mouth conspire with the most powerful urge to vomit. I can't speak.

"Okay, you've nothing to say? Dailess, are you pregnant?"

I drop my phone from shock and kick it backwards under my bed with my heel. How did my mother find out? I haven't even told her I had a boyfriend. At this point, who knows what her next move will be? Giant teardrops course down my face—I'm dead; this woman will kill me.

"Crocodile tears, heeh! So Amake Sally is a liar now? What's his name?"

"Andrew Michelo."

"Michelo? A Tonga boy? Does he work? Where does he live?"

My mother has caught me off guard. I struggle to focus between her flurry of questions pounding on me like bricks and my raging hormones.

I breathe in shakily. "An... Andrew is Tonga, and he works for his father."

"This Andrew, the Tonga boy, impregnated you? For what? For free?"

My mother continues to shout, hoping to *draw blood from a stone*. Frustrated, she takes matters into her own hands and yanks me from the bed. Determined to get the proof she believes I have tattooed on my person, my mother grabs my threadbare cotton night dress with all her might and rips it apart.

My mother gets away with a chunk of fabric from down the middle of my belly—the target of her mission. She grins and cries simultaneously, her facial muscles wildly twitching, not knowing which emotion to follow. I can't believe the dancing demon in front of me that triumphantly prodds my belly is my mother.

"Ehehe, look, what's this you're hiding?"

I summon every ounce of my strength to pull away from my mother and run past her as what's left of my night dress slips away from my shoulders. Thank God for my chitenge, which I hung on the bathroom door hook last night; I can cover myself.

But there's not much I can do for my nausea; I can't hold it any longer. My body convulses violently as the rush of vomit spews out of my mouth. Goosebumps mushroom all over my skin, and soon, my legs buckle. I drop to a crawling position, unable to support my weight.

Meanwhile, my mother, not ready to give up, chases after me, part of my night dress still in her fiercely balled-up hands. The cherry on her cake of discovery is my morning sickness sideshow, all the proof my mother needed to confirm Amake Sally's report.

From the horrific expression on her face, you can't tell this is the woman who gave birth to me. My mother stretches her lips and contorts her face into a loathsome horror mask I no longer recognise.

"Enhe! Look at your vomit! The *secret food* you *ate at night* is now open for all to see in broad daylight."

"Mummy, I made a mistake—I'm only human."

I sigh in despair. How can my mother poke fun at me now when I need her the most? My heart breaks into a million pieces— ones that not even time can claw back or mend. Aren't mothers supposed to love their children unconditionally? I have never felt so useless, stupid and unlovable in my life.

"Who's going to marry you now?

"Help me, mummy, please. Forgive me."

"Help you? Look what you've done. A *used* girl like you won't find a husband."

My mother's sharp cry pierces the air as she wails and stomps the floor like a widow bereft of her husband's love and devotion. Her racquet vibrates and sweeps my news into every crevice of our small five-roomed house.

It doesn't surprise me when my father drops his precious little radio to the floor and rushes to the bathroom. He's anxious to console my mother, who has begun to harmonise her tearful sobbing with the notes of a mournful *Ngoni* (Eastern Province tribal group) song. She raises her arms over her cornrowed head, cradling either side.

My father reaches for my mother's hand.

"Where is the funeral?"

"Funeral! Why a funeral?" She glares at him.

"Quietness, isn't that why you're screaming?"

"Radio Banda, you can't see this rubbish?"

"What rubbish? Isn't this how you behave when someone in the compound dies?"

"Look at this daughter of yours. She's pregnant at nineteen without a husband!

The nuances of my parents' marriage and how they communicate may not be that obvious to an outsider. One might quickly decide that my father's assumptions and questions are random.

Yet, he has nailed the hammer on the head about my mother's theatrics. Like her fellow church women at the UCZ, my mother is a *professional mourner*—she is the church's self-appointed *Chief Mourner,* who takes every death personally.

My father is intelligent and knows his wife's temperaments well. As such, he picks his battles carefully. Although he's gutted by what he has come to understand, my father knows that to fight his wife right now is a battle he won't win. If anything, it will escalate her aggression towards me.

"Quietness, let's discuss this without all this crying and shouting?"

"Radio Banda, what can you do about your pregnant daughter?"

My father deflects my mother's question. "Dailess, my dear, do you want a glass of water?"

"No, thank you, Daddy," I respond.

"Are you sure, my daughter?" my father insists.

"Radio Banda, there's no time for that water you're talking about!" My mother admonishes my father.

A glass of water would be heaven. But not at the risk of getting my eyes scratched out. My mother has by now become a *dangerous animal* that I must avoid at all costs. My father reads the room, too. It's a hostile ground. He knows that there is no way to reason with my mother without her kicking up a fistfight.

As my mother paces up and down, the already tiny bathroom starts to feel smaller, hotter and claustrophobic. It's impossible to breathe.

"Mummy, please let me return to my bedroom."

My mother looks at me and sucks her teeth. She's shocked that I dare ask to leave her *court* before the sentencing. "You think this is a game?" My mother pokes the side of my head. "At nineteen shuwa (sure)—what do you think the people at church will say? Shameful!"

"Mummy, I'm so sorry."

"What has your Tonga boyfriend promised you?" What Dailess, tell me?

"I have not spoken to him." My eyes stay fixed on the floor. I dare not look my mother in her eyes.

"Ohooho, you're playing with fire." My mother's eyes are bloodshot with anger. "Do you think there's a man out there who'll take another man's child?"

"I'll talk to Andrew. Please give him a chance."

"Talk to who? After he's *stolen* the goods?" My mother bursts into raucous and sarcastic laughter. "My daughter, that's why you must not have sex before marriage."

"Mummy, can I please go now?"

"Andrew Michelo, *ndi waku ma yadi uja* (That one is from an affluent suburb), my daughter, those people don't marry our kind. God is my witness!"

"Dailess," my father calls.

"Yes, Daddy. I'll get dressed, then come to you."

That's my father's way of telling me to leave my mother to her devices. Permission or not, I ran out of her *bathroom court* and back to my bedroom.

"Where're you going? Foolish girl!"

Five minutes later, I tiptoe out of my bedroom to sneak past my mother. There's no such luck; she's standing in the middle of the short hallway to the living room. I keep my head down and move as close to the wall as possible.

"Tell that foolish boyfriend of yours that he'll marry you. There're no free goods in this house. Stupid!"

Overcome with emotion, I drop to my father's feet and sob uncontrollably. I didn't plan for him to discover my pregnancy in such an embarrassing way.

"I am sorry, Daddy; I was going to tell you about my pregnancy. But I didn't know how. I was scared."

"Don't worry, my daughter. We'll find a way to survive this problem. Just focus on your college studies; that's the most important thing."

My father will never disparage me like my mother. But it hurts to know I have broken his heart. He doesn't have to say anything; I can see the suffering in his eyes.

"This too shall pass, my daughter," My father comforts me, his voice small and quiet.

"Thank you, Daddy." I squeeze his hand.

***

Shortly afterwards, my mother briskly walks into the living room with renewed purpose. She carelessly drops onto the edge of one of our only three chairs. My mother can be very calculated and unpredictable. My father and I look at each other, unsure of what my mother has up her sleeve. My father fidgets with the radio antenna while I nervously crack my knuckles, waiting for my mother to show her *claws*.

Without warning, my mother stands up and tightens her chitenge around her waist. A sign that she was ready for a scuffle. My mother drags me by my arm.

"Let's go!"

"Ouch, mummy, that hurts. Daddy, help me."

"Go where, Quietness? Where do you think you're taking my daughter?"

"Radio Banda, don't try to stop me; I'm warning you."

My parents lock eyes. I don't particularly appreciate where this is going. My father has had enough of my mother's uncompromising attitude. But unfortunately, my mother has never had much respect for him. Sometimes I wonder, would she treat him better if he had money, or is she just insolent beyond redemption?

"Quietness, if you want to go somewhere, feel free to walk out. But my daughter stays."

"That daughter? Useless, you can't even get *lobola* (dowry) for her now. She's *used*!"

Suddenly, there's a loud, determined knock at the door. My father and I jump in surprise. We look at each other, confirming that neither of us expects anyone. But my mother has a knowing smile.

To my horror, the door flies open, and my mother's UCZ *troops*, led by Amake Sally, push through the doorway. They storm in and take over like soldiers at an enemy camp.

"Amake Dailess, where is she?"

The intruders stomp around the room and gesticulate frantically at my father to let them have their way.

"Ba Radio, this is a job for women; let Dailess come with us."

"Quietness, we haven't even had time to understand your daughter's news. And yet, your arrogant friends are here to take over!"

It hurts to see how quickly my mother has made private business public news in Kamwala. Amake Sally, just like her daughter, can't keep a secret. My name must be on everyone's lips in every market stall in the compound. The unfounded, malicious and salacious stories that must be flying around are enough to make me move countries.

I dread the double standards I'll face—the men and the older women will strip me of any dignity I have left. I'll never be able to set foot in church without judgment. As for my innocent baby, already branded an outcast, they will *stand trial* and inevitably be found guilty of bastardism long before birth.

"Ladies, why are you here?" My father will not stand for the women's callousness and lack of respect.

"Ba Radio, we have an explanation..."

"Leave my house immediately!" My father interrupts them.

It dawns on me that when my mother was absent from the living room, she was rounding up her backup team. The UCZ women already know the *drill* and are now here to help my mother execute her plan.

"Radio Banda, listen to me. Are you going to marry your daughter?" My mother wags her finger at my father.

"We have to take her to this Tonga boy today!" Amake Sally backs my mother.

Outnumbered, my father knows he must think on his feet or lose his daughter to his wife's hasty and shady plan.

"Dailess, go to the kitchen, fetch the biggest *mwinko* (wooden cooking stick) and come and stand behind me."

"Iwe, Radio Banda! Iwe, you're not a man. A small Kabulonga boy *rapes* your daughter, and you're happy?" My mother, now a spotted hyena, gives my father a menacing head-to-toe-to-head look.

"Quietness, Banda, this isn't a rape case, you mad woman! Anyway, since you are so clever, where were you when this *rape* of yours happened?" My father chuckles derisively. "Don't answer—you were at a foolish funeral, crying the loudest!"

Again, my father is on point. My mother and her UCZ cohorts have made a *career* out of weaving in and out of hospital wards and funeral homes. *Oh no, have you heard? Mr X is dead, or Mrs Y is on her deathbed.* They spend tedious hours going through these morbid *revolving doors* throughout the year and neglect their homes.

"Radio Banda, tell me, what is this girl's future like now if this boy doesn't marry her?"

"Quietness, we must follow traditions to send word to the Michelos."

"No, I first want the *damegi* (damage) for my daughter; then we can talk!" My mother yells.

"Well, Quietness, that' won't happen today—*over my dead body*," my father shakes his head.

"Again, who's going to marry your daughter?"

"Let's first discuss the matter," my father pleads.

"No, no, no! I'll consult Ba *Nganga* (witch doctor), not you, Radio Banda. Useless man!"

My mother, contemptuous in her demeanour and twisted lips, flicks her fingers at my father. She dismisses him like a dirty fly in the Kamwala fish market.

On many levels, it is unfathomable and scary that my *holier-than-thou* mother believes God and Ba *Nganga* can co-exist. A so-called woman of God, my mother shamelessly compartmentalises her faith in the Almighty and the *Nganga*. She *runs* an interesting roster between the two, based on the nature and gravity of her problems, not forgetting how fast she wants results.

"Aren't you a Christian, Quietness Banda? Nothing good can come out of your voodoo nonsense."

"Voodoo! Radio Banda, you can talk to me about voodoo when that mother of yours is the chief *infwiti* (witch)!"

My mother has now crossed the line and hit my father *below the belt*. He raises the *mwinko* to smack my mother.

"Stop it, Daddy!" I scream and push my mother out of harm's way.

"Let's go, *Amayi* (mothers) and leave this stupid man!" My mother commands her friends.

The three women slide their *patapatas* (flip flops) back on their feet and hastily exit the house, intent on seeking consul from Ba *Nganga*. My father and I quietly watch my mother and her friends as they hurriedly stumble outdoors into the sunlight.

The three women sashay across the dry October ground as their patapatas rhythmically leave trails of little angry puffs of dust until they disappear. My father, defeated and downcast, doesn't try to stop them but gives my mother a nasty parting shot.

"*Fuseke* (forsake), Quietness Banda! Sleep in your Nganga's house; don't come back here. *Swaini* (Swine)!"

CHAPTER NINE

THREE KINDS OF MARRIED WOMEN

Saturday at last! I'm up early; what a relief that Francine will be here today. Finally, we can dig into what has got my son acting so strange. I've kept my distance from him as Francine advised. But that *grace period* is over now. It's time to join forces to find out what's eating Andrew Michelo.

Besides sorting out my son's woes, having Francine around will do wonders for me. It will help break the monotony in my marriage. Whenever Francine is here, it's like the *real* me comes out. We dress up to look and feel beautiful.

Today, I've decided to wear a lovely bright pink lipstick to match my blush pink linen dress and pumps. I'm a minimalist in jewellery; I like small, elegant, classy and expensive pieces. It does the job better than chunky and lumpy pieces.

My hair is manageable; I've got a beautiful wig from the ladies Wendy sent me during the week. The hair is so light it floats in the wind. I twirl in front of the big and, long mirror. There! I've still got it. Roger might have forgotten—what a mistake.

Francine and I keep each other on top of the game in fashion. She always says, as a married woman, the beauty queen inside you is your best friend, and you should never neglect her.

So, when in my sister's company, I've got to up my game. Francine has helped me grow even though she's my youngest sibling. Her approach to life and the way of doing things, mentally, physically and spiritually, is next level. You've got to love that about her.

I quickly tidy my dressing table and reflect on my marriage and life. Francine has played a significant role in keeping me sane and my head above the water. I've been very lonely in my marriage for a long time. But Francine's undying support and friendship have kept me going. She isn't just my sister, a blood relative—she's my soul mate.

On days when life gets too much, Francine helps me remember where I come from: my parents' home and their bloodline, as well as a wonderful childhood. A beautiful life lived with precious memories: uncomplicated—no Roger, his Mazabuka shenanigans, or mother-in-law drama.

In all my marital and emotional trauma over the years, the only thing I hear from Bana Chimbusa is: *Just be strong; you are not more special than other women. How do you think your mother did it?* It's the default answer for any woman who is a victim of a bad marriage.

Again, I wonder, does society not expect married women to tire of being strong in difficult situations? It's ironic, given the number of distressed marriages in Lusaka.

Where are we dropping the ball as members of this society? Is it that women aren't strong enough, that marriages are falling apart? Or that young men don't receive enough guidance on how to hold up their end of the bargain?

I know that Divorce isn't the answer, but a successful marriage requires a delicate balance—like in a business. For the investment to grow, both partners must keep their end of the bargain: time, money, dedication, loyalty, honesty, transparency, creativity—you name it. The company will collapse if one director keeps withdrawing without ever investing.

During the years of my fertility struggles and lowest point in life, Roger was always in *red*. It didn't help that Mrs Michelo wished for the failure of my marriage. It could go into *foreclosure*; she couldn't care less. My parents, hard as they tried to help, weren't strong enough a force for as long as my mother-in-law was against me.

And the silence, which is the *silent killer*. No pun intended. Long before I had Andrew, I had nowhere to turn besides my parents and Francine. I couldn't tell anyone about the emotional and psychological trauma my husband and his mother put me through. It was taboo back then, and it still is. *A good wife knows how to keep her mouth shut*, women are told repeatedly by the Bana Chimbusa.

Of course, no woman should be the *village crier* about her marital problems. But what are we supposed to do with our pain, seeing we aren't allowed to talk about it? Why does society shame us into silence?

It's mind boggling how many married women of all ages in Lusaka are going insane. Afraid to lose their marriages and society's approval, the lesser evil is the slow and quiet death from *sealed lips*. The silence is snuffing the spirit and life out of them.

It's no surprise to find sad, lonely women behind the beautiful tall gates and high walls that protect their sprawling mansions. The women drive around in expensive SUVs, wearing designer clothes and plastic smiles. They dare not admit the detrimental effects of keeping their mouths shut lest they lose the *ride and* the wardrobe—let's not forget the status.

But is the price of silence that chips away at the core of their being, day in and day out, worth it? The day always comes when they wake up too late, and there's nothing left to chip away. Where a beautiful and intelligent woman once existed, now lives a *zombie*. In turn, their husbands, crazy and cruel as f**k, then turn around and *fumigate* the *zombie* out of their homes to make room for a shiny replacement wife. There you go—done and dusted.

I used to be a *zombie* or nearly became one until I asked myself if my dysfunctional marriage was worth the self-inflicted *zombification*. I've taken a good look at Roger and decided no more. I've begun to question what a happy marriage feels like because I know it doesn't feel like mine.

The question is: I'm fifty-five years old—how do I want to spend the rest of my life? Is Roger the man who deserves to walk beside me till my dying day? Is he built for the long haul and my second act?

You might ask why I have waited this long. Good question. But I did it for Andrew to give him a stable home and upbringing—*chulila ing'anda* (endure trouble for the sake of your marital home). That's what Bana Chimbusa teach us. And I've done that to the best of my ability.

Now, I'm at a crossroads with tough decisions to make. Andrew will leave for England in January next year, three months from now. Roger and I will have an empty nest in every sense. The foundation of our marriage caved in long before the looming empty nest stage. We lost our way years ago, with little to say to each other—our awkward silence is deafening.

Worse still, *getting it on* is out of the window. The lack of intimacy, manifested in the prolonged dry spells in our sex life, is hard to ignore. It's a tight competition with the drought of the Kalahari Desert's winter months. Nowadays, Roger and I both have headaches—Nurofen Express is the *reigning King* on our shopping list.

Our communication is minimal and reserved for emergencies. Andrew is the medium we use in the case of idle banter. *Son, tell your mother to reconfirm my doctor's appointment*, or *Honey, tell your father I am off to bed.* The list is endless.

I've often wondered if there is a chance Roger and I can retrace our footsteps. But the road that our marriage has been on has too many *potholes*, and not all are worth a do-over. I'd sooner drive through the potholes in the Kalingalinga compound, Rainy Season floods and all.

The couple we once were is gone—Roger and April 2.0 at this late stage is a waste of time. Most of all, it's not worth the investment of the remainder of my life. There's more to life than Roger.

When it comes to it, my biggest hurdle is Roger's secret family. We don't talk about the matter anymore. Not in a big way. But I know he visits them and sends them money. I can't help but wonder what else goes on behind my back. Does he still have a relationship with the mother of his sons? It's hard to shut down the *noises* in my head—there are some ghosts that one just can't *put to rest*. The betrayal has damaged me more than I cared to admit to myself or anyone.

If you live in Lusaka, you'll agree that the city has a *kaleidoscope* of marriages: the good, the bad and the ugly. I have come to believe that Lusaka has three main types of married women.

The first is the *happily married* woman, like cousin Jennifer's thirty-eight-year-old daughter, Khetiwe. Genuinely happy, Khetiwe is intelligent, confident, and beautiful. She invests in herself as a successful business owner, constantly upgrading her skills.

Khetiwe chose well; everyone in the family knows that. Her husband, Samuel, is an evolved and confident young man. He believes in the merits of a solid, honest relationship with his wife. With a man like that by her side, it is no wonder she lights up and giggles like a schoolgirl each time I ask her about Samuel. Khetiwe is in love, but she also keeps it *real*.

Then there is the imposter of a *happily married* woman, a die-hard member of the infamous *Shipikisha* (marriage perseverance) Club. I call her the *married divorcee*. My friend Wendy Kandolo is a great example. An expert at adding water to her wine, she holds onto the shambles of her marriage as if it were life itself. *April, guess what? Justin and I are celebrating our twentieth anniversary. Can you believe it?*

With every anniversary that comes and goes, Wendy dims out all the lights in her life and career. She has to allow her beloved Honourable Justin Kandolo's persona room to flourish, a jerk who isn't easy to deal with. He is an arrogant Mr Know-it-all with a god complex, magnified by his new political career as a Minister and Member of Parliament.

Honourable Kandolo runs his marriage and household as he does his personal-to-holder government vehicle. No one has a say; everything begins and ends with him. The man takes up all the *oxygen* in his home. I find it silly that he instructs Wendy over mundane things like; *don't forget to put the fish in the fridge.* I mean, really? I would put the fish in his underwear drawer to teach him a lesson. Lol!

Wendy has to be the most tolerant wife I know because if Roger talked to me the way Honourable Kandolo talks to her, all hell would break loose. I've had the displeasure of witnessing some of their fights. Adults should be able to disagree without burning bridges or saying things they can't take back.

But oh no, not the almighty Honourable Kandolo: *F**k off, you b**h! I'll leave you and find a younger, more beautiful woman out there to f**k.* Who talks to their wife like that? Other times, I've heard Honourable Kandolo tell Wendy he did her favour by marrying her. A favour? What kind of logic is that?

It's strange how Honourable Kandolo gets away with such nonsense. He's ten years older than Wendy and doesn't fare well in the beauty department. Honourable Kandolo would be lucky to make the qualifiers list in the *Mr Zambia Contest*. If I were Wendy, I'd get him a full-length mirror for his next birthday, Christmas or Father's Day—and a smaller one for his glove compartment, but larger than his car rearview mirror.

Unfortunately, Honourable Kandolo's threats against his wife always work. Wendy hides whenever they fight, won't socialise and hardly picks up her phone. Whenever I call her during the weekend, I swear she talks to me from the bathroom or something. Why else is the water always running?

Wendy's favourite pastime, playing *Nancy Drew*, has recently intensified to keep up with her husband's skirt-chasing activities. She's on the verge of losing her mind, having used every trick in the book to find out who her husband's latest side chick is. Of late, she has befriended Honourable Kandolo's new Secretary and, cunningly, crowned her *Deputy Nancy Drew*.

I recall that during my fiftieth birthday party five years ago, Wendy attacked and beat the life out of Andrew's then-foolish girlfriend, Maria Sosala—the prostitute who robbed my son of his innocence. It baffled me how Honourable Kandolo did not intervene in the most embarrassing feline fight involving his wife. He sneaked out of my garden into his car on the street and left my friend behind. Horrific!

Wendy is like any other *married divorcee*—an expert at making excuses for her husband's physical abuse inflicted on her. She hides behind thick layers of full-coverage foundation to cover the bruises. Foundation companies should offer her shares in the business; that way, she can get the product for free.

Even in this October heat, she layers it on. I ran into her last week at the clinic. This time, even the fifty layers of foundation couldn't cover the bruise on her left eye. *Justin would never hurt me. He just pushed me by accident, and I fell. I must have tripped on my heels.* So, she claimed. Sigh!

What frightens me the most is how Wendy seems to believe her lies and overrates their romance. *Oh, guess what? Justin and I are going on a romantic trip to Cape Town*; she called to tell me two days after our accidental meeting at the clinic. I wanted to scream at her. *A romantic trip to where? With your black eye?* But instead, I said: *enjoy the vineyards. Take lots of pictures.* Go figure!

Lastly, there's the *married widow*—a dangerous and calculated woman. To be clear, her husband is not dead, but more precisely, she's a *widow in waiting*. The married widow has cut off the oxygen supply to *all things* hubby—she rarely asks him questions. The woman lets her husband roam around like a free-range chicken. To the undiscerning man, the married widow might seem small and as humble as a church mouse, *tamed* to perfection—the perfect wife. Again, big mistake!

My mother's youngest sister, Auntie Milly Kunda, at sixty-nine years old, is a *married widow*. She became that way through one of the biggest betrayals ever—our family is still nursing the collateral damage wounds we sustained.

My Auntie's husband of forty-five years, Uncle Billy Kunda, is a wealthy man. He owns one of the largest sunflower farms, which produces the country's best sunflower oil and margarine and exports to other African countries.

As successful as he is in business, being a faithful husband is something my uncle has miserably failed at. Even now, when all logic suggests Viagra has given up on him, Uncle Billy is still chasing all kinds of women.

Previously, Auntie Milly was a *religious* member of the Shipikisha Club—her husband could do no wrong. But the day finally came when Auntie Milly snapped at age sixty, gave up her Shipikisha club membership, and became a married widow. What changed?

Uncle Billy is very generous and looks after his wife well. But he forgets to draw a line where that generosity should stop. The licentious man of a hubby takes it too far and spreads his benevolence to areas outside his home. It's what finally broke the camel's back.

Once upon a time, Auntie Milly's favourite hair salon was a modern and upscale place called Go Girl Hair Salon. Joyce James, a beautiful forty-five-year-old divorcée with three children, owns Go Girl Hair Salon. Her mother, Auntie Sabina James, of mixed Zambian and Indian heritage, was Auntie Milly's best friend from Primary School.

Joyce, who grew up in my Auntie Milly's eyes, is her goddaughter—someone my Auntie has loved and cherished much like her own child. When Joyce launched her hair salon, it was a pleasure for Auntie Milly to support her goddaughter. She graciously had her network of wealthy women in Lusaka, including my mother, Francine, and myself, become loyal clients. For years, we all were happy clients of Go Girl Hair Salon.

As fate would have it, one day, Auntie Milly, intending to introduce a new client to the salon, dropped in unannounced. As she walked through the entrance towards the counter, she saw Joyce huddled in conversation with Mundia, Uncle Billy's driver.

Auntie Milly couldn't catch Joyce's words but caught Mundia's stage whisper as he explained that his boss had sent him to drop off a cheque. He continued saying that he would return with air tickets for Livingstone. Mundia insisted Joyce go to the airport and Uncle Billy would meet her there.

Foolishly, Mundia had his back on Auntie Milly. He was not ready for how he would be out of employment in an instant. A suspicious Auntie Milly, all elegance out of the window, dashed for the white envelope in Mundia's right hand.

Much to their horror, Mundia dashed for the door like a thief in a cassava plantation. He didn't wait to explain anything but shot out of the salon to the parking lot, where he cowardly sped off in Uncle Billy's car.

Filled with shame and regret, Joyce at once recanted. She tearfully explained to her godmother how *Uncle Billy* had been in a relationship with her for six years. He had invested in her salon business, paid school fees for her three children for years and bought her the mansion she lived in.

Later that evening, huffing and puffing, Auntie Milly confronted her husband with the cheque of K1,000,000 and Joyce's confession. As one could expect, Uncle Billy shamelessly denied everything, threatening to wipe Joyce and her mother out of business. How dare they make such shameful allegations? Useless women! Auntie Milly didn't buy her husband's defence but silently decided to bide her time.

Two days after the incident, Uncle Billy suddenly had a new driver called Minutemaid. Not sure what to make of the change, Auntie Milly decided to *Miss Marple* Minutemaid. The poor fellow caved under the pressure of Auntie Milly's relentless interrogation and ratted out his boss to the madam. Uncle Billy had fired Mundia and neglected to inform his wife about his course of action.

Auntie Milly wasn't the fool her husband took her for—she immediately understood the unspoken reason for Mundia's dismissal. From that time on, Auntie Milly permitted herself to check out of the marriage mentally and emotionally.

Betrayed beyond words, Auntie Milly bitterly mourned the end of her fifty-four-year friendship with Auntie Sabina. How could her friend not have known about this sordid relationship her daughter had been carrying on with Uncle Billy? And Joyce, a child she had helped raise, showered with expensive gifts, her goddaughter, what kind of sick betrayal was this?

Fast forward, Auntie Milly has remained adamant that she will not divorce Uncle Billy. One of them will die before that happens. She does all her wifely duties to the best of her ability. But she no longer asks her husband where he goes, what he does, or with whom.

Foolishly, Uncle Billy goes about Lusaka, prancing around like Eddie Murphy's *King of Zamunda*, believing he has his wife under control. How can he not see that the betrayal his wife suffered is something people rarely recover from? Auntie Milly lost a husband, best friend, and goddaughter in one afternoon. How can he think his wife's okay?

If anyone paid close attention to Auntie Milly's behaviour, they would know she carries a heart of dry molten lava. She believes her husband's misdemeanours have caused her to be the heartless woman she has become. His skirt-chasing no longer moves her—my Auntie is sure God exists solely to punish her husband, who is now seventy-five years old.

So, Auntie Milly patiently awaits the death of Uncle Billy, which she's sure will come before hers. She has convinced herself that her husband's estate is the prize to make the years of suffering worthwhile. It's no use telling my Auntie how messed up her plan is—isn't living in the present the purpose of life? And who can control another person's destiny? Who knows what God's plan is for anyone?

Oh well, *happily married, married divorcée, or married widow*, to each his own. Every married woman must find their balance and what works for them. As for me, I'm sure that the time to be a happily married wife has come and gone. Roger and his mother made sure of that. At the same time, I won't allow myself to become like Wendy, a married divorcée! The time has come for me to find out *who* I am, and I'll take it from there, with or without Roger.

The sound of the doorbell brings me back to earth from my reflections. Yay! Francine must be at the door. With a sudden burst of energy, I rush out of my bedroom to go and receive my sister. Roger and Andrew beat me to it, laughing and chatting with Francine in the hallway. I love the sound of my sister's laughter. She has always been the life of the party.

Francine smiles widely and lights up when she sees me. Overjoyed, I give her a big hug.

"Hello, baby sis, so good to see you."

"Oh, sis, I'm *feeling* this blush pink on you."

My sister and I laugh as I twirl to show off my dress. Francine then turns her attention to Andrew. She runs her hand through the top of his buzz cut.

"Boy, I swear you look more handsome each time I see you."

"Auntie Francine, I hope you'll stay longer than a week this time."

"I am a free *agent* for the next two weeks. Just keep the champagne flowing,"

I wink at my sister. "It's all stocked up for you."

"How's Michael doing?" Roger asks.

"He and the kids are still in London but doing great," Francine responds.

"You must tell him how grateful we are for helping Andrew with the scholarship," Roger says with gratitude.

Now that Michael's name has come up, it's an excellent time to ask Andrew about the scholarship. I discreetly wink at my sister to take the lead.

"Andrew, Michael said you received the scholarship offer last week. Did you get any communication from the university?" Francine casually asks Andrew.

Roger and I turn our attention to our son, awaiting a response. Andrew's eyes shiftily dart around the room, but he says nothing. His behaviour makes me nervous. My voice pitches as I imagine the worst.

"Andrew, what is it? Spit it out!" I demand.

"Calm down, sis; I'm sure Andrew can tell us what's going on," my sister says as she soothingly strokes my arm.

Roger jumps into the conversation. "Son, is there something we should know? Did you get the offer or not?"

Andrew avoids his father's gaze. "Ahem, I think I accidentally deleted the email last week. I thought it was spam,"

"Well, check your *Deleted Items folder*. Where's your phone?" Francine, always the Lawyer, interjects.

"The confirmation came to my work email account, but I haven't installed it on my phone. Also, I left my laptop at the office," Andrew replies.

My son's long-winded story doesn't make sense at all. At this point, we all know he's lying, which tells me there's something more sinister behind what's coming out of his mouth.

I yell at my son and throw him out of the front door. "Get your laptop, Andrew, and stop causing my blood pressure to rise!"

Chapter Ten

CHINESE WALLS

If I didn't know before, it is clear that my mother and Auntie Francine are on to me. They know I have the scholarship but want me to come clean. Uncle Michael had to have told his wife, who would have mentioned it to my mother. What they have not figured out yet but are getting close to is why I have not told them about it. The scholarship on its own is not a problem. Dailess is the main problem behind why I have been shady with my parents.

But after this afternoon's little ambush meeting, I know there is no way out. The honourable thing to do is tell the truth and explain how and why the two issues can't co-exist. If I'm open about it all, the burden of sorting things out will be lighter.

But again, I don't know how to sequence the information of what I already know. I feel mentally paralysed. The weight of the secret without anyone to confide in has taken its toll on me—my dizzy spells have become more frequent from lack of sleep, poor diet and extreme pressure. I must find David and talk to him. I can't take it anymore.

It has been some time since I last drove to David's house in Nyumba Yanga. I don't remember having such a hard time navigating the streets—frighteningly large, deep, and rugged-edged potholes have mushroomed in every direction.

I try to channel some famous Safari Car Rally champions and their obstacle-swerving moves to avoid damaging my father's car. I have enough trouble brewing. The last thing I need is to add a damaged car to the list of my sins. My father would have a fit. I swear he cares more about his cars than he does my mother and me.

Halfway to my destination, I call David to tell him I'm on the way. But there is no response from him—a good taste of my medicine, given my behaviour over the past few weeks. I pray to God that he is at home in any case. Otherwise, I don't know how to face my parents and Auntie Francine again.

Fifteen minutes later, I arrive at David's house and squeeze my car into his front yard next to his little yellow *banger*. My first thought is to examine my tyres to avoid any damage, if at all. Everything looks good with the vehicle—I can focus on my primary mission.

I approach the front door and knock a few times. The door is locked even though it looks like David's home, inside the house.

"David, are you in there?"

No one comes to the door, although I hear faint voices. "Open the door, bruv; I'm not playing with you!"

The fool ignores me. But I don't care how long it takes; I'll keep knocking until the clown opens the door.

David's house has two entrances; the second is around the back, closer to his bedroom. I'll try my luck with that one. I know that David is inside the house because his banger is here, and he drives it everywhere. It's unlikely he went somewhere on foot.

Hmmnn. Someone's in a good mood. The sound of smooth and romantic music *bleeds* through the open kitchen window that's ajar. It's Freddie Jackson's *Rock Me Tonight for Old Times' Sake*. I knew it! My thoughts don't have to wander far to piece the story together. Besides, David's nosey neighbour, Ms Aggie, doesn't need any encouragement to *spill the tea*.

"*Bwanji* (hello) Ba Andrew." Ms Aggie gives me a big toothy smile.

"Hello, madam," I respond flatly to steer the conversation away from where I think it's going. But no such luck.

"Your friend is enjoying," Ms Aggie continues.

"Excuse me?" I give her a stern look. But it's all lost on her.

She grins. "*Banzanu* (your friend) Ba David *bali na paate naka gelo* (David's hosting a party with a girl)," she chuckles with a mischievous glint in her eyes.

In other words, where is your girlfriend? Aren't you going to join the party? I ignore Ms Nosey Parker and continue to knock. Just as I am about to give up, David opens the door, bare-chested, unamused to see me. He wraps his arms tightly across his chest, looks me up and down, and sucks his teeth.

"It's you, wassup?"

"Hey, my man!" I offer my fist in greeting.

David smacks my hand down. "Seriously, bruv, you can't just show up here after being *MIA* for two weeks."

"Bruv, please hear me out; I can explain."

David shakes his head. "No way, man, all my calls have gone unanswered. That s**t ain't cool. It's not how we roll, bruv, or have things changed between us?

"Come on, man, it's nowhere near anything like that. I need your help."

David gazes at me for a few seconds, glances over his shoulder and then gives me a sheepish smile.

"Okay, make it quick; I have a party to return to—come inside."

It's dark and dingy inside David's crampy little house. It might be his idea of a romantic setting, but it just creeps me out. I try to sit on his two-seater couch. It's cramped with books, magazines, a bath towel and clothes. D**n! The whole place desperately needs a deep clean and tidy-up.

On second thoughts, it might be better to talk outside. Besides, the walls dividing the rooms are super thin. I don't want some random chick to eavesdrop on our conversation.

"Bruv, let's talk outside in my car?"

David gives me a sceptical look. "You show up unannounced, and now you want to call the shots for your little impromptu meeting?"

Okay, my friend is still smarting from my bad behaviour, and rightly so. I laugh to make light of the moment.

"Bruv, unannounced? Since when?"

"Starting two weeks ago, you set the rules. Besides, your queen won't let me come within three feet of your house. It's been years, remember!"

I don't want to argue with David; I need him to help me think things through.

"My bad, I admit, bruv. I'm sorry."

David relents. "Fine, let's go."

Back in the car, I get the air conditioning going and think about where to start. It shouldn't be that hard between us. That's what I like about my friendship with David. But the Dailess story is a tough one.

"It's Dailess, bruv."

David raises his eyebrows at me. "And? What about Dailess?"

I look straight at the dashboard of my car to avoid eye contact. The beads of sweat on my forehead rapidly team up and form little distributary rivers that meander down my face.

"She's pregnant."

David looks at me incredulously. I feel ashamed and nervous; no amount of shifting in my car seat could ease the sudden itchiness in my pants.

"Say something, bruv, please."

David thumps me on my back and laughs hysterically. "D**n! Congrats, my man!"

"Bruv, this s**t ain't funny. I haven't told my mother—I don't know how."

"Jeez! What's your bougie ass going to do?"

I look at David with a hopeless expression. "That's why I'm here. Help me think."

"But seriously, bruv, are you sure the pregnancy is yours? Not to dredge up the past, but think about Maria Sosala."

I let David's words sink in; his concern is genuine, and I have my doubts. But only because of how Maria *played* me. Dailess has some erking social climber tendencies, and it bugs the h**l out of me that she didn't tell me when she *knew* the condom broke.

Finally, I break the silence. "Do you think I should keep it quiet and smooth with Dailess, then have a paternity test when the baby is born?"

David sounds hard. "Bruv, are you for real? It doesn't matter if this baby is yours or not. You must *man up and dead* this s**t at once."

"So, you mean, like I should just deny it?"

"Bruv, Dailess is the real kick-in-the-butt type of chick. Hasn't it crossed your mind that she set you up?"

David's words strike a chord, and my temples pound as I take in the full extent of what that might mean. If Dailess were that shady, could I trust her with anything else? The last thing I want to deal with is another chick pulling the wool over my eyes.

"It has crossed my mind, bruv; Dailess' story doesn't track—for sure. But I don't think she's in Maria Sosala's league. That's a whole other level; a professional scammer, as you've always said."

David is still sceptical. "Still, bruv, what Kamwala chick does not want an address upgrade from a bougie Kabulonga baby daddy like you?"

"Well, then she pressed the wrong button because my mother has plans for me. There's no way she'll let me throw away my future to play happy families with Dailess."

David shakes his head. "Yep. This baby Dailess has you convinced yours is a one-way ticket to Mukobeko Maximum Prison—bruv with no parole."

I know David's right about Mukobeko. But that's where Dailess miscalculated. Rule number one: I'm *my mother's son*—my mother always comes first, above all else. All I care about now is doing what it takes to remain in my mother's good graces.

"Bruv, remember the scholarship I told you about a while back? Well, it came through; I bagged it."

David gives me a fist bump. "For real, man, there's your ticket; right there, take it and run!"

"Auntie Francine's husband, Uncle Michael, helped me through the process—another big reason I can't go to my mother with such a soul-crushing story."

"Humour me, bruv. What was your plan had Dailess not fast-tracked you into involuntary fatherhood? Where was this relationship going?"

"Bruv, I'm only twenty-one years old and three months into the relationship; what plan should I have had?"

David narrows his eyes at me. "Are you sure you didn't make any dreamy romantic promises? What made Dailess's sneaky little brain think marriage was on the horizon?"

"I'm a romantic guy, but I ain't stupid; I never discussed marriage with Dailess."

David looks amused. "Level with me, man; what's the difference? You wanted to marry Maria Sosala."

"Dude, you, of all people, should understand that. Maria was the first sex I ever had. So, of course, I wanted to marry her." David bursts into hysterics of laughter.

"Oh, and you're the one to laugh? "Didn't you want to marry that reckless *sugar mummy* of yours after a month with her in the sack?" I laugh.

"Man, I would have thrown my life down the toilet had her gangster husband not saved me by threatening to shoot me." Tears stream down David's cheeks as more laughter erupts from him.

"Bruv, the woman had four kids; one was your age!" I shake my head, looking back at the crazy period. "That s**t would have taken my life down the sewers with your ruined one."

"Remember, I wanted you to be my Chief Bestman." David laughs some more, holding onto his side.

"Bruv, my mother would have run us both through her meat mincer," I respond.

David wipes his eyes. "Okay, bruv, back to business. You've argued your case well, and the solution is simple. Put this Dailess chick in the *rearview mirror*. Don't tell your parents s**t about her—check out of town and go to England."

While David's idea might seem easy, it doesn't settle well with me. It also requires a tight strategy. I'm not sure I can pull it off.

"What should I do in the meantime, man? How can I prevent the pregnancy news from getting to my parents?"

"Plant a *Chinese Wall* between Dailess and your parents, simple as that," David responds.

"I have to act fast because Dailess' friend, Bridget, has repeatedly threatened to bring her to my parents' house."

"Bruv, it sounds like you must discipline both Dailess and Bridget. How can you let them walk all over you like that?"

"How exactly am I supposed to discipline them?"

"See, that's the problem with you right there. You're too soft and available for these chicks. Bruv, you need to lose your s**t on them, and it'll gain you some respect. I'm dead serious."

The Kalinga Linga gangsta in David is out on the loose. It is best to pretend I didn't hear what he said. I'd never raise a finger at a woman. My mother would disown me. As much as I think Bridget is out of control, I still need to manage my emotions. That's how my mother raised me.

"Bruv, listen to me, plan your exit out of this country fast, and don't look back; the rest will be history," David repeats. He can see that I ain't fully on board with his plan.

"What do I do about Dailess and the baby after that?" I ask, not sure I want to know the answer to my question.

"Trust me, these Kamwala chicks are so *thirsty* and cunning. Dailess will pin the pregnancy on some old *dwanzi* professor from the University of Zambia." David looks me in the eye. "The poor professor's wash-and-wear suits won't know what hit them!" David lets out a loud laugh and punches my shoulder.

"Nah, man—I'm not you. I can buy the Chinese Wall option. But I can't turn my back on my child. I don't want to become Roger Michelo 2.0," I try to make David see sense.

"You worry too much. Dailess is a tough cookie. She'll survive. Girls like Dailess never run out of options. Besides, Lusaka is full of sugar daddies; the world is her oyster."

My friend has always had a way of turning life's woes into something to laugh about. But in this case, I can't entirely agree with his sense of humour. It's disrespectful.

"Here's what I'm gonna do: I'll phone Dailess on Monday to meet in person and let her know I'll be there for the baby. That should *call off her dogs*."

David gives me a quizzical glance. "And the relationship? What's next?"

"Bruv, I know Dailess is after marriage. But that's out of the question, and so is the relationship. I don't want another broken condom situation. I've learnt my lesson."

"But seriously, man, put a clock on this s**t before it starts to mess with your head full time."

I know David is right. The longer I sit with all these secrets and plots, the deeper the hole. And the longer it will take to dig myself out of it.

"Thanks, bruv; I appreciate your support, *Uncle David*. You can go back to your party."

David doubles up with laughter. "F**k you, man!"

***

The drive back from David's house to my office in town is a smooth ride. On Saturdays, this time of the day, the traffic is easygoing. I arrive at my office in no time and efficiently carry out my mission. I have my laptop and two printed copies of my scholarship email. It'll help set things straight with my mother and Auntie Francine and keep my *Dailess secret* at bay.

After talking to David, I feel more confident and in control of my situation. My mother doesn't need to know about Dailess, nor does Dailess need to know about the scholarship—Chinese walls, *note to self*.

Back on our street, I park my car in front of our big black metal gates and close my eyes to say a little prayer. Talking to my parents and Auntie Francine about the scholarship should present a window to discuss my travel plans; I could leave for England in November instead of January next year. I already have my UK entry Visa.

An early departure won't solve the baby problem entirely. But it'll be easier to handle without it being a threat to my master's programme. My mother has invested too much in me to cut her plans short.

I open my eyes and am pleased to see Ba Bwezani's gummy smile. He's my *car whisperer;* he comes to the gate even before I arrive in front of it.

"Bwana Andrew, welcome home."

"Yes, boss, thank you." I cheerfully wave and smile at him.

I feel brand new after the *therapy* session with David and confidently swing through our front door.

"Mummy, Auntie Francine, where are you?"

The shrill laughter from the TV room tells me they are watching The Real Housewives of Atlanta—their favourite TV Show. And who knows how many bottles of champagne they have had? I'm not complaining because it all points to cheerful moods and no interrogation. I'm off the hook.

"Hi, Mummy; what's keeping you both so busy you can't hear me?"

"Oh, sorry, sunshine, you're back. We didn't hear you come in."

I grab the remote control to adjust the volume. "The TV is too loud, Mummy. It's not good for your ears."

"Hi Andrew, glad to see you back. Do you have the scholarship email with you?" Auntie Francine demands, her hand outstretched.

" Yes, of course. I printed out a copy for each of you."

The two sisters huddle together and read the email out aloud. Their eyes widen with excitement. I can already feel the pressure leave my body. Phew!

The two ladies scream. "Congratulations!"

"This calls for a celebration; where's Roger?" My mother walks away to find my father.

"Roger, hurry, our son's going to England. We have it in writing," my mother exclaims.

My father is beside himself but doesn't know how to show it. He sheepishly joins everyone and grabs my hand in a painful congratulatory handshake.

"Your mother and I are very proud of you."

"Thank you, Francine, for this gift. Please let Michael know how grateful we are."

My mother can't stop smiling and staring at me, her son. I feel like a celebrity.

Chapter Eleven

BRIDE IN THE MIRROR

Yesterday's events were off the charts! The worst Saturday ever—like an unhinged roller coaster, the day went from one disaster to the next. My pregnancy has turned into a nightmarish drama in which I've no power to control anything. I can't even protect my father, who I know will come as collateral damage along the way. If only I had stopped to think things through, I'd be telling a different story now.

Nothing is going as I'd planned; Andrew's disinterested, my mother's demons are out on the loose, and my poor father has to wade through a fire he didn't start. It's hard to believe, but my life is on an express train to *Nowhereville,* and I don't know what to do when I get there.

Worse still, my parents have brought their marital wahala to mine. One example is yesterday afternoon's drawn-out battle punctuated with the nastiest insults ever—fortunately, it was bloodless. After my mother and her troops realised victory wouldn't be theirs, the *Cold War* subsided, and the three women conceded.

But I think a more correct observation points to my mother's slippery character. She always has multiple cunning plans; getting ahead of her is impossible.

Yesterday afternoon, it wasn't so much that she accepted defeat as it had always been her plan to go to Ba Nganga. The three women had to have had a secret conversation before attacking my father. Their primary strategy was to secure the *damegi* and marry me off to Andrew with the help of Ba Nganga.

Later in the evening, when my mother returned from what she believed to have been a successful mission, another confrontation robbed our household of a peaceful night. My father and I had just sat down to eat some boiled cassava and have a casual banter when the crazy banging on the door startled us both.

It was my mother in a state of aggression. I wondered what she had done with her key and why she wasn't using it. My mother continued to bang on the door and unleash obscenities but with no reaction from my father. It's when I realised that my father had barricaded the door from the inside with an iron bar. It prompted me to go to the bathroom window for a little peep.

Under the moonlight, my mother's dramatic behaviour had already attracted a sizable group of spectators from the compound, especially women. My *finished* life was now on everyone's lips. We live in a part of Kamwala where the houses are tiny and tightly bunched together. There is no privacy; a person's dirty linen is everyone's business. There are no secrets, and integrity does not exist in most people's vocabulary.

The little gap in the window revealed familiar faces from the community, who gleefully took part in vile gossip about me. *Tsk, tsk! Have you seen her wigs and makeup? She is a fast girl, a prostitute.*

Some bystanders, convinced I was a bad influence on other teenage girls, insisted that I get kicked out of the Church. *At her age, with a pregnancy outside marriage, she will spoil our young daughters. Get rid of her, shameful!*

Others cupped their mouths, and their eyeballs popped out of their sockets in disbelief. *How dare she break the sanctity of our taboos?* No wonder my mother was determined to move heaven and earth to change my circumstances through marriage.

The unkind stories about my life were more than I could stand. I cried silently and returned to the living room to ask my father to let my mother in—if only to send those no-good Kamwala gossipers back to their stuffy homes.

My mother pushed the door open, panting and heaving quite dramatically. She was carrying a small reed basket, its contents concealed with a black cloth. After she had caught her breath, my mother declared that Ba Nganga had given her a perfect solution for my pregnancy.

My mother could barely wait to share her news. She launched into a convoluted explanation of how Ba Nganga had seen a bride in a mirror in a white wedding dress. More importantly, my mother insisted that Ba Nganga was sure I was the bride in the mirror. She claimed it was a water-tight deal, and there was no going back on the decision. Andrew and I would have a wedding in December if only I could follow the instructions Ba Nganga gave my mother.

Fortunately, my father, not ready to hear or participate in Ba Nganga's plot, politely suggested to my mother that we all go to bed. And that perhaps things will present themselves differently in the morning. My mother wasn't going to allow my father to usurp her plans.

Undeterred and without waiting for further input from my father, my mother once again took matters into her own hands. She thrust the contents of her basket, a bunch of dried leaves and twigs wrapped in a black cloth, into my lap. My mother's eyes glistened as she recommended I soak her miracle leaves overnight. She whispered that I must rush outside at 04:00 in the morning and bathe in the potion.

As you can imagine, it nearly put me in an early grave from fear, and my father lost it. He couldn't understand how my mother believed ba Nganga could guarantee my marriage to Andrew when her five sisters were all spinsters. The way my mother saw things was that my father was an obstruction in my soon-to-be Kabulonga life.

So, my mother upped the ante and produced two little male and female dolls made from sisal tied together in a black string. She forced me to a standing position and shot up my skirt.

My mother insisted that she tie the little dolls around my waist—again, as instructed by Ba Nganga. And that's when my parents turned our little house upside down, hurling insults and objects at each other.

Listening to my parents' shameless back and forth, I wondered whether the fight was entirely about me. Or did I come as a combo with their pre-existing marital problems? My father threatened to send my mother back to her parents in Chipata.

My mother said she didn't care because my father was useless to her anyway. He couldn't afford to buy her steaks like other husbands do for their wives. My mother claimed the last time she had meat in her diet was when she smelt it from the next-door neighbour's cooking six months ago. It was 02:00 hrs before my parents stopped their circus, and I could go to bed. Eish!

Back to the present, it is 10:00 hrs on Sunday. I didn't dare leave my bedroom, and after what I heard the Kamwala *Jury* say about me last night, Church is a no-go area. My mother has not come to crucify me for not going either. I'm sure she's afraid my presence would fuel the gossip and ruin her *good* name. I need some air; I'll sit outside and have tea.

Halfway to heaving myself out of bed, my phone rings. Group video call from the girls. Do I want to take the call? It could be urgent; maybe Andrew has been in touch with one of them. At any rate, it wouldn't hurt to pick their brains.

"Hello," I breathe heavily into the phone.

"I called you ten times yesterday," Bridget complains. Weren't we supposed to think of a new plan after Friday's meeting with that idiot boyfriend of yours fell through?"

Before I could answer, Sally proudly jumped into the conversation.

"BTW, the *cat is out of the bag* now. It isn't urgent to meet with Andrew anymore."

There is a moment of silence, followed by a flurry of questions from Bridget and Carol.

"What, where, when, and how?" They chorus.

I get a sudden rush of anger as hot tears burn my eyes. "Sally, who gave you the right to tell my story? You outed me to your mother after I told you not to!"

Bridget and Carol are astonished. "What? Sally, how could you?"

"What happened to our agreement to sleep over the issue and meet again today?" Bridget asks.

I harden my voice. "Well, *Miss-Everything-is-About-Me*, here, couldn't keep her mouth shut. What friend does that?"

"Your actions are below the belt, Sally. Dailess trusted you with her most private and sensitive information," Carol disapproves.

Sally defends herself. "I only told my mother..."

I cut her off. "Are you that naïve or just jealous and stupid? Can't you see that telling your mother *is telling my mother*?"

Bridget whistles slowly. "D**n Sally, you are a snitching b***h. It's about time you learnt to keep your entitled little behind out of other people's business!"

In Sally's book, she can never do wrong. She always has a good reason for her actions, no matter who the casualties are.

"You're just overacting; I did us all a favour."

Carol loses her cool. "Sally, there is no excuse for outing Dailess to your mother. How can we trust you to be part of our tight circle if you are a snitch, good reason or not?"

Sally shows no remorse. "You're all just cowards afraid to face the demon."

"You're mistaken about one thing. What's going on with Dailess right now affects the rest of her life. We must all try to be more sensitive in how we go about helping her," Carols says calmly.

Bridget has a rare moment of compassion.

"Sally, this poor girl hasn't even had a chance to sort things out with Andrew."

"Exactly! Every decision Dailess makes today will set in motion a chain of events that she may or may not be able to control. So, please be kind and show some respect," Carol adds.

Not wanting to face the consequences of her mess, Sally hangs up the phone without a word.

"Oh, no, she didn't! I can't believe the b***h just hung up on us. We need to add her to the call again," Bridget shouts, her voice frantic.

"Let it go. Dailess is here, and that's what's important." Carol sighs and brings us back to the main issue. "What I want to know is, where are things with your parents?

"My mother went to see Ba Nganga and claims she has a perfect solution."

"What?" Carol exclaims.

"What kind of a perfect solution can your mother possibly get from Ba Nganga?"

Before I could answer, my mother's angry footsteps cut my call to the girls.

"Guys, I've got to go. Quietness Banda is approaching." I finish the call, slide the phone under my pillow, and quickly pick up my bible.

My mother lurks in the doorway, holding two Chitenge dresses in her left hand and a small travel bag in her right hand. An angry and imposing figure, she looks me up and down and sucks her teeth to show her disdain.

"Ohoow, now you want to read the bible. Show me the chapter that says you can have sex before marriage?"

My mother pulls her mouth downwards and whips the air with the two dresses like a giant bird flapping its wings. She then strolls towards me and throws them on my head.

"Get up and put on one dress. The second one goes in your small travel bag; we must go somewhere. You'd better be ready at 15:00 hrs. Hurry up! Useless girl!"

My mother's sharp words send my mind on a roll. Go where exactly? To Chipata? Please let it not be Chipata; I pray but dare not ask my mother. After I violently resisted her Nganga's *bain aux herbes* last night, the woman is like a landmine on two legs this morning. She is ready to explode with any slight wrong move. In this instance, I choose life. It's wise of me *not to speak now and forever hold my peace.*

I pick up one of the dresses and slip into the cool chitenge fabric. My mother supervises my every move like a prison warden. Obediently, I stuff the other one in the small overnight bag and cross the room to my little wardrobe. As I reach for my makeup bag, my outstretched hand collides with my mother's backhand in a painful smack.

"Leave that nonsense behind. That's what got you pregnant in the first place. Colouring your lips all day like a hule!"

My mother rushes up to me to grab my small makeup bag and then pushes my tiny bedroom window open as far as it can go. She vigorously empties all my makeup outside and wags her finger at me.

"Let me catch you picking up that rubbish from outside; you'll see!"

This woman has no idea how many skipped lunches it takes to save up for one fake designer lipstick and foundation. But I calmly remind myself not to say anything. I sit down on my bed and pick up the bible again. My mother leaves and slams the door on her way out.

"Stupid girl!

Chapter Twelve

WHAT'S EATING ME?

My mother is a big believer in intuition. She stresses that it's how God communicates with us and helps us make choices that serve our higher selves. I have learnt to listen to my heart and soul when in doubt. It's God's way of shining his light upon our path, my mother always says. After my infamous break-up with Maria Sosala, my mother's words helped me get through my darkest days.

I had lost my way—the Honourable Kandolo's revelation was more than I could bear. I went off on the deep end. How could Maria have done me dirty like that? What young woman sleeps with a man old enough to be her father, then returns to me with a straight face? I lamented to my mother at the time. It took a while for me to heal emotionally and psychologically. Maria destroyed me.

As you might have already understood, manipulation is second nature to Maria. So, it didn't surprise me that she tried to fight for our relationship by whatever means possible. Maria insisted that we still loved each other. And that if we took a short break at the Royal Livingstone Hotel, we could rediscover our romance. Unfortunately for her, that was not the best suggestion she could have come up with. Was Honourable Kandolo going to finance this romantic getaway as well?

Maria is the type of woman who doesn't give up easily. She continued to mess with my head and claimed Aunty Wendy was a crazy older woman who had mistaken her for another chick. And that Honourable Kandolo was a useless philanderer who chased every young woman in town. The question was, how would Maria know?

What was most damaging was even though I knew Maria had lied to me, I kept second-guessing myself. Was I too harsh? Should I forgive her? I had to be strong and learn to choose better for myself, find healing, and leave Maria in the past.

I can hear my mother's words again this morning and wonder why now. Is my intuition at it again? I have tried to suppress the constant niggling feeling in the pit of my stomach. But like fresh seawater, it has relentlessly floated back to the surface each time. Dear God, help me figure this out. What's eating me?

After David and I met yesterday, it became clear that I could slow things down with Dailess while I manage my parents. If I left for England sooner than planned, it would be easier to handle my mother from a distance—over the phone. I can't look her in the eyes when she trusted me to be responsible with young girls.

Fortunately, I haven't heard from Dailess or Bridget since Friday. If anything, I expect to hear from them on Monday, but not today, on a Sunday. The only thing I must focus on today is convincing my parents about an early November trip to England rather than January next year. I must keep them sweet and relaxed before I sway them to see things my way.

While we all wait for our Sunday brunch, I join my father in the TV room. He's in a cheerful mood, which is a rare occurrence. Of course, only a football match between Arsenal and Manchester United can get through my father's emotional walls. I can tell by his ear-to-ear grin, the light beer in his right hand and the remote control on his lap that Arsenal is in the lead.

With the remote control within reach, one can expect my father to raise the volume suddenly if and when the Arsenal team scores. It's a strange habit, but my mother and I have long accepted some of his quirky ways.

It's a goal! My father exclaims and punches the air with his right fist. In the process, he spills his beer on the side table, which cascades onto the floor like a mini waterfall. I cringe as the frothy yellowish-gold liquid on the floor snakes towards my mother's hand-made Persian carpet.

My mother shouldn't find her rug stained and reeking of beer; there'll be no way to appease her. My father and I would have to pay dearly for it. He for the primary crime, the damage caused to the carpet, and I for the betrayal and obstruction of justice.

My mother doesn't expect me to ever cover up for my father in any way. I'm my mother's son—always on her side. Besides, I won't let my father put giant spokes in my mission. The happier my mother is, the higher the chance of getting what I want out of her.

So, I spring into action and go to the rescue. I quickly throw a bunch of serviettes onto the carpet as the beer seeps into its expensive wool and silk weave.

My father pats me on my back. "Thank you, son."

Really? It annoys me that he doesn't take his eyes off the TV screen. Oblivious to the damage before him, he feels around for another beer without a care. But I dare not complain because my father holds half the key to what I want, so I flash him a big smile instead.

"Anything for you, Dad."

"Today's going to be fantastic, son. Please, no sales calls. Let's enjoy our well-deserved break."

I punch the air. "Copy that," I try to match my father's enthusiasm. But my mind is elsewhere. I must seize this rare chilled vibe to launch my plan. I play out a few scenarios as I try to summon the courage to go for it.

"It's a goal! Yes! We'll win this match, son." My father's animated voice draws me out of my contemplation.

"What, who won the match?"

My father glares at me. "What's wrong with you? Aren't you watching?"

Any other time, I would have been right there, next to my father, equally psyched to enjoy the game. But right now, I have more important things to worry about, like why that nagging feeling is back in my gut. Again, what's eating me?

I rub my right eye as I feign pain. "Oh yes, I'm watching, Dad. But I missed the goal. A silly little beer fly flew into my right eye."

My father, too excited to care about random beer flies, high-fives me. "Don't worry, soon you'll be able to watch our favourite team in the stadiums in England."

Yes! It's now or never.

"I can't wait. It might be better for me to leave in November instead of January."

My father chuckles. "You reckon? Talk to your mother."

Distracted by the game before him, I'm unsure my father fully understood my request. Nonetheless, I'm relieved; a green light is a green light. I've secured my father's blessings; it feels so good that I can dance. The dark cloud that hung over my head has finally begun to dissipate.

I rush to find my mother and Auntie Francine. I've got to tell them about the good news before my father rescinds his blessings. I don't trust his mood swings. Eish!

The two ladies are in the kitchen, supervising our Sunday brunch preparations as they chat, laugh and sip their tea. It's a great day; my mother is in a celebratory mood. I got the scholarship; she's over the moon. My mother deserves every bit of happiness. The plans she's worked so hard for are now in motion. What's there not to celebrate?

I pause briefly in the doorway and think David was right about the Chinese wall. There isn't any room for Dailess in this scenario; my mother is a constant, and I've got to stick to the script between us. No doubt, this is my mother's moment, and when I've fulfilled part of what she expects from me, I can bring Dailess into the picture.

"Oh Francine, I'm super excited for Andrew. You know this will be his first trip to London; I should travel with him, don't you think?"

Auntie Francine claps in delight. "That's a wonderful idea. A holiday in London would do you good. When did you last go to the UK, April?"

My mother giggles. "All I know is that it's time to travel again. London, here we come! Drum roll, please!"

Auntie Francine turns around and sees me, her eyes gleaming with excitement. She waves to beckon me into the kitchen.

"Hi, Andrew, come over here. Your mother's very excited about your January trip. We're checking out airfares and schedules."

I rush over to hug and kiss my mother. "Oh, sweet! Is that what my two favourite women have been up to?"

My mother smiles; she's emotional. "Hello, young man, guess what? I'm going to travel to England with you."

"Wonderful, Mummy, that's great news. It'll be the first time you and I travel outside of Zambia together. And what better way to start!"

"Exactly; you and your mother can have our apartment in London until University begins." Auntie Francine is ever so generous.

I hug my Auntie. "Thank you, Auntie Francine, you're the best." I clear my throat and quickly turn to my mother. "Mummy, with Auntie's offer, we could travel in November, instead, more quality time together."

My mother looks discouraged for a fleeting moment. "Sonny, that's just around the corner. What about your father? Did you talk to him?"

"I wouldn't worry about Dad if I were you. He expects you to handle the travel plans," I distort the truth slightly.

It all comes down to how you interpret what my father said earlier. It sounded like he passed the responsibility for my trip onto my mother. That's how I conveniently understood it.

My mother makes the sign of the cross. "Well, in that case, November it is."

Auntie Francine adds the cherry on the icing.

"Let's all spend Christmas together in London. Michael and the kids would love that."

Sweet! Luck is on my side; everything is going more straightforward than I expected. With my travel plans sealed, this day couldn't be more perfect—I couldn't care less about what's eating me. I'll be long gone when Dailess and her friends next think of blackmailing me.

"Andrew, make sure you bring your office team into the picture. Otherwise, your father will kick a fuss. We don't need any party poopers," my mother warns. We all burst out laughing.

At 11:00 hrs, the sound of the mealtime bell interrupts our laughter. Ba Esther kneels at my mother's feet and proudly invites everyone to eat.

"Brunch is ready, madam."

"Thank you, Ba Esther. Did you ask the boss to the table?"

"Yes, madam. The boss is already at the table."

***

Our Sunday brunches are an event rather than a meal. From about 11:00 hrs to 17:00 hrs, the feast occupies a significant part of the day. A celebration, every brunch begins with Josephine Baker's *J'ai Deux Amours* classical song and delicious mimosa cocktails. My mother loves all things French.

"Mummy, you must have been French in your previous life," I tease.

"Ah, mon amour (my love), how I wish. But when you're in England, we shall make the most of the Euro Star and travel to Paris."

We all raise our glasses in a toast to Paris.

"Cheers!"

Our brunch menu is an exciting and tasty combination of Zambian, Italian, and French dishes—coc au vin is a staple. I can't wait to dig in.

My mother sounds like a food hypnotist. "Bon appetit. Remember to delve into the culinary journey with each bite you take." My mother closes her eyes as if in meditation. "Allow the aroma and taste to transport you to different places and connect you with diverse cultures."

"Mummy, these delicious Solwezi Dry Beans will take me to the North Western Province of Zambia," I chuckle.

Sunday brunch is the only time my mother does not chastise Ba Esther for making enough food to feed the whole neighbourhood. My parents have an open-door policy for their friends or relatives to drop in and eat with us without a formal invitation. But not today.

On Friday, I gave Ba Bwezani strict instructions not to let anyone through the gates, and my phone is out of commission for the weekend. I can't risk the likes of Bridget strutting in the living room like an apparition. I've got to maintain that Chinese wall—everyone can wait till Monday to see me.

My father flashes me a hopeful smile. "Son, I hope you invited some prospective clients. They're more likely to visit us at the showroom after an informal meeting during brunch."

"That's true, Dad. There's less pressure," I say and deflect the question. I then quickly switch topics to the banquet before us. "Mummy, this ritual never gets old, and I am hungrier each time than the last."

"About time; you haven't eaten much the last few weeks. I'm glad to see you bounce back," my mother scolds in jest.

I want to feel my mother's words in their truest sense. And yes, in a way, I have bounced back after seeing David yesterday. And today has gone well so far, hitch-free, except that feeling in my gut won't give me peace. I still don't know what's eating me.

Chapter Thirteen

KABULONGA, HERE WE COME

At 15:00 sharp, I grab my travel bag and lock my bedroom door. I must find my mother before she comes looking for me. Strangely, she still hasn't shared any information about her plans. Where are we going, and why must I take an overnight bag? But again, I'm in no position to ask questions; it's best not to tip the apple cart.

Our tiny living room is dark despite the harsh sunshine outside. My mother isn't there, but the closed windows and drawn curtains indicate she was there in preparation for the trip to *God knows where*. The house is unusually tranquil, given last night's battle for my so-called *mirror wedding;* I'm *a mirror bride* now. My mother intends to see to it that it comes to pass, even if it's the last thing she does on this earth.

It worries me that my father, especially, isn't in the living room. He spends most Sundays here, listening to Church music on his precious little radio. The radio now stands mute and forlorn on the old, weathered sideboard.

Everything is still; my parents might have silently agreed to have a *cease-fire*. Typically, their quarrels go on for a whole week. Unfortunately for me, our tiny house becomes a war zone with complex boundaries and shifting *enemy territory*—it complicates my life beyond anything one can imagine.

My mood perks up slightly. At last, there's a sign of life coming from the kitchen. It's my father, fussing with the door.

"Hello, Dad. The house is so quiet. Why is your radio not playing this afternoon?"

"Dailess, my daughter. I haven't seen you all day," he replies with his back to me.

My heart leaps into my mouth. "Daddy, what's happening? Do you know Mummy wants to take me to God knows where?"

"Go outside, my daughter; your mother's waiting for you. I'll join you in a minute."

My stomach lurches; this can't be what I think it is. Is my father sending me to the village in Chipata with my mother? Should I ask him again or wait for fate to reveal itself? I settle on the latter and leave my father to potter around the kitchen.

Terrifying memories of the only time I ever went to Chipata come flooding back. I remember wetting myself on the sleeping mat every night—I was always too afraid to use the pit latrine outside.

My village cousins would tell scary stories every night about lions that prowled around the huts and preyed on little children. I spent horrible nights clenching and unclenching my buttock cheeks to avoid two equally frightening *forces*—the fangs of the lions and my grandmother's wrath. As you can tell, my mother is *a chip off the old block*.

Throughout the night, I would pray for sunlight to stream through my grandmother's mud hut and save me from the two *beasts*. But at five years old, the nights were always too long for me—I never stood a chance.

While the lions never ate me alive, my grandmother might as well have done so. Every morning, she would inspect all her grandchildren. The bedwetters—I, being one of them, would get a good spanking; it left my small behind smarting all day long—such trauma!

The glaring sun outside is unbearable. I walk across the dry ground towards the roadside to find my mother. She's under a mango tree with Amake Sally and Amake Mwansa. They huddle together like spies as they whisper in hush, clandestine voices.

Why must we all wait outside without clarity about my mother's agenda? I realise, thankfully, that Chipata isn't part of this afternoon's plan. Otherwise, why is Amake Sally and her friend here? For all I know, my mother and her friends could be plotting my jail sentence, but I couldn't care less as long as I don't have to go to Chipata.

***

Ten minutes later, my father finally secures the front door and approaches my mother under the mango tree.

"Radio Banda, hurry up," my mother yells at him.

"Woman, shut up. This nonsense plan of yours had better work."

I watch my father trot to the roadside and hail a taxi, and it suddenly dawns on me that my mother's ambition is to take me to Andrew's house. My knees start to knock uncontrollably. What will Andrew think? Bridget had threatened to do the same, but I wouldn't let her do anything silly. With my mother, unfortunately, there's no dissuading her, and it's too late to warn Andrew. *Let the chips fall where they may.*

A run-down Toyota Corolla taxi comes along and skids to a halt in a massive cloud of dust. My father shakes his head and makes a last attempt to reason with my mother before we set off.

"Quietness, your plan is a bad idea. Besides, the car can't take all five of us. Do your friends have to come with us?"

My mother ignores him and addresses the driver instead. "Excuse me, can your car take five people?"

The driver scratches his head. "Aaah, Madam, please, this isn't a minibus. You'll pay extra for those two other Aunties."

"Quietness, you see now? Ladies, return to your homes; this is a family matter."

"Why? Why must we pay more?" My mother asks the driver.

"Madam, shocks are expensive. Are you going or not? You're wasting time."

Five minutes later, we all squeeze into the car. My father takes the front passenger seat while my mother and her two friends sit in the back—the skin on their bare arms clammy and sticky. I wiggle into the car to settle on my mother's lap.

It's such a tight space that my head hits the ceiling. Bits of old foam particles crumble onto my face. The car sags dangerously low from the combined weight of the human load, but that doesn't stop the plan. Kabulonga, here we come!

"Kabulonga," my father announces.

The amused driver gives him a quizzical look. "Aaah, boss. Where to in Kabulonga?"

My mother pokes me in the small of my back.

"Eeeh, Dailess, don't keep quiet now. Where does your silly boyfriend live."

I jump, and my head hits the ceiling again. "I'll direct you once we get to Kabulonga Supermarket."

"OK, sista."

The driver steps on the gas. My father panics, and sweat beads cover his upper lip.

"Slow down; we didn't agree on the fare."

"Boss, Kamwala to Kabulonga Supermarket is 120 Kwacha."

My father doesn't respond immediately but rolls his eyes backwards as he calculates how far his wallet can stretch. It's not hard to see that my *warmongering* mother's unplanned trip to the Michelos' house will undoubtedly burn a hole in his pocket. Left up to him, my father would rather not be in this old Toyota on a mission to ambush my boyfriend and his unsuspecting parents.

My father sighs. "OK, that's fine, keep going."

***

A while later, my mother shakes my shoulder as if she's unsure I'm still alive. "Dailess, wake up; we're at the Kabulonga Supermarket," she yells, her voice sharp and desperate.

I flip my eyes wide open and look around. I don't understand where we are. I turn to the driver.

"Yes, but this isn't where the Michelos house is."

"Sista, don't waste my time. You said Kabulonga Supermarket."

"No, I said I would show you the way once we get to Kabulonga Supermarket."

"Ah-aha, is this not Kabulonga Supermarket?"

"But this is inside the Supermarket parking lot; you could have stopped by the roadside." It irritates me because I'm sure it's the driver's way of pushing up the fare. "We don't need anything from this parking lot. Go to Roan Road and turn to your right; we can begin to look for the house from there."

For people like us, Kabulonga is a neighbourhood one rarely visits. It's a long way from home; unless you work or have relatives, you have no business being here. The streets look similar, which adds to the confusion of the already intimidated visitor.

My father glances around furtively like a thief amid a heist. "My daughter, are you sure you know where we're going?"

"Andrew told me he lives on Roan Road, and this is it, Dad.

Kabulonga has some of the most beautiful houses in Lusaka. The yards and houses appear impressively large to first-time visitors. Their high protective walls envelop them away from the passer-by's full view, which adds to the mystery.

My mother and her friends peer through the taxi windows like tourists as they point and marvel at everything in sight. They're enchanted to see the size of some houses in the neighbourhood.

Mesmerised, my mother briefly lifts her foot off the *gas pedal* of her Michelo *crusade*. "Dailess, is this a school?"

I smile. "No, mummy, it's a house."

Amake Sally is equally enthralled. "How many people live in this one house?"

"It depends on the size of the family. It can be two people or more."

I'm happy that I can be of touristic service to the ladies. My mother and her friends are short of words in their wondrous discovery. They nod and smile away like Cheshire cats. Andrew is the only person I know who lives in Kabulonga. To a degree, I'm just as curious as the Cheshire cats.

Since I met Andrew, I have hoped he would take me to his house to meet his parents. Is it a bad thing to long to be a part of his world? I would love to get out of Kamwala and join the high society of Lusaka. Is it wrong to think the way I do? Sigh.

Five houses later, we still drive around like lost elephants on Roan Road. Yet, we can't correctly identify the Michelo residence.

My father looks stressed. "My daughter, where're we?"

"I'm sorry, Daddy. I'm a little confused—I only have an old blurred photo on my phone to go by."

The driver pounds the steering wheel. "Sista, I can't keep driving in circles. Where are we going?"

As we make a sixth attempt to find the Michelo residence, I fear we might have to abort the mission.

My father shakes his head in despair. "Quietness, this is a poor plan; we're wasting money."

"Madam, your husband's right. I have other clients, and you must get out of my car."

My mother digs in her heels. "I'll walk if necessary, but I promise I'll find this house today. Rich people in kabulonga will know who Quietness Banda from Kamwala is."

The atmosphere in the vehicle is tense with opposing views. I wish I could get out because the endless merry-go-round has heightened my nausea. I'd give anything for the car to stop moving. With every speed bump and jerk of the vehicle, my guts threaten to spill out like torrential rain.

Despite the torture, I choose to bear it silently because asking the driver to stop for a few minutes is equivalent to putting spokes in my mother's plan. It's asking for war; any wise person must avoid it if they can help it. I say a silent prayer for God to give us a sign.

And then, I see Andrew's house as if in a dream. Triumph at last! I don't understand how we missed it. As I look at it now, it's a mansion that majestically stands on slightly raised ground. The magnificent building is a striking beauty amongst the other houses, with a thick white wall that sandwiches a massive black gate—the *holy grail* of the Michelo residence.

Excited, I slap the back of the driver's seat. "Stop here! I'm sure this is the house."

Startled, the driver abruptly slams the brakes with more force than necessary. We all scream as we lurch forwards. My father clings to the dashboard for dear life while my mother, consumed with intense fear, tightens her grip around my waist—more for her protection than mine.

She screams. "Don't kill us before I get the *damegi* for my daughter!".

Amake Sally and Amake Mwansa's horrified faces look like they'd just had a sneak preview of their funerals.

The driver doesn't offer any apology. He parks his decrepit car in front of the Michelo house as the toxic smell of burnt tyres chokes our nostrils.

"Boss, we are here, K200, please. I'm late now," the driver demands, thoroughly agitated.

My father clutches his chest. "Why have you changed the fare? Isn't this the same Kabulonga you said was K120?"

The driver raises his voice. "Boss, we went to Kabulonga Supermarket and five houses, wasting time and petrol. The K200 includes shocks for the car because of the two Aunties at the back."

My father tries to appease the man.

"Hey, my young brother, there's no need to shout or speak rudely over money. It's just money and not a matter of life and death."

"No *mudala* (old man), you can't be serious. If it's just money, why are you sweating? We all love money, mudala; money is a matter of life and death. Pay me, now!"

My father reaches for his threadbare wallet, stuffed with a few dirty Kwacha notes. His hand is unsteady as he discreetly counts his money. I'm saddened to see him face such humiliation in the presence of my mother's inquisitive friends.

My father clears his throat. "If I give you K200, my wife and I will be stranded here in Kabulonga."

"Mudala, that's not my business. My job was to bring you here. Haven't I done that?"

"Yes, we appreciate that. But I have to leave enough money to return to Kamwala."

Spit flecks fly out of the driver's mouth. "Aa-ah, Mudala, are you confused? How you and your wife will return to your compound isn't my problem. Pay me now, or you'll regret it, Mudala; I'm not playing."

"Let's not quarrel—why are you shouting?" My father replies with a tremor in his voice.

The driver wags his forefinger in my father's face. "Ohoo, Mudala, you don't know me. I'll teach you a lesson in front of your wife!"

My heart bleeds for my father. "Daddy, please pay the man. I'll reimburse you. Just let this man go."

My father takes heed and reluctantly pays the taxi driver. We're all barely out of the vehicle when the driver angrily skids off and douses us in more heavy clouds of choking exhaust fumes.

The man spits out of his window and shouts, "Cockroaches! Idiots!"

Gasping for winded breath, my mother, like a conquistador, stands triumphantly in front of the intimidatingly massive black gate of the Michelo residence. *Quietness Banda has arrived and marked her territory.*

Meanwhile, my eyes sting, and my ribs hurt as I try to contain my coughing fit from the polluted air surrounding us. As important as this mission is to my mother, it's most uncomfortable for me.

After such a long and unpleasant ride, we all need a few moments to compose ourselves. My father straightens his Sunday best suit; its shiny fabric looks more like *liquid plastic* from too much washing, sunshine and ironing.

My mother and her troops tighten their chitenge wraps, ready for war. I can no longer contain my nausea. My legs buckle as I drag myself to the edge of the sidewalk. Whose bright idea was it to call it morning sickness when, at nearly 16:00 hrs, I still have overpowering waves of nausea?

The loud bickering of my parents brings me back to earth. They can't figure out how to get past the gate that seals off the Michelos fortress.

"Quietness, we're here; this is what you wanted. How's your plan going to get us past this barrier?"

"Barrier or not, I won't leave this house without my daughter's damegi and *lobola* (dowry). End of the story."

"Is that what your witch doctor advised you, Quietness? The Michelos will call the Police, and I'm not going to Mukobeko Prison for you and your friends."

My mother sucks her teeth. "Why did you come if you can't help me get the *damegi* and *lobola*?"

"I came to protect my daughter. I don't trust you and your henchwomen."

"Go, Radio Banda, it's a free country. Go, we don't need you!"

"What do you think your stubbornness will do, Quietness? You'll embarrass our daughter. Even if the boy wanted to marry Dailess, he'd be afraid to do so because of you."

My mother gives my father a menacing eye. "Radio Banda, you're a fool. If you think this boy inside this mansion will get away with *free goods,* you don't know me well!" My mother heaves and paces like a caged animal. "Can't you see that this pregnancy has finished Dailess? Someone inside this mansion will pay!"

"Please, Quietness, let me come back with Uncle Broomson Zyambo to discuss the matter of the damegi."

"Never, never, never! Over my dead body. You shan't discuss my daughter's damegi with your greedy Uncle Broomson Zyambo. That man has no shame—he'll *eat the money*!"

I tune out my parents' senseless dispute. To help move things along, I bang on the gate with the palm of my hand, which achieves nothing except cause me excruciating pain. Impatient with my feeble efforts to announce our arrival and my parents' drama, Amake Sally takes matters into her own hands.

Without warning, she picks up a big rock and bangs on the metal portal. The explosive noise throws my parents into silence and increases my jitters.

"Amake Dailess, be serious; we didn't come to play," Amake Sally says as she gathers rocks in a pile.

The clanking of chains rings out from the other side of the gate. "Hello, who are you please? Can I help you?"

I have never met Andrews' parents before but have seen his father from afar, and the voice behind the gate can't be Mr. Michelos. It sounds like one of a much older man—Ba Bwezani! I smile as I recall the fondness with which Andrew speaks of him.

My mother isn't amused. "Oh, look at her smiling now—foolish girl! So, you can laugh now, Dailess? Wait until you have a baby without a husband. Let's see if you'll laugh."

"Please, can I help you?" Ba Bwezani repeats, his voice getting louder.

"It's Radio Banda and family," my father says.

"Radio Banda...from where? My boss isn't expecting you. Go to his office on Monday, please. Not here."

My mother loses her patience and pushes my father out of the way to inch closer to the gate. "We want to talk inside, open for us now."

As if weighing his words, Ba Bwezani takes his time to speak. "There's no one for you to talk to here."

"No one to talk to? So, no one made my daughter pregnant? That foolish boy inside the house raped my Dailess!"

Ba Bwezani panics. "No, Madam, this is a mistake. I'm sorry I can't let you in. Please leave immediately."

There is nothing that my mother likes more than a challenge.

"Amayi, let's teach this man a lesson!"

"Please, my people of God, don't cause trouble. You can talk to the boss on Monday."

"I will climb this gate!" my mother threatens.

"Quietness, shut up and stop that nonsense!" My father restrains her.

Ba Bwezani sounds stern. "You have the wrong address; please go away."

"Dailess, call Andrew; tell him we are here, and he must let us in." My father commands.

It's not such a great idea to call Andrew. Firstly, there's little chance he'll pick up the phone. Secondly, the last thing I want my parents to witness is Andrew's rejection of me. There's only so much humiliation I can take.

My father narrows his eyes at me. "Dailess, didn't you hear what I said?"

"Yes, Daddy. I'll do so now."

I wish this day could end as I dial Andrew's number three times, and there's no answer each time. It does not escape my mother's eye. She looks at me up and down in disdain, then cackles in mockery.

"Amayi, look at your niece. *Shuwa shuwa*, we have come to talk to a boy who doesn't even pick up the phone when his foolish girlfriend calls."

My father looks sad, but my mother thinks there must be another way to make Andrew respond. She grabs my phone and hits the redial button. But still, there's no answer.

Amake Mwansa is impatient.

"Amake Dailess, don't waste time with that stupid phone. Find some bricks, and let's break this gate."

The three women proceed without caution and savagely hurl rocks at the giant metal. Blow after blow, chipped bits of black paint fly about, revealing the grey metal beneath it. The combination of the clamorous racquet of rock against metal and the women's roaring tumult travels far. It's loud enough to wake the whole neighbourhood.

My father summons every ounce of authority left in him. "Quietness, who'll pay for this vandalism now? The Police will arrest you. Stop it!"

"*Fuseke* (forsake), Radio Banda! Rich people have already vandalised your daughter. I tell you, someone will die today!"

Tempers fly uncontrollably, a cue for my parents to start an unsightly *dog fight* before the Michelo house. Amake Sally and Amake Mwansa, who don't need the invitation to join the kerfuffle, viciously attack my father in solidarity with my mother. A crowd of passers-by quickly gather like red ants to cheer and jeer at the four shameless adults.

I look around frantically; if only someone could help free my father from this gang of women. But no one makes any attempt to stop the fight. To everyone, it's like any other street fight—*entertainment!* I have no choice but to break up this Sunday afternoon *horror show* myself.

"Mummy, stop, stop it! Let me talk to the man behind the gate. I know his name."

My mother doesn't answer me but signals her henchwomen to let my father go. I take it as approval to approach the gate and speak to Ba Bwezani.

I put a smile in my voice. "Ba Bwezani, how are you, sir?"

His voice softens. "Aah, *iyee* (oh) madam, you know my name!"

"Yes, sir, I do. Andrew talks about you all the time. Please tell him that Dailess Banda is here with her parents."

Ba Bwezani is friendly but firm. "Madam, you can see Bwana Andrew at his office tomorrow."

"Sir, you're like my grandfather; show pity on me. I'm carrying Andrew's child."

Ba Bwezani lets out a cry in shock. "Nooo! A baby for Bwana Andrew, are you sure?"

"Yes, sir—please, help me."

"Ha! I have to get the boss, not Bwana Andrew. My God, my God—it will kill his mother. How can I tell them this news?"

"Please, sir, we'll be grateful if you can bring Mr Michelo Sr." My father pleads.

"OK, give me fifteen minutes. The name is Dailess Banda?"

"Yes, sir, thank you."

And so, we wait with bated breath.

Chapter Fourteen

THE CHICKENS HAVE
COME HOME TO ROOST

Our Sunday brunch went by fast today; it finished earlier than 15:00 hrs when, typically, the last guest leaves at 17:00 hrs. With a bit of help from my *partner in crime*, Ba Bwezani, I carefully orchestrated a guest-free event. By 14:30, my parents, Auntie Francine, and I had all savoured our meals, thanked Ba Esther, and gracefully left the table.

We have all moved to the TV room to enjoy the cosy ambience of a leisurely Sunday. The glow and tranquillity of this time of day is heaven. Everyone seems at peace, no pressure.

Sprawled across the soft embrace of the couch, I drift in and out of a soothing nap. My mother and Auntie Francine's cheerful banter and laughter are a sweet lullaby. They have picked up the London trip discussion from where they left off earlier.

Across the room, reclined luxuriously in an armchair, my father has succumbed to a deep sleep. His mouth is slightly ajar, and he snores gently while his left arm loosely hangs on the side of the chair.

It's a perfect time to unwind and leave all my cares behind. But from the corner of my eye, I can see Ba Bwezani through the glass doors. As he waves to catch my attention, it strikes me as unusual behaviour. But I figure whatever it is can wait.

I discreetly signal Ba Bwezani to wait till later to talk to me, but that doesn't work. If anything, he attempts to approach the TV room but loses his nerve midway and awkwardly turns back. But not before my mother sees him.

"Come back here, Ba Bwezani. What's got you behaving this way?"

Ba Bwezani turns back to approach my mother, and he kneels at her feet, head cast down. He does not speak for a few minutes, but his weird energy beckons our attention. We are now all alert and look at each other, unsure whether to laugh or be concerned.

My father is impatient. "Do you have something important to say, Ba Bwezani? If not, please don't disrupt my sleep."

Ba Bwezani stutters. "Bwa...Bwana Andrew..."

"What has my son done that has got your tongue tied?" My mother sharply demands.

Ba Bwezani stares at me long enough for our eyes to lock. There it is! The thing that won't give me peace—the mysterious unease deep in my gut. I can see it in Ba Bwezani's eyes.

Ba Bwezani shifts his gaze to the floor. "Bwana Andrew, you have vistaaz."

I sit up on the edge of the couch. "What, me? Who is it?"

OMG. Deep in the pit of my stomach, a chilling wave of desperation uncoils. It's like a sinister serpent has engulfed every fibre of my being. I attempt to stand up, but my legs wobble like jelly and betray me. I collapse back onto the couch, forced to remain seated. *Lord, please help me*—my mind freezes, I can't think.

My father misses my fearful demeanour. "Andrew, this might be one of our clients; what do you think?"

My mother sees through me. "Visitors, clients, whoever, I don't care—Andrew, what's going on?"

"But we always receive guests on Sundays; what has changed?" My father asks, perplexed.

Meanwhile, Ba Bwezani doesn't attempt to leave the room. Instead, he looks at my parents and solemnly shakes his head. Something is wrong, but my parents take a while to *come to the party*.

Auntie Francine *cracks the code*. "Look, it can't be regular visitors," she addresses my parents. "Ba Bwezani knows more than he is letting on but is afraid to say so."

"Andrew, spit it out! Who's at the gate?" My mother's voice is shrill with fear.

I shrug my shoulders. "Ba Bwezani, tell the visitor to meet me at the office."

My father raises his voice. "Son, go to the gate and sort out your rubbish."

The air is tense and filled with nervous trepidation as we wait for what happens next. All I can think of is I might wet my jeans if the ground doesn't magically open to swallow me.

Ba Bwezani intervenes. "No, Sir, you're the father of Bwana Andrew. They want you."

"Who, they? Please stand up, Ba Bwezani; I must understand what you mean. Is it the Police?" My father demands.

"No, sir, but we have a big problem at the gate."

"Very well, Ba Bwezani, take me to the visitors."

My life is over! Could it be Bridget? She's cantankerous enough to show up at my house unannounced. What am I going to do? My mother and Auntie Francine look at each other, their eyes glazed with worry. But no one says a word as we all wait in the formal living room for my father to return with the mystery visitors.

***

It feels like a century has passed, but ten minutes later, my father returns with a string of strangers. At least, I think they are until the young woman who half-stumbles into the room looks up and holds my gaze.

Goodness! It's Dailess! What the f**k!! *The chickens have come home to roost.* My heart drops to my shoes like a bag of solid cement, dragging my stomach along, and everything goes black.

I have heard that near-death or out-of-body experiences, although rare, happen. I've heard stories of people who say they died, went to heaven, and returned. Tales of such incidents are a mystery to the living and will remain so until the end of time. But this afternoon, that narrative has got my name on it.

Lying here on the floor in my semi-conscious state, I'm unsure if I'm dreaming or dead—it feels close to what a near-death experience might be like. I feel lightheaded, and my body is like a cloud floating around aimlessly in the sky.

But I can hear everything—Doctors say *hearing* is the last sense to leave the body while dying. Around me, there's a flurry of activity, which I'm a part of and yet detached from, like seeing myself in a movie.

"Hurry, lay him down in the prone position," my father gives snappy instructions. "Son, say something; can you hear me?"

My mother's words echo as if from a distant world. "Lord, please help me. My son isn't breathing. I can't lose my only child!"

"April, stop the drama. Our son isn't dead. He's breathing all right. Can't you see that he's just in shock, and that's why he fainted?"

My father's words offer my mother no comfort—instead, her *mother-hen syndrome* kicks in, and she's ready to fight the world. "Get away from my son!" My mother snarls like a wild animal.

"Your son? Look what he's brought into this house. April, this is all your fault. The way you coddle this boy is what's caused this calamity."

"Francine, please take over. Roger knows nothing about being a mother."

Auntie Francine tries to find calm in the chaos of the Michelo-Banda circus. "OK, you two, you can play the blame game when your son comes round." Auntie cuts to the chase. She then turns to instruct Ba Bwezani. "Please bring the big fan closer. And Ba Esther, wring a face cloth in ice cold water and bring it to me, hurry!"

Auntie Francine lifts my feet to put two cushions underneath for support while my mother tenderly cradles my head. My father isn't impressed.

"April, your son had better sit up and explain who these people are!"

***

Disoriented, my eyes finally open. The room is full of the same people I remember seeing for a few seconds before I blacked out. So, I wasn't dreaming, after all. In an ideal world, the so-called visitors should have left and returned at another, more convenient time. Unfortunately, they're still here, ready to launch an attack.

Still nursing my blackout, I continue to observe the room. Dailess, the last person I expected to see, is on the floor in the middle of the room—a far picture of the girlfriend I know. I hardly recognise her dressed in an oversized chitenge outfit and her strange hairstyle—*sans* (without) wig.

I don't know anything about hair styling, but Dailess's cornrows look like they have *seen better days*. Coupled with the *au naturel look* (no makeup), I might have walked past her. The man and woman beside each other appear familiar; I've seen pictures of them. They have to be her parents.

Mrs Banda catches my eye. Her face twitches as she throws me a menacing look. "Iwe, you're Andrew? You think my daughter is for you to use for *free*?"

Mr Banda put his right forefinger to his lips. "Quietness, stop it, let me talk."

I glance over at my mother; she rolls her eyes in a fury. It's one thing if she has to discipline me, but it's another when someone attacks me. Mrs Banda is *playing with fire*.

"Excuse me, Madam, I'm April Michelo, Andrew's mother. Welcome to our home." My mother pauses to compose herself. "You and your husband can speak on behalf of your daughter directly with Andrew's father and me. Don't you ever address my son again!"

Mrs Banda sucks her teeth. "Aa-ah, we know you and your type; today, you'll see what will happen in this beautiful home of yours."

My father stands up to take control. "Mr Banda, can you kindly explain why you and your wife are here?"

Mrs Banda doesn't allow her husband a chance to speak. "You can't see my daughter? We want to collect the damegi and discuss marriage." She folds her arms across her chest. "Your young man has *used* and spoilt her life!"

My parents, Auntie Francine, and I all gasp in unison. The mention of the word marriage adds *electricity* to the atmosphere and changes the direction of the meeting. My mother immediately crosses the room towards the door.

"Mr Banda, please take your ladies and leave my house. We understand you feel aggrieved, but you must send a representative to discuss the matter of damages."

Dailess' mother glances at the two ladies beside her. An unspoken pact of malevolence passes between them. And before her husband can respond to my mother, Mrs Banda unravels.

The woman dissolves into tears; her anguished wail shatters the air as if to summon demons from some evil source. Mrs Banda then stands up and starts to sway and dance like she's at a witches' sabbath. With an uncanny synchronicity, the other two women join their ringleader; they scream and convulse their bodies like backup singers in a nightmarish girl band.

The air thickens with an evil energy that chills the bone, sending a foreboding sense of darkness over our heads. In the pandemonium of such madness, no one can get a word in or penetrate the unholy veil the three women cast upon the room.

Had I known about this side of Dailess' mother, I would never have looked at Dailess twice. How could I have not tried harder to learn more about her background and family situation? If the baby she's carrying is mine, this demon in front of me will be my child's grandmother. The *satanic show* is enough for me to know that Dailess is more than I bargained for.

My father clenches his jaw. "Mr Banda, control your wife. We are Christians and don't believe in the ritual she's engaged in."

Dailess' father doesn't respond but clasps his mouth, his eyes wild with fear. His right leg shakes erratically like a malfunctioning electric device. It points to more ominous trouble on the horizon. As abruptly as she started, Mrs Banda halts her performance to address my father. She surprises us with her choice of words.

"Who'll marry my daughter? No man wants to marry a woman with a *bastard*!"

"Mr Banda, we have just discovered your daughter's condition. Give my wife and I a chance to discuss the matter with our son," my father says, ignoring Mrs Banda's rant.

"Yes, sir, we want to do things properly. Quietness, let's leave now; we can return another day."

Mrs Banda sees red. "Sir? What, sir? Radio Banda, don't confuse things. You're not at ShopRite. Mr Michelo isn't your boss!"

My father shakes his head, irritated. "Madam, please follow your husband and leave my house!"

Mrs Banda digs her heels in. "No, follow him where? With no damegi?" She laughs and slowly brings her hands together in sarcastic applause. "If you don't pay, your son will pay another way."

"Quietness Banda, stop it! Let's follow our traditions to get the damegi."

"Radio Banda, remember what the mirror *said*? I won't take Dailess back to Kamwala. She is in her *new home* now."

Auntie Francine realises the situation is now out of control, and in a quick-tongued manner, she asks the unwelcome guests to leave.

"Ladies, quick, stand up, Mr Banda, you're all trespassers. Take your daughter and come back only after you have secured an appointment. Otherwise, I'll have you arrested."

Mrs Banda cackles like a jackal. "Arrested? Who is getting arrested? The rapist there or me?" She wags her finger at me.

"Quietness, what's wrong with you, woman? Uncle Broomson will handle this matter!"

By now, it's evident that the Bandas aren't on the same page, and Mrs Banda's erratic behaviour shows a lack of planning. But that does not deter her. She has smelt blood and is circling like a ravenous shark.

"Madam, whatever your name is, I'm not going anywhere." She shouts at Auntie Francine. "And you, Radio Banda, I'll *finish* you if I hear you mention that useless, greedy Uncle Broomson of yours again."

Auntie Francine retrieves her phone from her handbag. "Mrs Banda, this isn't an idle threat. It is my final request to you to leave this property. You have no right to be here. I'll call the Police to arrest you for trespassing."

"Police or no Police, Dailess will remain here. You don't know me!"

And without warning, Mrs Banda stands up and summons her friends. "Amayi, it is time to bring *HIM* in."

Stunned into silence, we look at each other. Who is *HIM*? We are horrified when Mrs Banda and her *bandmates* start chanting, leaping, and dancing in circles like demons cast out at an exorcism ritual. The eerie sound spewing out of their mouths gets louder when they suddenly fling themselves to the floor with a thud.

We all silently watch in fear as their chests rise and fall. While rapid, short breaths escape their flared nostrils, accompanied by a spooky, hair-raising rattle of wheezing and panting.

We mistakenly thought the scariest part was over. So, it is a shock when Mrs Banda suddenly shifts gears and barks instructions in some jibberish language with an eerie sound. The three women change the rhythm of their movement and sound as they pick up speed and writhe like a dying person trying to ward off death.

Finally, the *voodoo troika* reaches a crescendo and calls my name in a triple chant. *Andrew Michelo, Andrew Michelo, Andrew Michelo.* Their strange male voices send shivers down my spine as goosebumps sprout all over my body and face. I have never felt such terror in my life.

"Mr Banda, take your wife and your daughter. Don't ever come back here again!" my father shouts.

"I'm sorry, sir, it's too late. My wife has instructions from Ba Nganga, and only he has the power to stop her."

I fear for my life and hold on to my mother's arm. Wasn't Mrs Banda supposed to be a Christian woman in the UCZ? How could she be the same person Dailess describes who visits the sick and preaches in the community?

My mother is livid. "Get out of my house, you wretched animals of the underworld!" She picks up a floor lamp and lifts it high to deliver a blow at Mrs Banda. "I will crash that nasty mouth of yours if you ever mention my son's name again!"

Things are getting out of control, and Ba Bwezani manages to restrain my mother just in time. "Iyeee, Madam, no, don't do this."

My father grabs Mr Banda by the collar. "Take your wife and daughter and get out of my house. I won't ask you again."

A frightened Mr Banda staggers and stumbles over his wife's outstretched legs. Unmoved by the threats, Mrs Banda displays a renewed vigour and enters a trance. She jerks her head as far back as possible, arches her spine and lifts her back off the floor, supported by her heels and the back of her head. Her two friends join her and lie on their sides in a foetal position, one on either side of Mrs Banda.

With her eyes shut, Mrs Banda speaks in a voice foreign to her natural one. It's a man's deep, bellowing, and raspy sound in which she delivers a *message* like a medium at a séance.

"*HE* says, Andrew Michello, your son, will marry our daughter, Dailess." Mrs Banda's eyes bulge from her skull as she scopes our faces. "*HE* warns that no power on or below the earth can remove our daughter from this house."

My mother stands up, her legs and hands visibly shaking from fear. "Ba Esther, Ba Bwezani, please help us to get these people out of our house now!"

As Mrs Banda continues her creepy monologue, the other two women, curled into a foetal position, make weird sounds of a newborn baby. The dreadful mimicking stops abruptly; the three women start to hum and form a queue facing the exit.

"We're leaving and won't look back or return here again. We've completed our job, and *HE* is pleased." Mrs Banda concludes.

Like warthogs in the wild, the three women walk briskly in a straight line and leave my parent's house without a backward glance. The strange evil force they conjured trails and propels them out of sight.

For a moment, no one speaks—we all look at one another in disbelief. There was no mistaking the sense of fear that still hung in the air. I look at my mother, her hands clutching the base of her throat in shock. I can't describe the concoction of emotions that grip me. How could I do this to my mother? It breaks my heart.

My father is no better. He rapidly opens and closes his mouth like a dying fish on the banks of the Kafue River. Auntie Francine paces the room, her hands on top of her head. What's happening to us? Did Mrs Banda bewitch me and my family?

Dailess is still in the same position on the floor, sobbing. She picks up the edge of her Chitenge dress and wipes her tears and snot. Anger wells up in me; what else is she hiding? Why didn't she ever mention how *creative* her mother was?

I've heard countless stories about Mrs Banda's church work. But not one story about her voodoo skills—it's not something one forgets to mention. So, what's the purpose of Dailess' crocodile tears? Is it because her mother has blown her cover, or what? I'm confused.

It's hard to read Mr Banda's mind. With his elbows on his knees, he cradles his head in despair. Oddly enough, he stands up to leave but doesn't invite Dailess to do the same. Mr Banda doesn't say a word or even look at his daughter.

Auntie Francine, determined to end the nightmare, grabs Mr Banda by his arm. "Whoa! Hang on a minute, Mr Banda; no one is marrying anyone today or anytime soon. Take your daughter with you."

We all pray Mr Banda has more sense than his wife. Alas! He, too, leaves and doesn't look back. Like a ghost, in the middle of the night, he floats across the yard and vanishes behind the gate and onto the street.

I look over at Dailess and see fear and desperation in her eyes. But she does not attempt to follow her father. What does Dailess think this means? I stand up to go over to where she is sitting on the floor. But Auntie Francine signals me to stop.

My father is frantic. "What are we going to do, Ba Bwezani? Do you understand what Mrs Banda means?"

Ba Bwezani twitches his eyes. "Boss, you must make the family happy,"

"What does happy mean?" My father asks.

"Don't worry, boss." Ba Bwezani reassures my parents. "I'll bring elders from Eastern Province to talk with you and madam before you meet the Bandas again."

"Andrew, my dear boy. What have you got us into? What will we do with this girl?" my father slumps into the *fauteuil*.

The two of us may not always agree. But this time, my father is right to question how I allowed such trouble to come to my parents' doorstep.

My mother screams in anguish before I can say anything. Her cry is sharp, gut-wrenching and rips through the room in a way I can never forget. I attempt to put my arms around her, but she shrugs me off and lets out another hair-raising and blood-curdling scream. "Andrew, my *ibeli*, my *kasuli*, why have you brought witchcraft into my house?"

My heart stops. I watch my mother slowly rise from her chair as if she has tons of bricks on her shoulders. Without a word, my mother walks out of the living room, crying like an injured animal—she's inconsolable. The last time I heard my mother weep like that was when my father's secret surfaced and changed her world.

"Auntie Francine, I'm so ashamed of the pain I've caused our family. My mother will never forgive me, will she?" I pray that my Auntie can help make things better.

Auntie Francine closes her eyes and nods. "I'll take care of your mother. Let's meet tomorrow morning with clear minds. We have a long and treacherous journey ahead of us."

Chapter Fifteen

ROCK BOTTOM

Once again, my life just zoomed past me, lost in the turmoil of events. It has grown a pair of wings, taken off and left me stranded in the chaos of the unknown. The *script* I had meticulously written is out of the window, and right before my eyes, a succession of wild events have reduced me to a helpless spectator of my existence.

It's like I'm in a movie in a supporting role—the leading lady's best friend. I've lost control and am back where I started—fighting to claw back anything that can help get my feet back on the ground. I've never felt so weak and alone, with no idea how to get out of the trenches. And yes, rejected by everyone, it's official; *my life has hit rock bottom.*

As much as I would like Andrew to marry me, it was wrong to ambush the Michelos. What a bonkers idea this was. Not that I had a choice in the matter, but in my naivety, I secretly thought the plan might make Andrew fess up to our circumstances. I had pictured the four parents in a conversation regarding their children's future—not to say I expected the discussions would ever be peaceful.

The way I saw it, a more likely worst-case scenario, was my mother's corrosive character getting in the way. Her overbearing, manipulative, argumentative, rude antics would have been the biggest problem. It's who she is, and I can live with that. But my mother took things to the next level in a way that might have killed my chances with Andrew.

I know my mother believes in the powers of Ba Nganga; she always has. It's not something I'm proud of, but it's also not my issue to change. I've been running away from it since childhood—it's my biggest secret. The only other person who knows about my mother's ways is Sally. But only because her mother is an accomplice. Otherwise, Sally would have already submitted my secret to the local media outlets.

But even as much as I am aware of my mother's ways, I wasn't ready for the *voodoo freak show* that she and her friends put up for the Michelos. There's no return from that; it's not something I can explain away to Andrew.

The consequences are irreversible; indeed, it is a game-changer in how things will play out going forward—and not in a good way. Lord knows what they all must be thinking.

So why would my mother think dumping me on the Michelos was the best way to resolve my issue? I'm sitting in a pathetic heap on the floor like a bag of rotten *Solwezi* beans that no one wants to buy. I can tell by the look in Andrew's eyes that it's over between us.

Besides, with Andrew's mother weeping like she did, I have little chance of becoming a beloved daughter-in-law. So, what exactly was my mother's point? Where do we go from here? I have never felt this downcast in my life.

My father might have known about this sneaky strategy but chose not to snitch. And to be fair, it's not that I think he agreed with my mother. He couldn't have stopped her; it would have led to more trouble. My father has never been able to control my mother.

My mother's rough and urgent plan to ambush the Michelos was wrong on many other levels. Talk about my appearance—doesn't the packaging count in a sales pitch? I would say yes, 100 per cent. Yet, my mother robbed me of the chance to make a good impression.

How I look now isn't how I imagined I would ever present myself to Andrew's parents. It's a far cry from the Pinterest mood board I created! I may not have deep pockets. But had it come to it, I would have planned something. A quick rummage through my mother's salaula bales would have done the trick.

Packaging aside, my mother has said her piece. She won't rest until she gets what she wants—a son-in-law. My mother never wants me to *darken her doorstep* without a husband, a pact she made with her Nganga.

At the risk of repeating myself incessantly, everything loops back to the messed-up strategy. You don't attack future in-laws with voodoo and hope to get a marriage out of it. How am I supposed to make Andrew marry me?

From the look of things, climbing Mount Everest will be easier than getting Andrew to any wedding chapel. I saw how quickly he disappeared into their precious mansion's belly without a word to me. That's not a dude who's about to get hitched. No way.

The voice of Andrew's Auntie rescues me from the gloomy thoughts that have hijacked my mind. I don't know how long she has been calling for my attention. But the concern on her face is very telling.

"Young lady, can you hear me? Are you okay? Get up and come with me."

"Sorry, madam, I didn't hear you."

"It's okay; call me Auntie Francine. You were far away—I get it, you're tired; it has been a long afternoon," she kindly responds.

I don't know if it's her soothing voice, but something in me breaks. Naked in the worst possible way, all the emotional walls I had built around start to fall brick by brick. I don't know where or how I can begin to rebuild a stronger version of the current mess that I've become. For the first time, I know what heartbreak might feel like. The pressure in the middle of my chest alone is enough to make me stop breathing. My world has literally come undone.

As I rise to my feet, I pick up the hem of my chitenge dress to wipe away the tsunami of tears that threaten to erode my face. My right leg seems to have gone to sleep, and I struggle to stand up and drop into the armchair next to me.

Auntie Francine grabs my arm. "Oh dear, take your time."

I smack my leg to jumpstart the blood flow. "I'm sorry, I think I can walk now."

"Aww, I don't blame you. You've been on the floor in the same position for hours. Come with me to the kitchen."

Despite my sadness, I take in the comfort and luxury of the Michelo home. I'm amazed at the kitchen's size, cleanliness and smell of cinnamon-scented candles. Ba Esther flashes a warm smile as soon as she sees us. She looks so neat in her uniform.

"Hello, Auntie Francine; I have set up dinner for you and the young lady."

"Thank you, Ba Esther." Auntie Francine walks around the table and pulls a chair. "Dailess, make yourself at home. You must be hungry."

"Yes, thank you very much."

Auntie Francine opens an expensive-looking bottle of chilled Chardonnay white wine for herself. In my condition, she offers me a glass of orange juice with lots of ice. She serves both the wine and juice in crystal glasses. I like her style—the few minutes I've been with her feel like taking a crash course in the *art of fine living*.

I gulp my juice down a little fast. I've had nothing to drink since we left Kamwala in that horrendous taxi.

Auntie Francine gives me a look of concern. "Oh, you must be very thirsty. Do you want some water?"

I stammer as I try to suppress a burp. "Yes, ple...please," I reply, tears welling up in my eyes again.

"Dailess, you know that the strength to get back on your feet lies within you. Don't wait for anyone to save you," Auntie Francine tries to soothe me.

"It's just so hard, and I don't know where or how to start," I sniffle.

"Stay open and listen to your heart. The answer will come to you. I'll give you a book to help you get through this," Auntie Francine offers.

We enjoy the rest of our dinner with intervals of awkward small talk and polite laughter. Thankfully, Auntie Francine steers away from anything personal or what happened a few hours ago. She is either the most courteous person I've ever met or simply disinterested in what's happening. But from what I have heard about her as a successful lawyer, neither of those possibilities makes sense. I think she's sassing me out. Yeah.

After dinner, Auntie Francine hands me a bag of toiletries and shows me to the guest bedroom. A beautiful scent of lavender candles hits me as soon as I open the door.

OMG, is this where the rich and famous of Kabulonga sleep? Gosh, I'm in heaven. With all this beauty surrounding me, I've every incentive to quit my pity party. Will you look at that bed? A double bed! Ha! I can't believe this enormous bed awaits me, a simple girl from Kamwala!

The bed has four large pillows and a soft lavender-coloured bedspread—perfect for sweet dreams and a restful night. I knew I would one day ditch my creaky old single bed in Kamwala, but I didn't expect that day to come today and this way.

I smile. "Do I get to sleep in this room?" I can't contain my excitement.

"Yes, of course. I've also put a change of clothes for you in the bathroom."

Auntie Francine's words sound distant. My attention is elsewhere, engrossed in the elegance of the entire room, and for a moment, I don't have a care in the world. Maybe, just maybe, my mother's rough way of doing things is paying off. Leaving me behind wasn't such a bad idea after all. I think the baby and I will be okay.

"Are you alright?" Auntie Francine asks.

She hands me a piece of paper with the family's Wi-Fi details.

"Here, in case you need to make some calls."

"Thank you ever so much for the hospitality."

"Not a problem. Good night." Auntie Francine closes the door behind her.

I am so happy that I could dance but also confused. Does this mean the family accepts me, or what? I need to call my girlfriends to bring them up to speed. It's free Wi-Fi; I might as well make the most of it. But I have to exclude Sally from the call. Stupid *Judas Iscariot*!

Carol is the first one to answer. "Hi, Dailess; you never call this late on a Sunday. What's going on?"

"Hi Carol, thank God you're there. Let's wait for Bridget to pick up."

Bridget comes to the phone, breathing hard. "Hi guys, phew! What's up?

"Hey you, what's with the panting? Carol laughs.

"My phone was at the neighbour's house, charging. I had to run to get the call."

"Bridget, did you forget to pay your electricity bill?" I chuckle.

"No, our whole side of the street is in pitch darkness."

I jump right into why I called. "I am at Andrew's house," I whisper.

"This time of the night? What? Wait a minute, are you serious?" Carol asks.

Bridget is excited. "Let me come and *sort out* those worthless bougie people? Give me five minutes to grab my wig!"

"No, listen, guys, the very light version of what's happened is my mother and her friends bought and left me here. I'm not to go back to Kamwala without a husband."

Bridget whistles. "Whoa, Dailess, from *zero to a hundred per cent*, how?

"My mother, as you know, can be unpredictable and strong-willed. It's a long story. You'll get the blow-by-blow account when we meet. For now, I just wanted to let you know where things are. No more secrets."

Bridget laughs. "Girl, I've met your mother. And Sally's mother is a bad influence on yours. I can't imagine what *wahala* must have gone down in *bougie land*."

"Sweetie, why isn't Sally on the call?" Carol sounds concerned.

"Sally's a backstabber. Besides, she set everything in motion and already knows what's happened. But I can't let her in on my thoughts or plans from now on. It's very thorny out here after my mother's attack. I must tread very carefully—so let *Judas* go."

"OK, it's a pity things have soured between you two. But I respect your position," Carol replies.

Bridget clears her throat. "Forget Sally. What's Andrew's take on everything? Are you guys finally on the same page?"

"Yes, what did he say? Did he apologise for last Friday?" Carol chimes in.

I suck my teeth. "Girl, the boy fainted as soon as he saw me; how was he going to talk to me, let alone apologise?

"Seriously!" The girls scream with laughter and call Andrew names.

I whisper into the phone. "Shush, shush, ladies."

"What? You be quiet yourself. It's not as if anyone can hear us," Bridget protests.

"You have said nothing about his parents; what are they like?" Carol asks.

"Girl, his mother is a *queen bee,* and Andrew's tied to her apron. She kept fawning over him, and he lapped it all up like a little boy!" I suck my teeth again. "I can also tell you that there's gonna be a fierce *tug-of-war* between my mother and Mrs Michelo."

"I get the picture. It can't be easy for you," Carol sympathises. "But try to get on Mrs Michelo's good side. She might be a good person despite her tight relationship with her son."

Bridget disagrees. "Nah, such people don't budge unless they get their way." She pauses. "Girl, if Andrew ever marries you, get rid of that silly bond with his mother."

It is just like Bridget to think along those lines. If it ever came to it, Bridget would help me work out a ploy that separates mother and son.

Carol isn't having it. "Seriously, Dailess, how are you comfortable plotting to deal with Andrew's mother in her own house?"

"I am in one of their spare bedrooms, and nobody can hear me."

"Dailess, it is just a matter of respect. Mrs Michelo doesn't have to hear you for you to behave appropriately," Carol scolds.

I'm convinced Andrew would have taken my pregnancy differently if it weren't for his needy mother. So, although I know Carol is right, I don't let her know; I change the topic instead.

"Guess what? I'm lying on a to-die-for bed as I am talking to you. I never want to return to my tired, worn-out little single bed in Kamwala." "I could get used to this kind of bougie living."

"Girl, if I were you, I would hold on to that spare bedroom and enjoy it for however long it lasts," Bridget says.

I have dreamed of a better life since I was a little girl. It is time to change the narrative. My parents found a home and settled in Kamwala. Years later, I came along as their only child, and we still live in the same little house. That cycle ends here with me.

Chapter Sixteen

MY SON IS ALL I HAVE

If anyone understood how deeply I love my Andrew, they would know better than to cross my path. There isn't anything I won't do to protect my boy. Even animals in the wild know that to threaten their young is to ask for war. I will be damned if I let anyone ruin Andrew's life. Witchcraft or not, I'll leave no stone unturned to protect him, single-handedly if I must.

I don't know what else happened after those wretched women left this afternoon. I had a massive headache after all that voodoo performance. I took two painkillers and fell asleep for four hours. I have not spoken to or seen Francine and Andrew.

Restless and unable to sleep anymore, I look at my husband and gently nudge him. "Roger, are you awake? How did we miss the signs of Andrew's struggles?"

My husband does not respond. Besides his snoring, he doesn't appear to hear me or move. How can he sleep soundly after such a crazy day? Dailess and her lunatic mother don't make for a good night's sleep.

I snap my bedside lamp on. "Roger, wake up! How does it not bother you that we have a random pregnant girl in our house?"

"April, I agree Andrew completely blindsided us. We were ten steps behind. But it's 23:00 hrs; the sensible thing to do now is go to bed!"

From his response, I can tell he heard me the first time; he was ignoring me and, as usual, burying his head in the sand. Of all the times to dismiss me, now isn't that time.

"Roger, aren't we going to talk about it?"

"No, April, you amaze me. Where's the mystery in what has happened? News flash: your *Fabergé egg* of a son had sex. Very soon, he'll be a father and a husband and you a grandmother. Get used to it!"

"Are you serious? There's no way I will allow my son to become a husband to a girl whose mother is a self-professed witch. How have you made peace with that?"

Roger is adamant. "How often have we talked to Andrew about the risks of unprotected sex? We can't be responsible for his choices."

"Is that all you have to say, Roger?"

"Well, if you insist, I *must say* you have a busy schedule ahead of you—a lavish wedding to plan, and might I add, as a *grandmother-to-be*, you must adjust your lifestyle. How's that for something to say?"

Angry tears well up in my eyes. "Roger, I am amazed that you think I should be the only parent to take an interest in Andrew's problem. What father detaches himself from such matters?"

Roger covers his head with a pillow. "Look, you should know when to accept defeat. Unless you plan to yank the baby out of that poor girl's uterus, there's no solution!"

I savagely rip the pillow away from his head. "The question is, why are you so quick to accept defeat? Is it because you have options?"

Roger scrambles to a sitting position, suddenly alert and wide awake. "What's that supposed to mean, April?"

"Well, you've two other sons in Mazabuka. If this silly girl and her parents were to bring harm to Andrew's life, you have options. Unlike you, *my son is all I have.*

Roger throws his arms up. "That's just the problem with you, April. Everything I do or say, right or wrong, leads to Mazabuka."

"That's because Mazabuka broke us. Let's face it, Mazabuka and all your foolishness is a big white elephant in the room—it won't leave no matter how hard we try to get rid of it!"

"For how long, April? It doesn't matter how much I grovel at your feet. You'll never forgive me. Does one not get points for *good behaviour*?"

"You just don't get it, Roger. It's not about how sorry you are, let alone my forgiveness. Mazabuka changed the *DNA* of our marriage. We can never get back to who we were. Not in this lifetime. You and your other family robbed me of the happy marriage I should have had!"

Roger gives me a side glance. "It's not my problem that my other sons are successful."

Ouch! Roger's words, sharp as a razor blade, slice through my heart. "That's below the belt, and you know it. Are you saying Andrew is unsuccessful, and those *bastards* of yours are better?"

Roger laughs sarcastically. "Andrew has made a girl pregnant and ruined his life. The boys in Mazabuka haven't brought any pregnant women home!"

"Let me help you rephrase that sentence. Andrew, *like his father*, made a woman pregnant. And *like his father*, he has ruined his life and must live with the consequences!" I fume.

Roger deflects. "What about Andrew's scholarship?"

My voice is harsh. "What about it? Nothing has changed. My son's going to England as planned."

"April, listen to yourself. Your son isn't going to England anymore. Who is going to look after his girlfriend and baby? You? I find that hard to believe."

"I'm warning you, Roger, if you don't negotiate a deal that gets this girl out of my house, I'll return to my parents."

Roger snaps back into a sitting position like a jumping jack, his snarky words suddenly out of the window. "What do you mean, April?"

"Let me spell it out for you. When Andrew leaves for England, I'll go with him. Once back in Zambia, I'll pack all my stuff and return to my parents' home. You and Dailess can then freely live happily ever after in this house!"

"Yes, April, I get it; your father is rich, blah, blah, blah."

"So, I guess I've given you fair warning."

I storm out of the bedroom and quickly saunter to the guest room to talk to Francine. I hope she's still awake. I rush through the dimly lit hallway. The polished black and white tiles feel cool under my bare feet, soothing and therapeutic.

As I make my way to the guest bedroom, my stomach growls. The noise across the hallway reminds me that I have not eaten or drank anything since the brunch.

I knock on Francine's door and poke my head around. "Sis, are you awake? Can you talk?"

Francine turns on the bedside lamp and yawns. "Hey, sis, sleep is a struggle after what we witnessed this afternoon."

I am so grateful to my sister. If anything, she's the one person I trust to be by my side regarding Andrew. I need her support more than ever.

"Where's the young lady, Francine? Please tell me she left with her father."

"Don't worry about any of this, April. Dailess had something to eat. I settled her in the second guest bedroom and gave her a change of clothes."

"Thank you, sis. I don't know how to repay you."

"I've instructed Andrew not to talk to Dailess until the three of us have spoken."

"That's important. Did Dailess say if she planned to return to kamwala?"

"April, we've got a long battle ahead of us. The Bandas, as you saw, aren't interested in an unwed pregnant daughter."

"My son isn't marrying anyone anytime soon. But we've got to find a way to do right by Dailess and the unborn child," I reason.

"That Mrs Banda will sell her daughter to the highest bidder with some loose change. Right now, that man is Andrew. But yes, April, we say NO to marriage."

"Francine, that's why Dailess can't stay here. Mrs Banda knows there'll be no return if that baby is born while her daughter is in this house."

"You've got that right. One can hardly throw out a young mother and her newborn baby. Not to mention a baby with blood ties to our family."

"Yep, if we aren't careful, that woman will soon organise a Chilanga Mulilo (the Bemba traditional premarital degustation feast) for my poor son."

Francine laughs. "Well, nowadays, it's a gimmick that the woman's family use to pin a potential groom down."

"On that note, today, the Bandas took us by surprise. It must never happen again. Francine, we must plan carefully to avoid anything they might throw at us."

"Don't worry about any of this, sis. I won't lift my eyes from the chessboard. It's our turn to say, *checkmate*."

My mind returns to Roger and our disagreement, and I wipe fresh tears from my eyes. "Roger and I aren't on the same page."

"What do you mean? He should take the lead on this matter. How does he plan on conducting the *damage* discussions with the Bandas?"

"I swear if Roger doesn't do right by Andrew, it will end our marriage. I won't have him deferring the matter to Ba Bwezani. The man offered to help, not to take over the problem."

"Or worse, still, his mother," Francine adds.

"In his opinion, Andrew must take responsibility for his mistake and get married."

"Sis, you must put your foot down. Andrew's got a bright future and is about to go to England for further studies. Doesn't your husband see that?"

"My sentiments exactly; we must keep him out of the loop of *all things Andrew*."

"I'm disappointed he can set his son's ambitions so low."

"All Roger cares about are his Mazabuka bastards!"

"The problem with your husband is that he doesn't know where to draw the line. Andrew is your Achilles heel—as such, he'll always be collateral damage in your disagreements with Roger."

"Can you believe Roger compared those fools to my Andrew? The cheek of it all!"

"Okay, sis. Forget about Roger and his Mazabuka bastards. I'll think of a plan and call in some serious favours."

"Whatever it takes, sis, I trust you. I owe you big time, little sis; good night."

Chapter Seventeen

I'M SORRY MUMMY

Today has to be the worst Monday morning possible. Built on the echoes of yesterday's venomous events, the prospects for the day changing aren't promising. I scratch my head absently, confused and mentally exhausted—it's incredible how swiftly my life has changed in the last twenty-four hours.

Everything has come to a head, and like unwanted visitors—shame, desperation, failure, and hopelessness—have gathered, uninvited, on my doorstep. Their imposing presence looms, and I wonder how and what it will take to get past these relentless intruders.

I've learnt that no matter how hard you run or hide, your secrets will always find you at the most inconvenient time. In hindsight, I now know I should have jumped ahead of my Dailess issues and not run around with secrets that attracted more lies.

It's simple. Had I told my parents about Dailess, yesterday might have gone better. My parents would've been better prepared and spared the horrific ambush, except for the chilling voodoo session Mrs Banda unleashed on us. That was totally off the charts.

Unfortunately, in my cowardice and determination to manage my *time bomb* of a secret, I have fed my parents to the wolves. My mother's tortured scream is still ringing in my ears. And the whole night, I mentally replayed the image of her walking away in tears, broken beyond anything I could have imagined.

I regret that I pushed my parents into the position of underdogs in so far as the pregnancy battle is concerned. It will require all hands on deck to come out from under the Bandas' thumb.

But where do we begin? Right now, I feel like a punctured tyre, deflated, with no idea what will happen next. The temptation to go back to bed and feign illness is overwhelming. Perhaps everything will go back to normal while I sleep.

But how much sleep will it take for Dailess to disappear from my life, to never have ever met her? Or for me to arrive in England, magically, with no baby mama issues? I know that I can't hibernate in my bedroom all day. It will just cause my mother more alarm. I have to get up and face the music.

First things first, if I'm to manage this day, I must take care of business and clear my work schedule. It'll help keep my colleagues in check and minimise unnecessary phone calls.

I also don't need my father breathing down my neck about work, in addition to yesterday's disaster. I must be one hundred per cent back on my feet to deal with this Dailess s**t storm. Otherwise, I'll get caught with my pants down again and lose all control—as it is, I'm already drowning.

I dial Jordan's number and prepare to sound upbeat, to cover up all traces of misery.

"Hello, Jordan, wassup, my man!" but my voice is thick with panic, sounding desperate and awkwardly louder than I intended.

"Hey, bruv, what's going on? Everything all right?" Jordan asks, alarmed.

It's 06:00 hrs, which is too early for my phone call. I never call our staff outside office hours.

"Yeah, bruv, sorry to call you this early. It's nothing serious, but I want to give you a heads-up. I won't be in the office today. It's my grandmother again."

Eish! I'm tired of my own lies. When will it stop? I've lost track of what I've said and to whom.

Jordan senses the despair in my voice.

"Is there anything I can do to help?"

"Not really, Bruv. But I need you to hold down the fort. Ensure everyone pulls their weight, or my old man's gonna lose it."

"Of course, man, you don't need to worry. Best wishes to your grandmother."

"Yes, thank you. It's tough on my poor grandmother."

"Aww, sorry to hear that. Nothing too serious, I hope?"

"No, not at the moment. Our family doctor is on top of things. But thanks for the concern, bruv."

"Andrew, before you go, you said we should tell you when we had out-of-town clients. We have two deliveries scheduled for this afternoon. Should I ask the delivery team to wait for you?"

I suppress a scream. Oh, Jordan, last week, I would have sold my kidney for an opportunity to do an out-of-town delivery to avoid Dailess and her friends. So much for great timing! "Nah, man, let them go ahead without me. Thanks for the heads up, bruv. I've gotta run now," I reply.

Even with the office agenda out of the way, fear and shame still have my mind in a stranglehold. I'm unprepared to face my parents and Auntie Francine this morning. But what's the worst that can happen that hasn't already happened?

Dailess and family busted my *hide-and-seek* game, but I still feel the weight of the fracas. The pain I've caused my mother and the shame of lying to her is a heavy burden to shoulder. Will she ever trust me again? It was never my intention to disappoint her like this.

The remorse I feel for what has happened aside, a part of me resents Dailess. I never expected her to *do me dirty* like this. It takes two to tango, for sure. But Dailess has a lot of power play in this pregnancy saga. She wrote the script of our lives and set it in motion without my knowledge.

The deception and manipulation are something I would expect from Maria's playbook. But not from Dailess? How come I didn't know that the condom broke? And seeing she knew, why didn't she tell me there and then? We could have talked about it from the beginning and managed the narrative. Sadly, we're both in free fall, with no guarantee of a soft landing.

Finally, I summon enough courage to leave my bedroom and shuffle down the hallway like a zombie towards the dining room. Ba Esther's usual sumptuous breakfast banquet awaits, but I've got no desire to eat anything. The last time I ate something filling was yesterday's brunch before the s**t hit the fan. Today, though, like it or not, I must stuff my face to have the energy to deal with the Dailess nonsense.

My mother and Auntie Francine are already at the table beside each other, their voices low and sombre. Dailess is nowhere in sight. Thank God.

My father has also made himself scarce. He must have skipped breakfast to avoid discussing yesterday's event with my mother and Auntie Francine. *I have an early start today, April.* My father might have announced—his code language for *my position still stands, and I don't want to discuss it.* My parents aren't good at not letting the sun go down on their anger.

From my father's absence at the breakfast table, I'm sure it will also be a late night at the office—his ticket out of what's happening at home. My father would rather *ostrich* himself during difficult family discussions than get involved or, in this case, take the lead. This morning, though, if one gave my father the benefit of the doubt, his absence could mean one of two things.

The first scenario could be that my parents might have had an in-depth discussion last night about Dailess—and might have agreed my mother would manage matters today. But as much as I would love for this scenario to be accurate, it's a stretch.

My parents have failed to hone the art of communication. The expression *middle ground* does not exist between them. Someone always has to lose. They disagree on the simplest things; they hear what the other is saying but make no effort to understand. My parents talk to each other but stopped communicating a long time ago.

The other scenario could be that their conversation might have gone wrong, and my father might have decided to secretly bring his mother into the picture—a recipe for trouble. He defers everything he can't resolve with his wife to his mother, Grandma Selina. She is my father's ultimate ally in all things against my mother.

Constantly waging war with my mother, Grandma Selina has unfinished business with her daughter-in-law. She relishes every opportunity to tear my mother down.

As I walk towards the table, my mother stares at me. There's so much sadness in her eyes. She must have cried the whole night. What's the protocol for comforting your gutted mother after you've knocked up a girl?

My mother's voice shakes with emotion. "Andrew, my dear boy, look what you've done. What are we to do?"

For a split second, I stand motionless and stare back at her. I struggle to find the right words. "*I am sorry, Mummy*. I didn't mean to cause you so much pain."

"Son, unfortunately, this situation goes beyond how sorry you are. We have some tough decisions to make."

My mother embraces me, and together, we weep in silence. Of all the trouble I imagined I might get into, this wasn't it. It was never on my radar. David's, perhaps. But not mine. What, though, could I have done to stop it?

Out of respect, Auntie Francine allows a few minutes of the mother-son *crying session*. But the pragmatic lawyer in her has got to get things moving.

"Okay, sis, let's be strong and push past the tears. We've got bigger fish to fry. Andrew, sit down."

I look around the room. "Where is Dailess? Is she still here?"

My mother and Auntie Francine look at each other.

"Son, Dailess isn't going anywhere. Not on her own, at least. We've got to appease her family. But even that's complicated, considering Mrs Banda has her sights set on you as a husband for her daughter."

"I'm sorry, mummy. I don't know what happened."

"Like your mother said, forget how sorry you are. How long have you known about Dailess' condition?"

"Just three weeks now, Auntie Francine. I've been in the dark all this time."

My mother raises her voice. "Andrew, I don't want us to cry over spilt milk. But how many discussions have we had about safe sex?"

"Believe me, Mummy, even I don't understand how Dailess got pregnant. We used protection each time, and she was also on the pill. Or so she said. But now Dailess insists that the condom broke, and she'd stopped taking the pill."

Auntie Francine frowns at me. "We believe you, Andrew, but Dailess' explanation sounds shady. She likely planned the whole thing."

My mother narrows her eyes. "What bothers me, son, is your choice of women. First, it was that loose Maria and now this manipulative Dailess, with a sorcerous mother to complete the picture. Why can't you find a decent, honest girl?"

"Dailess seemed like a nice girl. I had no way of knowing everything I know now."

"Andrew, what your mother means is that there's a pattern to the kind of women you pick, and it's concerning."

"Son, we talk about everything, yet you didn't tell me you were dating. How much could you have known about Dailess and her background?"

"I wasn't hiding her Mummy. But out of respect for you, I wanted to see if the relationship had a future before bringing you into the picture."

I wish I could explain to my mother and Auntie that the dating pool is complex nowadays. It's tough to know who's who and what their genuine background is. Everyone is *window dressing,* as David likes to call it.

When I met Dailess, she was just like any other girl. I had no reason to suspect anything. It's not like I could've rolled up to her and said: Hi, Dailess, is there a chance you might trick me into becoming your baby daddy? Or: Hi, Dailess. Does your mother conduct Voodoo rituals? No way, she would have thought I was a weird nutjob.

Auntie Francines gives me a stern eye. "Andrew, if you respect a woman, you won't be in a rush to jump in the sack with her."

"Yes, you should have waited until you knew more about her background. Who exactly is Dailess? Do you know?" My mother asks.

"Mummy, things happened so fast in the three months I've known her. I'm failing to piece the puzzle together," I explain.

"But then again, son, why did you let things get out of control like this? I didn't like those people in my house at all."

My mother and Auntie have a point. There's so much I could have done differently. Had I been honest about my relationship in the first place, they might have helped me question things about Dailess that didn't add up.

"I'm sorry, Mummy and Auntie. I know I've put you in a difficult position; I should have come clean from the start."

My mother frowns, her eyes dark with worry.

"My dear boy, if you haven't known Dailess long, coupled with the *wishy-washy* story of how she got pregnant, are you sure the baby's yours?"

"Mummy, I don't want to say Dailess is a bad girl. But I don't know what to think for the same reasons you find this situation dodgy."

"Andrew, don't be naïve. Dailess doesn't have to be a bad girl to want *a leg up* in life. Good people do bad things when they're desperate. But, yes, we smell a rat with Dailess' story; it's questionable and calculated," Auntie Francine adds, pacing the room.

"Exactly, son, that's why you've got to try to understand someone's agenda. Boys like you with a good background are prey to all these lost young girls."

"Oh, Mummy, how can we tell if the baby is mine? I'm ashamed that I even have to ask. But it's a valid question."

Auntie Francine looks me in the eye. "Listen to me carefully, Andrew. Only Dailess knows who the father of the baby is. You won't know until the baby is born and you've taken a paternity test."

"But If I'm not sure the baby is mine, why does Mrs Banda expect me to marry her daughter?"

"Unfortunately, Dailess has picked you as her baby daddy, and her mother believes her," Auntie Francine responds.

"Son, I disagree with Mrs Banda's *colourful* way of doing things. But she's fighting for her daughter's future just as I'm fighting for yours. So many young people forget the sacrifices their parents make for them," my mother explains.

Panic and fear grip me again. I can hardly breathe. "Does that mean you want me to marry Dailess, Mummy?"

"No, not at all—over my dead body! But Mrs Banda and I have the right to fight for our children. If the baby turns out to be yours, we shall look after it— but nothing more."

In my mind, the idea of single parenting takes me to another level of panic. I wish I had the resilience of my mother's brother, Uncle Patrick. After the untimely death of his wife, my uncle became an instant mother to his daughters, all under the age of ten.

"Mummy, what if Dailess's parents push the baby onto me full-time? How am I to raise a child on my own?"

"My dear son, whatever you do, you don't want to be like your father. Children are a gift from God, not something a parent hides." My mother takes my hands in hers. "You must step up and do whatever it takes to ensure this baby, if yours, is okay."

"Andrew, you know your Uncle Patrick's situation. He embarked on a new parenthood journey with his daughters, trusting God and his instincts," Auntie Francine adds, to drive a point home.

"If you became a *mother* and father to your baby, you would experience new challenges but also discover priceless joy and happiness," my mother encourages me.

It's true, now when I think of it, Uncle Patrick is one of the best *mothers* I know.

Auntie Francine hardens her voice. "Did you say anything about your scholarship offer to Dailess?"

"No, no way. I didn't tell her anything about it." Both women let out loud sighs of relief, and Auntie Francine shifts the gears in the conversation.

"Great, keep it that way. I think I have a plan. Sis, the two of you must follow my lead without asking questions. For now, Andrew, you've got to talk to Dailess—we need to know what we are up against."

My mother lowers her voice to a whisper. "Listen, Andrew, your father might bring his mother into this discussion. Don't tell her anything we have discussed this morning. That includes your father."

"I hear you, Mummy."

"By the way, don't tell Dailess you have questions regarding the baby's paternity. At this stage, she's vulnerable; you don't want her to feel like you're rejecting the baby too. Let's cross that bridge when we come to it."

I look at my mother and think about everything that has happened. I feel incredibly fortunate to be *my mother's son*. Heaven knows what I would have done without her.

Chapter Eighteen

TAKE THE BULL BY ITS HORNS

I've been ghosting Dailess for three weeks—I've avoided her calls and used up every excuse in the book not to see her. I couldn't face the problem, and now the situation has dealt with me. But coupled with what I now know, the stakes to get out of my mess have escalated.

So, today is the first time Dailess and I will talk about our *so-called baby* since the news broke. Thanks to Mrs Banda and her friends, yesterday was a day from hell. And it wasn't the right time to have a meaningful conversation with her daughter.

I take a deep breath as I walk down the hallway to the spare bedroom where Dailess is. But I wish with every fibre that I didn't have to see her. I feel like I'm on a long and possibly dangerous journey—set on a thorny and unpredictable path. I didn't sign up for this, but it's where things are now.

So, mentally, I'm all over the place. I've tried to psyche myself up and allow motivational lines to run through my head. *A man has got to do what a man has got to do*. But a large part of me isn't buying it. I'm still terribly anxious about what lies ahead. But it's too late to be scared. I have no choice but to man up and *take the bull by its horns*.

My emotions aren't doing any better. I feel angry, frustrated, betrayed, disrespected, and trapped—everything rolled into one. I don't know what to say to Dailess except that I don't want to marry her. Not out of malice or lack of a sense of responsibility. But shouldn't we both get a chance to choose our life partners?

My mother has taught me the importance of exercising my freedom of choice in every circumstance. Being chosen is not enough; it has to go both ways. I have to be able to participate in important decisions such as marriage.

So why doesn't Dailess care that I'm not choosing her? How does she not know that there are two sides to choosing? If what you want doesn't want you, how is that a good choice for you?

In too big a hurry to get things her way, Dailess forgot that the relationship must grow organically. Someone should have told her that no relationship built on lies, tricks and games can survive the test of time. I can't get past everything she has presented before me; together with her mother's voodoo antics, my mind screams, RUN!

I whistle softly to calm my nerves as I approach the bedroom. Dailess isn't expecting me this minute, so I try to tiptoe, but my Air Jordans soles squeak loudly against the polished tiles. I slow down and stop a few feet from the door. My heart beats so loudly as terror runs through my body, that I briefly consider turning back.

But that's not an option anymore. It's now or never. Anything short of that will land me more trouble with my mother and Auntie Francine. I can't afford to get on their wrong side any more than I already have. So far, they've been amazing and have given me unconditional love and more understanding than I deserve. I won't let them down.

After a few deep breaths to steady my nerves, I knock on the door and hesitantly reach for the handle. I tentatively peek through the door. My voice wobbles. "Hi, Dailess. May I please come in?"

"Yes, come in," she says, her voice soft and sad.

As I enter the room, I recall how demure Dailess's voice can be—how it had me fooled. My eyes land on her in an armchair, looking out the window pensively. I wonder what's going through her mind. Does Dailess think she has carried out her mission?

Lying on her lap, face down, is an open book by Iyanla Vanzant, *The Value in the Valley*. Auntie Francine must have given it to her to read last night—a good move. My mother, too, loves Iyanla Vanzant. She got me to read the same book a few times; its message, like the title, never gets old.

Dailess slowly stands up, nervous, cracks her knuckles, and clears her throat. Together, it makes a strange cacophonous noise. In better times, we both might have laughed at that. But now, it's just another unpleasant sound devoid of humour. Neither one of us speaks, and time stands still. Awkward. Eish!

Dailess pats herself gingerly to smoothen her clothes. She looks better than she did yesterday. The chitenge dress is gone, thankfully. She is now sporting one of Auntie Francine's designer dresses. It looks great on her. But still, no wig, not that I expected Auntie Francine to share hers. I owe my Auntie so much; she has been very gracious.

I look around the room, not sure where to settle my eyes. The vibe between Dailess and I is super weird. We both feel the breakup premonition, the unspoken understanding that the end of our relationship has come. It's no longer about who did or said what. There's just too much that one can't change.

Dailess's mother, for a start, who she is and will always be, is a deal breaker for me. We must address the obvious—the room will explode with unspoken words and unshared emotions if we don't speak. So, I go first.

"Hello, Dailess; how are you? Did you have a good night's sleep?"

Dailess looks away from me and doesn't respond. But she gives me a cold and brief handshake; our hands barely touch. I walk over to the bed and gently lower myself onto the edge while she flops back in the armchair, clutching the book to her chest, her eyes cast to the floor.

There's more silence between us. I contemplate taking responsibility for my part in this calamitous situation. It might pave the way for a more amicable discussion between us.

My voice cracks. "Ahem, Dailess, I sincerely want to apologise for not making a greater effort to see you before today. I needed time to clear my head."

"Time? Time to clear what head? You have embarrassed me with my friends and both our parents."

"Dailess, it took you two months to tell me anything. I've only had three weeks with this news. So, excuse me if I'm not moving fast enough for you. I've got to play catch-up."

"Catch-up or not, that doesn't give you the right to ghost me!"

"But it gives you the right to hide the pregnancy? Besides, I tried to meet you and your *committee* last Friday?"

"Yes, when you pretended you couldn't find parking at Levy Junction Shopping Mall?" she scoffs.

"No, Dailess. When you allowed your crazy friend Bridget to think and act for you. Did I not suggest we meet in the car park?"

"The agreement was to meet all four of us at Rio Restaurant. Not in the stupid car park. My pregnancy is private!"

"Private, what do you know about privacy when everything in your life, you decide and do by committee?"

"What do you mean? The girls were there to give me support!" She yells.

"Dailess, has it ever occurred to you that this *fast food combo* girl group of yours is exhausting? You can't expect me to be in a relationship with you and your friends. It's equivalent to dating a *quartet* where three women in it have no business with me."

Dailess glares at me, her nostrils flaring. She knows I'm right but won't admit it. I guess it all doesn't matter anymore. At this point, I need to stick to the script my mother and Auntie Francine gave me.

"Okay, that aside, Dailess, what's the plan here?"

"What do you mean? What's the plan? Isn't it obvious? I'm keeping the baby,"

"I wasn't suggesting otherwise. But it's my right to ask what you had in mind when you came off the pill and when the condom broke, as you say."

"Andrew, none of that matters anymore. Didn't you hear what my mother said yesterday before she left?"

I stare at her in disbelief. "We all understood what your mother wants, but marriage is out of the question."

Dailess stands up and paces the room. "You think you can make a girl pregnant and just walk away?"

"I didn't just make a girl pregnant. Dailess, you made sure you got pregnant."

"I've already explained to you what happened. What more do you want?"

"You surprise me, Dailess. What about your college education, your future? Don't you want to do something with your life first?"

To my surprise, Dailess shouts back, her voice thick with desperation. "You promised to get me a job at your Dealership. Was that a lie?"

"No, Dailess, I can't be your *begin and end all*. The Dealership is my father's business. Besides, I might not be here by the time you graduate."

I knew I had said too much when those words rolled off my tongue. Without warning, Dailess grabs the collar of my t-shirt and yanks me. I stagger backwards and clumsily grab her forearm for support—my weight throws us out of balance.

"Won't be here? Where will you be, Andrew?"

"I might find a job elsewhere in another town."

Dailess crosses her brow. "Which town? We live in the capital city where the best job opportunities are, so why would you live elsewhere? What aren't you telling me?"

I struggle to keep the argument under control. "Hey, easy. Keep your voice down. You're in my parents' house; have some respect!"

I try to free myself from her grip. But Dailess pulls my collar tighter around my neck. I have never seen her behave this way; entirely out of character.

"Get off me; what's wrong with you?"

"I'm sorry, but what are you hiding from me?"

I would tell Dailess about my scholarship and plans if things were different. But where we are today, my obligation to her starts and ends with the baby. Why can't she see that she's throwing away her future for marriage to a twenty-one-year-old guy? One who has also yet to figure out his life. What do I know about being anyone's husband?

"Dailess, I hate that we find ourselves in this situation. But this baby will need both parents to have stable lives, whether we are together or not."

Dailess is too angry to see my point. "We're a couple with a baby on the way. We must talk about where you are going to live and work!"

"Why do you think you can decide everything in my life? I'll inform you of my plans if I choose to. But last I checked, we weren't married, so I don't need your permission."

I'm amazed at how stunned she looks in response to me. But what comes out of her mouth next is even more shocking.

"Tha... That means you don't want to marry me?" Dailess asks with tears in her eyes.

"You say that like we've discussed marriage before. Dailess, even in the best of times between us, marriage isn't in my cards for me—not for another ten years."

"So, you plan to walk away while my life goes down the toilet?" She responds, her eyes wild with anger as they search my face.

"I care about you deeply, and my family will support you and the baby during your pregnancy. When the baby arrives, I'll do my part. I'm not walking away from the baby."

"So, I'll be stuck with the baby as a single parent?" Dailess asks.

"If you're honest, we could have avoided such *accidents* had we stuck to both methods of contraception."

"Andrew, please, I can't return to Kamwala with an illegitimate child. My mother will call me today. What am I supposed to tell her?"

Without warning, Dailess throws her hands over her cornrowed head as a piercing scream escapes her lips. With each deafening scream, her emotions become palpable, and my heart bleeds for her. But there's no way under the sun that my mother and her entire Mulenga family would ever get past the voodoo. It's bad enough that I caused us to *rub shoulders* with Mrs Banda.

Now, angry tears stream down Dailess's face as her cries become more desperate. They reverberate past the open door and down the hallway. My mother must have heard the distressful crying, for a curious Auntie Francine appears at the door.

"Guys, guys, guys, keep your voices down. The whole of Kabulonga, to the Supermarket, can hear you."

"I'm so sorry, Auntie," I respond.

Auntie Francine pushes the door open and rushes over to Dailess.

"What's going on? Are you okay?"

"Auntie, Dailess and I have talked. I've told her marriage is out of the question, hence the tears."

Auntie Francine signals me to stop talking. She takes Dailess by the elbow, steers her to the armchair, and hands her a box of tissues. "Calm down, Dailess. This amount of crying isn't good for you or the baby."

Dailess contorts her face in frustration. "So, Andrew gets to walk away scot-free into a bright future, and all I'll get is the debris of shattered hopes and dreams?"

"It's sad to see young girls like you saddled with pregnancies they aren't prepared for. But marriage isn't the solution." Auntie Francine looks at both of us. "For as long as this baby shall live, neither of you'll get away scot-free."

"Dailess, we both have a duty to our child, but it won't always be equal responsibilities," I add.

"My mother won't accept anything less than marriage. I've already told you I won't return to kamwala without a husband!"

Funny, until now, I never knew Dailess could be stubborn and unreasonable. She behaves like her mother in a way that doesn't comfort me. I can smell her fear, and I'm sure she can smell mine. It's intense as we fight for our separate interests—Dailess marriage and I, my bachelorhood.

Auntie Francine takes Dailess' hands.

"You're so young; what do you know about marriage? It's not something you get entangled with just because you're pregnant. It's not enough, and it'll never be."

"So, who's going to marry me now?"

"I can't answer that question. But I can tell you that the Michelo family will discuss with your family to see that you and the baby receive the financial support you deserve."

"No one will marry me with another man's child," Dailess responds, not taking in what Auntie Francine's telling her.

"It worries me that your education and personal development don't seem a priority to you. Is there anything you want to do with your life besides marriage?" Auntie Francine asks.

"My mother's priority for me is marriage; nothing else matters—education or whatever!"

"What your mother understands is one thing. But you must be the best version of yourself in preparation for motherhood." Auntie Francine replies.

Dailess is silent, but from the look on her face, one can tell that her mind is boiling. The temples on the side of her head pulsate like drum beats at a traditional ceremony. She is a woman scorned who doesn't need encouragement to explode.

"Do you know how often your nephew sneaked me into the house of that stupid friend of his, David?"

"Dailess, you weren't a virgin when I met you. Did you ask your previous boyfriend to marry you?" I demand.

The more Dailess protests, the more I'm convinced she set me up.

"Why are you in a rush to get married to me? I doubt your twisted ambition is genuinely about the baby—the poor child is just a means to an end."

Auntie Francine raises her hand. "Shush, both of you. There's a reason why abstinence is best before marriage. You both *made your bed and must lie in it*. No amount of mud-slinging will change your circumstances."

Dailess folds her arms across her chest.

"I won't leave this house. You can call the Police if you want. I don't care."

Auntie Francine snaps. "*Mukashana* (young lady), don't forget this isn't Andrew's house. His parents have been kind enough to let you spend the night and give you the comfort you deserve in your condition. Don't cross the line."

"Dailess, my Auntie is right. You can't just decide to live here. Don't you have relatives who can take you in if your parents' house isn't an option?"

Dailess tries to guilt-trip me. "So, you want your child to be born in Kamwala?"

But I won't fall for it. "No, Dailess, the baby will be born in the fee-paying maternity ward at University Teaching Hospital."

"No one is trying to *throw you under the bus*, Dailess. Your father promised to come back with his uncle to discuss your condition. The Michelo family will care for your maternity needs and general well-being." Auntie Francine adds.

"My mother said Ba Nganga saw me wearing a wedding dress in a mirror," Dailess argues.

"Goodbye, Dailess, I won't come back here. I can't engage you and your mother's Nganga story anymore. I'm sorry that things have ended this way between us."

As Auntie Francine and I leave a wailing Dailess behind, I know putting the ghosts to rest won't be easy. Seeing how determined Dailess is to become my wife, it'll take a sophisticated game plan that goes beyond the child's birth.

Chapter Nineteen

IT'S NOT WORTH THE TROUBLE

As Auntie Francine and I hurriedly leave Dailess' room, I can't help but wonder what my future looks like. But whatever that is, I know it's more complex than I could ever imagine. My brain is on fire as I try to figure out the twists and turns ahead of me.

Am I the only young man in Lusaka whose relationship and sex life is this complicated? Other than the obvious, I don't know if I could have done anything to prevent Dailess' surprise pregnancy. Perhaps I could have paid more attention, but to what? To something I didn't even know was an issue?

I'm ashamed of how royally I've let my mother down. My baby mama saga has to be her worst nightmare next to my father's Mazabuka sins. It kills me that I've no clue how to make things right. I was naïve to think the discussion with Dailess would go well for as long as I promised her financial support.

But rightfully or wrongfully, Dailess has her eyes set on marriage to me—I'm her chosen *vessel* that will give her the life she has dreamed of. With such ambitions and her mother's evil ways, we have a two-headed monster. I shudder to think how this story will end.

I've no doubt my mother and Auntie Francine will go to the ends of the earth for me. But no matter what anyone does for me, only I can pull myself out of this muddy puddle I've created. My life's on a path where everything my mother has taught me is the only ally to get me through. Otherwise, even with the support of those who love me, I'll sink and disappear in Mrs Banda's world of dark shadows and obscurity. I'm seriously f**ked.

Back in the TV room, my mother nervously paces up and down. She rushes to meet Auntie Francine and me and throws her arms around us in a tight embrace. The corners of her mouth quiver upwards into a strange smile. Her lips tremble and show more sadness than mirth.

My mother's face looks unfamiliar, a weak reflection of her true self. The rapid flutter of her eyes tries to shut off her tear ducts as she puts on a brave act. But I know she's dying inside, fearful that the evils of darkness orchestrated by Mrs Banda will take her only son away.

Seeing my mother like this breaks my heart into a thousand pieces. No matter what it takes, I must make things right with my beloved mother.

"I take it things did not go too well in there?" My mother's anxious voice greets us. "I could hear Dailess crying from here."

"Sis, we've got a bigger problem than we thought." Auntie Francine responds and takes my mother's hand. "The girl wants marriage, and her mother's vicious aspirations don't help matters."

"Auntie Francine's right, Mummy. The girl you saw yesterday, meek and humble as a church mouse, is now a vicious feline, ready to claw her way into marriage."

"My darling boy, what have you gotten us into?" My mother despairs as she lowers herself into a chair. She appears tired and clings to Auntie Francine for support. "Where do we go from here?"

"Mummy, I don't want to get married." My voice trembles and rises as I speak. "There's nothing I did or said to Dailess that might have encouraged her in any way."

"Andrew, you're way too nice and naïve. You really must learn how to read women." My mother shuts her eyes to control the onset of fresh tears. "Have you forgotten your experience with that wretched Maria Sosala?"

"We need a quick solution. Lusaka's full of treacherous women." Auntie Francine racks her brains. "For the likes of Maria, you were a *beard*, and for the Dailesses, you're *security and a bougie lifestyle* on two legs."

My mother and Auntie are right. How do I always pick the troublesome girls? Between Maria and Dailess, it appears there's a lesson I'm missing because I've been scammed back to back.

"I don't believe I am about to ask you this. What does that nasty friend of yours think?" My mother muses.

Really? Wow, my mother must have hit a new record of desperation.

I wink at Auntie Francine. "Mummy, you mean David Likezo, my cantankerous friend, the one you said you couldn't stand?" I tease her.

"Well, I've got my reasons. But yes, David's more streetwise than you are, son. He might help us learn more about Dailess' family and background."

"An ear to the ground is crucial to moving forward," Auntie Francine exhorts. "No more surprises."

***

The clock on the wall strikes 13:00 hrs. Where did the time go? I can't believe it's afternoon already. What a morning we've had. The door to the TV room opens, and Ba Esther kneels in the doorway. Seeing her sends a message to my brain, and my tummy lets out an eager rumble.

"Lunch is ready, madam. Please come to the table." Ba Esther announces, her eyes cast on the floor, respectful of my mother's sombre mood.

"Let's eat; we need the energy to deal with Dailess and her aspirations to become your wife, Andrew." My mother shakes her head in sadness.

"Thank you very much, Ba Esther." I give her a polite smile.

The aroma of village chicken stew hits my senses when we get to the dining room. My stomach rumbles again as Ba Esther removes the covers from the serving dishes to reveal the rest of her handiwork. She has a buffet of dried fish, beans, impwa (small green aubergine), chibwabwa (pumpkin leaves) and nshima, a traditional thick porridge made from a mix of ground maize corn and cassava flour. There's nothing like a home-cooked meal.

Auntie Francine does a little happy dance. "Let's enjoy a stress-free lunch—a little break from Dailess."

"Francine, you've always danced for food since you were a little girl," my mother teases. But something tells me this isn't just about Ba Esther's culinary skills."

"You brought me here to help solve the problem, didn't you?" She chuckles.

"Whatever brainstorm you've had, it had better work." My mother laughs.

***

We have barely sat down, and the front doorbell rings ten minutes into lunch. All three of us startle and exchange puzzled looks. My hands start to tremble as I put down my serviette. Who could it be? I pray to God it is not Dailess' mother and her entourage. I cannot take another voodoo session from her today or anytime soon.

My mother half rises from her seat, unsure if she should go to the door herself. She looks at me, and her smooth face gives way to a furrowed brow.

"Ba Esther, check who's at the door. If it's Mrs Banda, please do not let her in the house."

"I'm not expecting anyone, Ba Esther," I add for good measure.

Our eyes are still glued to the French doors, anxious to know who the unannounced guest is. None of us wanted Mrs Banda back, but my mother, Auntie Francine, and I gasp to see my father walk into the dining room with Grandma Selina in tow. We didn't expect my father for lunch, let alone his mother. The room whirls around at high speed as we try to regroup and mask our confusion and disapproval.

Who would have thought my father would rope his mother in my *mess* so soon? Grandma Selina's presence is poor judgment on his part. Why the rush? At this rate, things will blow up in our faces. D**n!

"Grandma! You're here!" I exclaim and scramble to my feet. My mouth attempts to curve into a joyful smile. But it settles in a miserable expression between a smile and a cry. So full of self-importance, my grandma doesn't answer me. Instead, she turns away from me to address my mother.

"Ah-ah, April, you look surprised to see me. Is there a problem?" Grandma Selina raises her once-thick eyebrows, now grey and thinning rapidly with old age.

My mother struggles to sound sincere. "Not at all, Baama (mother). Roger didn't say anything, that's all. It's not a problem."

"What you mean is that my son needs your permission for me to come to his house?" Grandma Selina spits out her words.

After so many years, it's uncanny how Grandma's adversarial relationship with my mother has never waned. Her poison is still as alive as it was thirty years ago. It seeps through her skin and pollutes the air—in comparison, the stench of a pile of rotten fish smells like roses. The woman is impossible to please. Eish!

My mother's voice falters as it collides with Grandma Selina's abrasive booming tone. "Forgive me, Baama, I just wa..."

"You *just wanted* what, April Mulenga?" She attacks and switches to my mother's birth name with a condescending slur to her words.

Grandma Selina can't help but *dig* at my mother. Oddly enough, she doesn't see my mother as part of the Michelo family. For that reason, combined with her super shady remarks, it's hard to include Grandma Selina in family meetings. She'll happily drag my mother through the mud.

Look at us; we're already on a slippery slope, guns drawn and ready for war, long before we get to the real issues. Someone should do something before someone loses an eye.

"Madam, I'll bring some more plates," Ba Esther suggests, suddenly bursting into the room.

Something tells me Ba Esther was behind the door listening to this hateful conversation. Ba Esther has never liked Grandma Selina's oppressive attitude towards my mother. For this reason, she has always been protective of my mother.

"Yes, please, Ba Esther, thank you," my mother responds, misty-eyed with gratitude.

It upsets me that my father is oblivious to Grandma Selina's *corrosive* behaviour. Everyone can see what a scam she is and how she has robbed him of any chance at happiness with my mother.

"Baama, please have a seat here next to me," my father makes an exaggerated display of grand hospitality.

"Roger, who cooked this food?" Grandma scowls and pushes her plate away.

"Baama, Roger and April have had Ba Esther cook for them for years. Today is no different," Auntie Francine jumps to my mother's rescue.

"That's because your sister is lazy and can't cook!" Grandma Selina hisses.

"With all due respect, Baama, April's the one who has taught Ba Esther how to cook—the same food that has nourished your son, Roger, for years. As you can see, it hasn't killed him." Auntie Francine retorts, unapologetic for defending her big sister.

There is strength in numbers. It's time to add my two cents to defend my mother. As I open my mouth to speak, my father frantically signals me to stop. I ignore him.

"Grandma Selina, if my father had told my mother you were coming, she might have personally cooked your favourite dishes."

"Roger, you see this rubbish. Even this boy expects you to get permission from his mother for me to visit my own son!" Grandma Selina, spitting mad, glares at my father.

"Let's eat Baama. We've got a lot to talk about," my father responds, raising his hands like a referee at a boxing match. I knew it! He brought his mother for backup. We shall see whose mother wins—his or mine.

***

After lunch, we all move to the TV room, which, though roomy, feels tight and short of air. What with Grandma Selina hogging the space and taking up all the oxygen. She believes her words carry more weight than anyone else's—including mine, whose problem we're here to address.

"Everyone, my son, Roger, has brought me here today because Andrew, you're in trouble. You've made a girl pregnant; is this true?" Grandma Selina asks. She squares her shoulders and towers over me like a High Court Judge.

"Yes, Grandma. My girlfriend's pregnant. But my parents can manage the matter between them. My father shouldn't have bothered you with my problems," I respond.

"Young man, you shan't talk to me like that! Your mother can't handle anything; your father brought me here to take charge," Grandma snaps to cause fright.

"I mean no disrespect, Grandma. All I need is a chance to discuss the matter with my parents together," I stand my ground. I won't let an enemy of my mother take over the direction of my future.

Across from me, my father moves to the edge of the couch and makes a futile effort to harness a conversation that has gone rogue.

"Son, go and get Dailess to come and meet your grandmother. We think you should get married," my father says.

"Over my dead body!" My enraged mother declares. "Roger, we are not going to introduce Dailess to anyone. Besides, you and I are Andrew's parents. How does Baama come in?"

"The same way you brought Francine into the discussion?" My father retorts.

Auntie Francine stares at my father in shock. How could he hit below the belt after all she and Uncle Michael have done for me?

"Everyone, please! Let's all take a deep breath and think before we all say things we can't take back." Auntie Francine reasons.

"No offence, Francine, if my mother can't speak, neither should you," my father defends his point of view.

"Firstly, Roger, you can't compare my presence in your home to ambushing your wife with your mother's visit." Auntie Francine confronts my father. "And here's the difference: I'm on your side. Your mother has never been on my sister's side."

"Truthfully, Dad, Grandma Selina has always stood in the way of you being a good husband to my mother; why is that?" I add to drive Auntie Francine's point home.

"This family you married into is a problem, my son." Grandma Selina pokes the air with her forefinger with fury. "Your wife and her sister are like your proud, good-for-nothing Bemba mother-in-law."

My mother can no longer contain herself.

"Roger, I request you excuse your mother from this discussion. Andrew is an adult. Let him tell us what he wants to do."

When opportunity knocks, it is best to yield.

"Thank you, Mummy." I stand up and take a deep breath. "Grandma Selina, Dad, I've only known Dailess for three months. Marriage's out of the question."

"Oh, no, you plan to bring a bastard into this family?" Grandma Selina scowls at me. "Your brothers in Mazabuka have never disgraced the Michelos."

"With all due respect, Grandma, how different are your Mazabuka bastard grandsons from my unborn child? So yes, my bastard will be part of the Michelo family, like every other bastard."

"Roger, have you heard this rubbish from your son's mouth?" Grandma Selina stomps her foot.

"As for your glowing reviews of your beloved grandsons, Grandma, what exactly do you want me to do about that? Jump into the Victoria Falls in self-pity?" I poke the bear.

My father, unable to control his mother or me, coughs loudly to drown out our voices. It beats all logic because it was his idea to include his *demon* mother in my private life.

"Baama, Andrew has made a mistake, but he's a sensible young man," my mother tries to smooth over the rough conversation.

"That's true. I've got a scholarship to pursue a master's degree in England, starting in January next year," I say proudly.

But to my surprise, my father shoots up from his seat like a man on fire. "Let's continue this discussion tomorrow when everyone is calmer." My father grimaces like one attacked by a colony of red ants but is afraid to scream. "Baama, let me show you to your room."

It takes a minute for us to figure out why there is a sudden change in plans. But we don't have to think too hard because Grandma Selina brings us all up to speed, much to my father's chagrin.

"England? Who's going to England?" Grandma Selina turns to her son.

My father, nostrils flaring like a hippo in distress, stutters. "It's Francine; I mean...it's Michael who arranged it."

"Roger, speak properly. Francine, Michael, who arranged what? Tell me, who's going to England?" Grandma Selina demands.

What an interesting observation. It dawns on my mother, Auntie Francine, and me that my father hadn't told Grandma Selina about my scholarship, yet she knew about Dailess. Oops! It looks like the *hyena* has just *outed* its cub. I watch my father squirm in his pitiful charade and decide to put him out of his misery.

"Grandma, I'm the one off to England." I pause for effect to enjoy the look of the rude awakening on her face. "I got a scholarship for a master's degree in Climate Change."

"No, no, no, you? Why you? What makes you so special?" Grandma Selina rants nonstop. One might conclude we have utterly different blood running through our veins.

Grandma Selina's jugular veins look ready to burst through the sides of her wrinkled neck. "You went to good schools, live in this beautiful house, work at your father's company, and now you get to go to England? What about your brothers?" Grandma demands.

"Baama, I'm sorry my son hasn't explained himself properly," my mother pleads.

Grandma Selina comes undone; she can no longer hide her anger and failure to see sense. "Shut up! You think I don't know you are the reason Roger doesn't spend money on his other sons and me?" Grandma Selina comes undone; she can no longer hide her anger and failure to see sense.

"Please, Baama, Roger and I won't pay a penny towards Andrew's education in England. My sister's husband, Micheal, helped Andrew get a scholarship."

"Oh, Mummy, Grandma Selina thinks you and I are the biggest mistakes of Dad's life. It's a conviction she'll take to her grave. So please don't stress yourself. *It's not worth the trouble,*" I console my mother and take her hand.

"What April is saying, Baama..." my father's voice trails off, cut short by Grandma Selina's wrath.

"Roger, tell the truth. How much money will it cost you to send this boy to England? Grandma Selina is relentless.

If Dailess and her troubles had us all in a deep hole, we all just sunk further down. It's hard to tell who's doing the digging. Is it my father and his mother or my mother and me? Whatever the case, my mother and I must get out of the *trenches* fast and throw my father under a moving fast goods train.

"Dad, you've already trusted Grandma Selina with my private life. Why is it difficult for you to explain my scholarship?"

"Andrew, please, this doesn't concern you," my father snaps.

"Really? Roger, how or why would that be so?" My mother questions.

My father is at wit's end. "Baama, you don't understand how these things work. I won't have to pay a single Kwacha for Andrew's university fees in England."

"Your sons in Mazabuka, Roger, you have two sons in Mazabuka! When will they get to live like April's son?" Grandma Selina demands without any shame or guilt.

"Baama, please! Francine's husband, Michael, the British man, has been very generous with Andrew. Michael doesn't know about my sons in Mazabuka!"

"Oooh, Roger, because of this woman, you've hidden your sons from the white man?" Grandma Selina shamelessly spews more poison. She clings to the Mazabuka boys like it's her passport to insult my mother at will.

What hurts more than anything is her catalogue of issues against my mother. They run longer than the river *Nile*—from the fact that my mother is of the Bemba clan, her miscarriages, and my late arrival into this world. Not forgetting the Bemba crown, she insists my mother has bestowed upon my head. Yet, my mother keeps trying to win Grandma Selina's love. It's not worth it.

"Roger is right, Baama," my mother tries to back my father's account with zero success.

"Rubbish, you think I don't know your tricks, April?" Grandma Selina decides to switch tactics to remove attention from the fact that her son, my father, disagrees with her. "What do you have to say now, April? Your son, the accidental egg and child, has brought shame to the family."

"Baama, what do you have against my son?" My mother finally rages. "Is it because Andrew is a living testimony of my fertility? Tell me because I don't understand how a grandmother can hate her grandchild this much!"

"Fertility? A fertile woman doesn't give her husband five miscarriages." Grandma Selina's putrid words hit everyone hard. It's shocking.

"Baama, control yourself. We've heard enough hurtful words come out of your mouth." Auntie Francine strikes back and puts Grandma in her place. "This isn't your house. You must give respect to your son and his wife."

"Without my sacrifices, Roger wouldn't be where he is today!" Grandma rages at the top of her voice. "April can't be the one to enjoy my hard work."

"Roger isn't your husband, Baama. Leave my sister alone!" Auntie Francine chastises. "My husband worked hard to get your grandson, my nephew, a scholarship; what can be so bad with that?"

Grandma Selina looks Auntie Francine up and down and curls her lips into a detestable grin.

"Look at her. You useless woman married to a foolish *mukuwa* (white man), rubbish woman."

"April, how has your marriage lasted this long with a mother-in-law like this?" Auntie Francine fumes.

"If your sister is tired, she can leave. There're plenty of women waiting to move in with my son." My Grandma Selina's hatred would give Mrs Banda's voodoo a run for its money.

"April, I'm sorry I can't stand such poison." Auntie Francine gives me a serious look. "I'll take Andrew and return to my house this evening. We won't spend one more night here for as long as your mother-in-law and Dailess are in this house."

Yes! That's my Auntie, my champion! I look at my mother, and she smiles back in agreement. My father tries to open his mouth to speak, but Auntie Francine cuts him short.

"Roger, effective today, Andrew will no longer work at your car dealership."

My father's eyes dance around in desperation. "Francine, Andrew can't just quit like that; what about the marketing strategy he has been working on?"

"Dad, last Monday, you practically fired me. When would I have implemented the marketing strategy you never allowed me to design in the first place?"

"Roger, for whatever reason, you've always behaved like Andrew was a charity case at the dealership. A favour of sorts that you have extended to him," my mother adds salt to injury.

"Dad, you'll be fine. I'll prepare handover notes for Jordan." I look at my Grandma Selina as I speak. I want her to understand that her sting can't hurt me. "Besides, what difference does it make now? I'll leave in three months."

"Roger, perhaps Baama is right. It's time you brought your Mazabuka *duo* into the family business," Auntie Francine says sarcastically.

"Get out of here, all of you. Leave my son alone!" Grandma Selina, a sore loser, yells.

"Roger, listen to your mother." My mother shakes her head in despair. "We've spent the last three hours arguing about things that don't count. Was it worth it?"

My father has no words. What he thinks doesn't matter at this point. Grandma Selina has drawn a line in the sand; she'll never be team April or Andrew. It's hard to imagine how my father can be okay with such divisive behaviour. Granted, he doesn't overtly encourage it, but he makes no effort to stop it. Grandma Selina's malice must work in his favour.

My mother, Auntie Francine, and I leave the TV room. We're happy to give mother and son a chance to lick their wounds. Once outside, I'm glad to have escaped the confines of the TV room. With everyone disagreeing, it felt like a prison of negative emotions.

Out here in my mother's garden, it's peaceful, and I feel liberated. I'm grateful for Ba Bwezani's enormous, beautiful umbrella trees. Their sprawling branches offer a refreshing sanctuary of soothing shade in this hot weather.

Ba Esther appears just in time. I could use a cold drink. "Can I bring the usual for you, madam and Auntie Francine?" She asks, and then turns to smile at me. "And a mosi beer for you, Bwana Andrew?"

"You read my mind, Ba Esther, thank you."

Pleased with her hosting skills, Ba Esther sashays back into the house to fetch the drinks order.

Away from my father and his mother, it gives the three of us a chance to go over what should happen next. It worries me that my father prefers that I marry Dailess. Why would he choose that for me after what we all saw yesterday? Even in the best of times, Mrs Banda would be a challenging *taste to acquire*. Our marriage would be doomed straight out of the gate. My father must know deep in his heart that his decision is wrong—except Grandma Selina's word is *law*.

"Mummy, you have to stand up against Dad and Grandma. Otherwise, the two will feed me to the Banda wolves."

My mother rolls her eyes. "Son, one doesn't need a crystal ball to see how wrong your father is."

"If it did happen, your marriage to Dailess would be a life of hardship. Auntie Francine cuts in." No young man can cope with Mrs Banda as their mother-in-law?"

"I know. Relationships are tough enough as it is." I add.

Ba Esther returns with our drinks and snacks, with Ba Bwezani in tow. From the look in their eyes, I can tell they've just had a *sidebar* about me. Ba Bwezani towers over us and then clumsily throws himself at my mother's feet.

My mother abruptly puts down her glass of white chardonnay. "Oh no, not again, Ba Bwezani. What is it this time?" She clutches her chest in fright. "Please don't tell me Mrs Banda is back at the gate?"

"No, madam, I want to tell you something." Ba Bwezani hesitates and swallows hard. "Please forgive me; I don't want to insult or scare you."

"Just say what you want to say, Ba Bwezani." My mother panics.

"Mrs Banda is a dangerous woman. You must take her seriously." Ba Bwezani raises his arms above his head. "In the compounds where we live, many evil things happen to young men involved in unwanted pregnancies."

Scared out of my wits, I stare at my mother, who stares at Auntie Francine.

"What must we do, Ba Bwezani?" my mother asks.

"Madam, the most important thing is for you to hold onto your son."

"Explain what you mean, Ba Bwezani? Auntie Francine asks.

"Don't let Bwana Andrew marry Dailess. Otherwise, you'll be feeding your only child to the forces of darkness."

"My God! Ba Bwezani, please don't scare me. How can we keep Mrs Banda away from my son?"

"Madam, remember Dailess is their only daughter. For poor people like me and the Bandas, marriage is a way of survival for the whole family."

"But Ba Bwezani, you just said Andrew shouldn't marry Dailess." My mother sounds puzzled.

"What I mean is, if you can't give Bwana Andrew to the Bandas, what can you give them in exchange?" Ba Bwezani emphasises.

"It makes sense, Ba Bwezani." Auntie Francine adds.

"Yes, they will ask for a lot of money. It would help if you made them happy—especially the father's family. If they're happy, eventually they can control Mrs Banda." Ba Bwezani smiles.

"But wait a minute, we aren't sure it's Andrew's baby?" Auntie Francine litigates the issue.

"Madam, nine months is a long time." Ba Bwezani looks Auntie Francine straight in the eye. "Mrs Banda can cause a lot of damage. Don't wait to prove anything."

"But we can't accept the pregnancy now, then later say no?" My mother makes a good point.

"Let me speak like your father, not your servant." Ba Bwezani stands up and places his hands on his heart. "Please put out this fire before we start seeing unexplained disasters. Bwana Andrew is your only child."

"I understand, Ba Bwezani. Thank you very much for your guidance." My mother responds.

"April, it's urgent to support Dailess as agreed earlier." Auntie Francine says.

"I agree, Andrew, we shouldn't raise the paternity issue. For now, let sleeping dogs lie," my mother says.

"Madam, Bwana Andrew must leave the house. Traditionally speaking, if he lives under the same roof with Dailess in her condition, it's marriage." Ba Bwezani has never looked this serious.

"Common Law marriage. Excellent point, Ba Bwezani. We must avoid cohabitation between the two." Auntie Francine pulls Ba Esther's close to her. "Please pack two suitcases for Andrew. I'll take him with me this evening."

"Thank you, Auntie, for the offer to take me in with you." I finally speak, alarmed after listening to Ba Bwezani. "But will Dailess live with my parents until she gives birth?"

"Madam, prepare to hand over Dailess to her parents when they return with Mr Banda's uncle." Ba Bwezani addresses my mother.

"Mummy, that's a battle requiring a strong *army*, including Ba Bwezani," I add.

"Eish!" We all sigh.

Chapter Twenty

HE WHO SUPS WITH THE DEVIL
SHOULD HAVE A LONG SPOON

Sleepovers at Auntie Francine's are always a blast. Last night, we arrived at her house in New Kasama at 19:30. Ba Eunice, Auntie's ever-cheerful housekeeper, met us at the door with a warm and inviting welcome. There was no way to miss the aroma of the sumptuous meal she had prepared.

Auntie Francine and I made our way to the dining room at once. Ravenous, we couldn't help but savour every bite—given that Grandma Selina had soured our lunch earlier in the day. We later closed the evening with a chilled bottle of Veuve Clicquot. Why not?

For once, this morning, I feel chilled as I languish in the king-sized bed in the fancy guest bedroom. What a luxury! It's been forever since I was this relaxed. I stretch my arms and think I've got a lot to be grateful for, even though I haven't fully figured out my future yet.

But I know that with my mother and Auntie Francine on board, I'll be okay, no matter what life throws at me. I'm happy to part ways with the emotional doom that has kept me paralysed for weeks.

I wonder about Dailess for a few minutes. Strangely enough, I haven't heard from her. Not that I want to. But does she know I left the house by now? If not, it's just a matter of time before the *penny drops*—and her mother finds out. Mrs Banda will soon realise her strategy of a Common Law marriage for her daughter has collapsed. And that will open a whole can of worms.

For this reason, Auntie Francine has forbidden me to talk to Dailess any further. Yesterday morning's disastrous meeting with her was all my Auntie needed to see the red flags littered everywhere.

A part of me feels sorry for Dailess. But if I called her now, it would muddy the waters unnecessarily. Things are complicated enough as it is. I can't give her what she wants. Marrying Dailess out of pity would be unfair to her and our unborn child—a train wreck waiting to happen.

And my mother. My dear mother—all alone with my father and Grandma Selina. I can't understand why, after so many years, my mother still must walk on eggshells around Grandma Selina.

My father has made big mistakes in his relationship with my mother—his illegitimate sons, for a start. But one might even say he can't change that. The second mistake is his unsettled spirit in the marriage. My father has failed to be a dedicated husband, a comforter and a protector to my mother. Grandma Selina won't allow it.

Why did my father bring his mother home yesterday? What did the two of them have in mind? Whatever the case, Grandma Selina's plot to send me off into accelerated matrimony and fatherhood fell flat. And there's no room for negotiation.

Sadly, Grandma Selina doesn't *wear* defeat well. If you check-mate her, you can be sure you'll become her mortal enemy. The woman can hold grudges longer than an Alaskan wood frog can hold its pee. Your name will go into her black book without the hope of an eraser setting you free. One can expect that yesterday afternoon's *downfall* has left a bitter taste in her mouth. My mother won't hear the end of it.

A knock at my door interrupts my reflections.

"Good morning, Andrew. Did you have a good night's sleep?"

"Morning, Auntie. I'll be with you in a minute."

"Good, breakfast is ready."

***

After a quick cold shower, I hurry out of the bedroom to join Auntie Francine. She's already at her desk, working on her laptop. I admire how composed, organised, and on top of things she always is. Auntie Francine would never have been in my situation if she were a guy.

"That was quick, Andrew."

"Auntie, I'm not like you and Mummy. You take forever in the bathroom." We both laugh.

I have a lot to be thankful for. Auntie Francine's decision to bring me to her house was a power move. The last thing I want is to *play house* with Dailess under the supervision of Grandma Selina. God forbid!

"Auntie, you're heaven-sent. You did well to rescue me from Grandma Selina."

"I did it for both of us. Your Grandmother could've swallowed me alive, given half the chance," she responds, her eyes glazed with mischief.

Before I can sit down, I suddenly remember my luggage in the boot of Auntie's Porsche Cayenne.

"Auntie, can I please borrow your car keys? My luggage is still in the boot."

"Oh, don't worry about it. Ba Jeremiah will bring it in for you when he returns." Auntie Francine motions me to sit down. "He took the car for service."

"Okay, no worries, I'll wait. Besides, I'm hungry."

"I've laid out some of Michael's clothes for you to choose from."

"Thank you, Auntie. I'll get changed then."

"Yes, be quick. Don't let your breakfast get cold," Auntie Francine says. She doesn't look up from her laptop.

***

When I return to the breakfast room, ready to chow down my food. I'm surprised to find Auntie Francine all dolled up—looking fly. Where's she going? If she mentioned it earlier, I don't recall.

"I didn't know you had work today, Auntie?"

"I don't. But your mother will be here shortly." Auntie Francine turns her back to me and reaches for her handbag. "I've got a few errands to run this morning."

"Great, at least I get to see Mummy. I was worried Dad and Grandma Selina might have torn her to pieces."

"Nothing can keep your mother down until she's sure all is well with you," Auntie Francine reassures me.

***

My mother breezes into the house fifteen minutes later. She offers a broad smile. "Hello, my beloved."

It warms my heart to see her. "Mummy, there you are. I've been worried about you!"

"Fear not. I can handle your witch of a grandmother," my mother hugs me.

"Did Dailess leave the bedroom at all yet?"

"I don't think so," my mother replies, changing the topic. "Your Auntie needs a ride into town. We can't keep her stranded after all she has done for us, can we now?"

"That's right, you owe me," Auntie Francine chuckles. "We're off into town."

"Okay. I could go with you if you don't mind?" I rise from my chair.

"No!" Both women respond in unison. I'm puzzled. What's with the chorused answer—I wonder what the two sisters are up to.

"Invite your friend David for lunch. He'll keep you company while we're gone," Auntie Francine greenlights.

I hesitate. Since when has it been okay to mention David's name, let alone invite him to the house?

"Go ahead; I've let David out of the *doghouse*." My mother chuckles. "He can't corrupt you beyond the damage Dailess has caused."

"True dat!" Auntie Francine says and sends us into a chortle.

I'm unsure what to make of all this lightheartedness. But I know these two women's behaviour is cagey enough for me to think something's up. What could that be?

I get back to my breakfast after my mother and Auntie leave. The house is quiet except for Ba Euniece's humming. Afterwards, I wander into Uncle Michael's library. I've got to fill my unplanned free time. I could read a book or call David to come over. The latter is more appealing—my friend will keep me busy.

***

Three hours later, David pulls up in his good old faithful banger. It looks out of place in Auntie Francine's beautiful driveway. I rush out to meet him and give him a fist pump. "Hey, bruv, what took you so long?"

"Dude, I'm on a tight budget." David chuckles. "Bruv, the fuel cost from Chudleigh to New Kasama is no joke. I had to make a plan," he complains in jest.

"Dude, what were you doing in Chudleigh?" I ask, even though I'd rather not know. But David, being *David,* he tells me anyway.

"Bruv, there's a married chick I've been seeing for the past two months. She's *unhappily* married to some good-for-nothing Bally." David cackles like a jackal.

"What's with you and these unhappily married women you keep picking up? And bruv, the emphasis is on the words *unhappily married.* Really, bruv? Why would you buy that s**t?" I reproach him.

"So says the guy who got sneaky Dailess knocked up," David sniggers.

"Touché!"

"Besides, I'm not trying to marry this chick, bruv. Again, I keep telling you, it's a *situationship.* I know it, and the chick knows it—everyone's happy," David says with a smirk.

"Fair enough, bruv. Come on inside."

I lead David into the lounge. He whistles and walks around gingerly as if stepping on hot coal.

"Sweet! Whose crib is this?"

"Auntie Francine and Uncle Michael's."

David stops like he's about to bolt. "Hey, hold up, bruv. You're sure your queen won't show up with a gun or something?"

"Chill, man. My mother is cool with you," I smile to appease him.

David furrows his brow. "Woah, hold up, not so fast, bruv. After all these years, what changed?"

"I'll tell you all about it; let's go and grab lunch first."

My friend looks sceptical but follows me to the kitchen anyway. I know the suspense is more than he can handle. But lunch is just the bait I need to get David to do as I ask. He wolfs his food down like a man who hasn't eaten in days.

"Bruv, I can see *Ms Chudleigh* hasn't been feeding you," I ask in jest.

"The chick tries, but you know I can't fully relax in her home." David laughs between mouthfuls. "Her Sugar Daddy of a hubby might suddenly show up."

"Risky! That's a lot of *chopping*, bruv." I respond.

"Dude, his *wife* and his *food*." David cackles, unmoved by how dangerous and inappropriate his dalliance is. But it's no use saying anything. David lives for this type of *situationships*.

My friend's so-called situationships sometimes mask his fears, given his background. What's he afraid of? Love? Whatever it is, this kind of news shouldn't get to my mother's ears for whatever reason. She'll have us both thrown in jail.

Lunch between us goes by very quickly. It's not like when I eat with my mother and Auntie Francine. Right now, we're just two young guys sharing a bite. And besides, David seems on edge.

"Dude, chill, you're not in Chudleigh—what's with the fidgeting?"

"Bruv, spill the tea; that's why you called, not? I must get back into town soon." David responds as he impatiently glances at the time on his phone. "Come on now. Hit me with the short version."

Typical David.

"Grandma Selina ambushed my mother, Auntie Francine, and me yesterday afternoon. She and my father think I must marry Dailess."

"Woah, slow down—this s**t is *deep*, bruv. News travels fast in your family. How did your grandma even know about Dailess?"

"Long story. But after I left your place on Saturday, all seemed cool with my parents." I pause, and David watches me intently.

"Shockingly, on Sunday, Dailess, her parents and a voodoo entourage *landed* unannounced at our house. Bruv, no jokes, they busted our family time after brunch."

"Man, I thought I was the one with the exciting life. I told you that chick Dailess was nothing but trouble. Too eager to exit the compounds."

"I hear you. But wait, there's more to this mad story," I say, annoyed.

"Bruv, just don't tell me you've decided to get hitched to that chick."

"Of course not! Just listen. Mrs Banda and her crazy friends then performed some voodoo s**t in the middle of our living room."

David stares at me, his eyes wide in disbelief. I lower my voice and slow my words for dramatic effect.

"Dude, get this. Then Mr and Mrs Banda and their wretched support system all left. They refused to take Dailess with them."

"Wait, that chick is at your queen's house right now?" David asks and abruptly jumps to his feet. He ducks his head as if he has just dodged a bullet.

"Yes! Dude, the Bandas want a ring on their daughter's finger."

David is silent, a rare occurrence. His eyes dart around the room as he digests the news about how quickly things in my life have gone south.

"And later, that's when your grandmother came in," he asks.

"That's when my father brought her into the picture. He didn't consult my mother or me. I can't understand why he needs his mother like that," I say, frustrated.

"Bro, that's some messed up s**t. Your old man could have *skipped a beat,* for sure," David responds. He then pats me on my back with a cheeky smile. "But when it comes to his mother, you and your old man are very alike."

"Bruv, my mother teaches me to be an upright and responsible young man. I look up to her. My father, unlike me, is afraid of his mother, who's impossible to please. Where's the respect in that?"

"Either way, you and your old man are lucky in the grand scheme of things. You have mothers who care about you. Mine tossed me out and never looked back."

David is not the sentimental type of guy. Far from it—I'm taken aback by his words.

"I'm sorry, man. I hear you. I wish things were different for you and your mother was still in your life. I know that when it comes to mine, God gave me the best."

David changes the topic and assumes his armoured personality. "Look, man, back to your s**t storm; what does all this mean for your scholarship?"

"Plans are still on track. Thankfully, everything was set in motion long before I met Dailess. There's no way my mother will let me give up on my education."

"Your queen is right, bruv. Dailess is a *noose* around your neck. She'll end your life!"

"How can she not want more for herself? How can a man she's known for only three months be enough for her? Eish! Bruv, if I have a daughter, I'll teach her straight out of the gate to choose herself over anything and anyone."

David nods. "Yeah, there's more to life than a forced marriage. But few chicks get that."

I click my fingers in David's face. "But guess what, I quit my job too!"

David laughs and gives me a fist pump. "Dude, your old man must have *hit the roof!*

"Why should he? He's always firing warning shots—boy, am I glad I left on my terms."

"Good for you, bruv. But I've got to run now. Let's meet at the weekend. I need a blow-by-blow account of your drama," David says, heading for the main door.

"Sure! Thanks, bruv."

I quickly shut the front door to keep the heat out and move back to the library. Uncle Michael has a beautiful collection of books on the Beatles. It's like a mini museum. I've all the time in the world to devour everything the library has on this iconic band. I also plan to visit Liverpool to understand where they are from. Fascinating!

***

Oh my! I must have fallen asleep. My mouth is open, and there's drool running down on the left side. I wipe it with the corner of my shirt. Apart from the hazy figure of my mother in front of me, I have no idea where I am. I can hardly make sense of her words.

"Andrew, wake up! Who sleeps like this in the middle of the afternoon?"

I jump up with fright. "Ahh, Mummy, you're back," I say, stretching my body.

Auntie Francine joins us in the library. "What time did your friend leave?"

"About an hour ago. Mummy, David always thought Dailess was trouble."

My mother deflects. "Let's go and see your grandmother."

"Oh no, Mummy, I'm not returning to see Grandma Selina. Wasn't that the point of Auntie Francine bringing me here?" I complain.

"She means our mother, silly," Auntie Francine says and laughs.

I haven't seen Grandma Bertha and Grandpa Simon in a while. I love them to bits. But I'd die of shame if going to see them meant coming clean about my *sins*.

I reluctantly stand up, and in a shakey voice, ask, "Mummy, do we have to tell Grandma and Grandpa about Dailess? I'm not yet ready for their heartbreak."

My mother looks me in the eyes. "Son, your grandparents will always love you, no matter what happens. You're alive and healthy; that's what counts. Dailess isn't the end of the world."

"And we won't share anything about her yet. What's the point?" Auntie Francine reassures me. She grabs her car keys and motions us out of the house.

"How does one explain the voodoo episode to your grandparents?" She continues.

"Andrew, the most important thing for me and your Auntie is to ensure your life stays on track. What's happened can't be reversed. You have to keep moving," my mother says, worried about my well-being.

"At eighty-five, your grandparents can do without the stress, as your mother has pointed out," Auntie Francine adds.

"Quickly, go and freshen up; your grandpa Simon is a spiffy man, as you know. We don't want you showing up looking less than perfect," my mother says.

Auntie Francine rushes me out of the room. "Andrew, I'll take you to a work function later as my plus one. Change into one of Michael's suits. Hurry!"

***

Feeling handsome and confident, I join my mother and Auntie Francine outside a while later. They're ready to roll. Back from car service, Auntie's Porsche Cayenne is in front of the garage—how I'd love to take the beauty for a spin. I mean, why not? Plus, I look a million dollars. There's nothing like the feel-good high from driving a cool car. I usually go around in luxury cars at my father's Dealership. But we have not had a Porsche Cayenne before.

"Auntie Francine, do you mind if I drive you and mummy in your car?" I ask, fingers crossed.

"Sure, be my guest. That was the plan, anyway. I've still got a lot of things to juggle," she responds eagerly. Sweet!

It's just after 14:00 when we get to Great East Road. Thankfully, it's not that busy this time of day. Great East Road is tricky to navigate. There have been countless fatal accidents that have occurred.

I'm generally a careful driver, but with my beloved mother and Auntie in the car, I've got to pay extra attention. I look at the back of the car through the rear-view mirror and think, these two women are the VVIPs of my life.

"Andrew, can you please head to the airport," Auntie Francine interrupts my thoughts. She has been on the phone for the last ten minutes.

"What about Grandma and Grandpa?" I ask, surprised by the change of plans.

"We can see them on the way back," my mother quickly responds.

Auntie Francine puts her phone in her bag. "That was my husband. We must pick up a friend from the Airport. The gentleman will be on the 15:30 flight this afternoon," Auntie Francine clarifies.

"I am at your service, Auntie," I eagerly respond, happy to take the car for a much longer drive.

We arrive at Kenneth Kaunda International Airport within fifteen minutes. It's been ages since I had any business here. Everything looks impressively different and improved.

"Auntie Francine, what would you like me to do?" I slow down the car.

"Drive to the parking lot. We must allow time for the gentleman to clear Immigration and Customs," Auntie Francine says.

Thankfully, there is plenty of parking. I find a nice spot under a tree to avoid the scorching sun.

"Andrew, be a sport; go and receive the gentleman. Here are his details," Auntie Francine says, and hands over an A4 paper that says Phillip Branson.

"Anything for you, Auntie," I chirp as I get out of the car. I take the A4 paper with me. The bold black marker print makes the writing stand out. Mr Branson won't miss me.

"Andrew, take a mask with you. COVID-19, as you know, is not entirely behind us," my mother says. She sounds worried and hands me a pack of five masks and a small tube of hand sanitiser.

I chuckle at her. "Mummy, do I need all five masks at once?"

"Andrew, not everything is a joke," she retorts, her expression subdued. I'm surprised by her snappy reaction.

"Mummy, I'll be careful. Besides, as Auntie says, I only must meet Mr Branson and bring him back to the car. I'll be back in an instant," I reassure her.

The Airport is on the up and up. The waiting area is clean and roomy, with comfortable seats. Security has tightened—gone are the days when folks with no business at the Airport loitered around all day, all night—from pickpockets, hawkers, and *curious foxes* who live vicariously through passengers on international flights.

The Airport used to be a mess of activity. One shouldn't forget the number of dubious men who took their clandestine romantic partners on *Airport dates*. I can't understand why any dude would do that.

Picture this: the dude doesn't even work at the Airport, he can't afford an air ticket for the girlfriend to go anywhere—what's the point? Watching planes take off and land over a meal of sausage rolls and meat pies was the highlight of the date, in the perfect hide-out. Very shady and old-fashioned if you ask me.

The human sensor on the sliding doors goes off again. As much as I love this technology, the beeping sound has me on edge. I have no clue what Mr Philip Branson looks like. Any white man walking through those doors could be my guy. It has been twenty minutes, but no one is interested in my labelled A4 paper. But then I see Auntie Francine approaching.

"Hey, Auntie, our Mr Branson hasn't shown up yet. Do you think he has issues with Immigration?"

Auntie Francine has a weird expression and, more importantly, seems distracted. What's got into her?

"Auntie, are you with me? Do you want to sit down?"

"Andrew, come with me for a few minutes. Let's go and find your mother in the departure section," Auntie Francine says and takes my elbow.

"What about Mr Branson?" I ask.

"Just come with me," Auntie Francine responds, looking slightly shifty.

I can see my mother from a distance. She's talking to ground staff and handing them a bunch of documents. I've never been more confused, except in the case of Dailess and Maria's shenanigans. What's going on? Is my mother leaving?

"Auntie Francine, please explain what's happening. Is my mother flying off to somewhere I didn't know about?" I ask as panic sweeps into my veins. My heart pounds so loudly that I can hear it.

I don't wait for my Auntie's response. Nothing at this moment matters. I must get to my mother and stop her. Why would she leave the country without telling me first? Without a care who's looking, I break into a sprint, confused. I would crumble if my mother suddenly went away.

As I get closer, the two big men standing close by her move to walk away—and OMG, my two suitcases! They were in the boot of Auntie Francine's car. She said Ba Jeremiah would take them out and bring them into the house. But that never happened. What's going on here? My knees start to tremble.

Wait a minute—I'm wearing Uncle Michael's borrowed suit, looking smart; now it makes sense. I slow down to a light trot and watch as my mother looks at me teary-eyed.

"This is it, son. It would be best if you went away," she says.

"Mummy, go where?" I ask, just as Auntie Francine catches up with us.

"You're going to England tonight on the 19:00 Flight. Michael will meet you at Heathrow," Auntie Francine says.

I'm so stunned and at a loss for words. I have so many questions, and my emotions are all jumbled up. Should I be happy or sad?

My mother points to a uniformed ground staff. "The kind lady there has your passport and one-way ticket; she will take you through," my mother says, her voice breaking with sadness.

"What about Grandma Bertha and Grandpa Simon? What will you tell them?" I ask, feeling like a small boy anxious about the imminent separation from my mother and family.

"My darling boy, as the saying goes, *He who sups with the devil should have a long spoon*, my mother says.

"What she means, Andrew, is that you can't be in the same space as Dailess, her sorcerous mother and friends, and hope to come out of this madness unscathed," Auntie Francine quietly explains.

"You must exercise caution and keep an impossible distance between you and those opposed to your wellbeing. If not, Mrs Banda will hunt you down, and who's to say what she could do to you? Andrew, you are my only child," my mother says, her eyes red as she fights off more tears.

"And the baby, Mummy? How will I know it's mine for sure? And if it is, Mrs Banda might make access impossible."

"Don't worry about your unborn child. I'll do everything in my power to look after Dailess. We shall find a decent way to ascertain paternity when the baby arrives. For now, let's take it one day at a time," my mother responds.

"It will be well, Andrew. Have a safe flight. We love you," Auntie Francine says, and for the first time, she shows emotion as she hugs me tightly. She has been so strong for my mother and me.

"Travel well, Andrew. May the Almighty protect you and give you wisdom. You're my only child, my Ibeli and Kasuli. I love you so much, Andrew," my mother says, giving me another big hug.

"Goodbye, Mummy, bye Auntie. Thank you so much for everything."

"Be good, Andrew, for yourself but for your mother too," Auntie Francine says.

"Always, Auntie. I'm my mother's son.

Chapter Twenty-One

"FINAL BOARDING CALL"

Finally, I arrive in the departure lounge and collapse in the nearest seat to catch my breath. Is this how anyone's life can change—I swear, I will never take anything for granted again. You never know what lies around the corner. If someone had told me three weeks ago how different my life would look today, this minute, I might have laughed in their face.

Everything is surreal; with today's events topping the charts—I'm at the airport about to catch a flight to London. There's a considerable lag between where my body and mind were *last seen* versus my reality this minute. I've pinched my arm several times to check that this isn't a dream.

I dare not think of the disaster waiting to happen when Dailess finds out I've left the country. She'll be livid beyond imagination. My departure is one turn of events her mother will never understand or be able to control. Mrs Banda and the vengeful *demon* in her won't take the matter lying down.

The woman will search country-wide for a Witch Doctor with the most potent and dangerous Voodoo spells to bring me back to Zambia—possibly on a witch's broom. My mother and Auntie Francine were right; only mountains, valleys, and seas between us can save me from the wrath of Quietness Banda.

My father is the least of my worries. He won't be surprised by my disappearance. Years of experience have taught him that when it comes to me, my mother will always be ten steps ahead of him. But he'll be in a *hot mess,* though, as far as his mother is concerned. Eish!

But most of all, Grandma Selina will take her frustration out on my mother. It will infuriate my grandmother that her most detested daughter-in-law got away with it again. First, the marriage to her son and now, my escape from the country.

Within that whole hullabaloo, Grandma Selina's greatest regret will be the lost opportunity to shove my mother's face in the dirt. Dailess' pregnancy and an interruption in my further education would have played into her trap. Let me tell you, Grandma Selina will find someone to scotch for her nasty loss in her own silly game.

Grandson or not, in her twisted mind, my misfortune would have been fodder for salacious gossip about my mother. I can almost hear her snarky voice, deep in slanderous conversations with random relatives. *From the beginning, I told Roger that no good could come out of his April. Now look at her son, just as useless as the mother, making young girls pregnant all over Lusaka.* Oh well, let her rant and rave. My mother will pay her no attention if I'm safe and out of reach.

I would have loved to say goodbye to my colleagues at the dealership. They will die of shock when they hear of my sudden departure. Eish! I smile as I imagine them huddled around Belita's desk, trying to scoop the dirt on what *really* happened. They'll chinwag for days! But such is life; one can't stop people from talking; it's human nature.

As for my work, I'm glad I had a call with Jordan on Monday. He and I have worked very closely since he joined the company. He'll easily slide into my role and pick up from where I left off. They'll all survive; it is not the end of the world. I suspect my father will regret not letting me implement my marketing ideas.

Out of nowhere, there's a loud commotion around me—it snaps me out of my mind-wandering. People hurriedly grab their hand luggage and tug their little children along as they dash out of the departure lounge. I'm now alert as the Tannoy sound echoes across the room. *Attention, please; this is the final boarding call for the flight to Dubai. Passengers, please proceed to the boarding gate.*

I'm confused—final boarding call? When was the first one announced? A sharp terror rips through me, and my heart thumps so hard I'm afraid it'll burst. *Lord, please let me not miss this flight.* I hastily grab my belongings and sprint to board the plane.

I pant my way to the boarding gate and dash past to the plane. Huffing and puffing, I then rush up two stairs at a time to the entrance, sweat profusely running down the sides of my face. Phew! I try to catch my breath to calm my heart, which, out of panic, is working harder than it should. At the top of the stairs, I look around me and feel a rush of euphoria as I admire the plane, a *giant insect with wings* about to fly me into my future.

The cabin crew cheerfully greet me. "Welcome on board, sir; 40A, please proceed to the left."

"Thank you very much,"

What a bunch of charming and well-mannered people. They seem like the happiest folks in the world. I shuffle with difficulty through the aisle to my seat. It feels like everyone is striding through quicksand. It's a chaotic sight of anxious passengers with bulky hand luggage and distressed babies everywhere. Everyone is impatient, and tempers fly across the cabin.

A lady behind me nudges me on my shoulder. "Why have you stopped? Move!"

"I'm sorry, where am I supposed to go? I can't get past the people in front of me," I try to explain to the lady. She angrily rolls her eyes at me. The woman must be having a bad day, so I ignore her.

Meanwhile, my phone vibrates in the inner pocket of my jacket. Not sure where my seat is, I decide not to take the call. Worst of all, it could be Dailess. Has she discovered I had left home yesterday evening? Well, now isn't a good time for that conversation. It can wait until I get to the other side.

Finally, I spot 40A—great! It's a window seat. I quickly exit the aisle and heap my hand luggage on the empty seat beside mine. Ever so thoughtful, my mother has packed a delightful collection of miniature travel items—toiletries, a hairbrush, hand wipes, hand sanitiser, socks, snacks, and a *Welcome to London* book.

There's also a long list of *Dos and Don'ts*, things to watch out for, etc. What would I do without my beloved mother? I smile and hastily shut my hand luggage as my phone vibrates again. It's my mother, thank God.

"Hello, mummy. I'm sorry I missed your call earlier. The flight is full; it looks like a mass *exodus* of Zambians. To get to my seat through the cabin aisle was worse than walking through Lusaka Inter-City Bus Terminal on a rainy day," I chuckle.

"We've been worried about you. Are you okay? Have you seen what's in your hand luggage?" my mother asks. Her voice sounds strained.

"Yes, thank you. It's a well-thought-out little package. The *Welcome to London* book is genius. It'll keep me occupied, and by the time I land at Heathrow, I'll have a PhD in the City of London," I say with an exaggerated enthusiasm. It's all to try to calm my mother's nerves.

"Okay, Dr *London City*," she says with a little laugh.

"We're still in the parking lot. We won't leave until your flight takes off," Auntie Francine says, joining the call.

"That's very kind, Auntie."

"Andrew, don't you worry about your mother. I'll look after her. As for you, your Uncle Michael and little cousins will be at Heathrow when you arrive. They're very excited. You'll be in good hands, "Auntie Francine reassures me.

I can see a flight attendant trying to catch my attention from the corner of my eye.

"Sir, can you please switch off your mobile phone and put your hand luggage in the overhead locker," the lady instructs.

"Okay, mummy, you heard that; I must go. I love you both very much."

I obediently hung up the phone and put it away. The cabin crew turn off the lights, and we soon take off. How magnificent Lusaka is in this aerial night-time view. Eish! I draw a sharp breath. What a beautiful country.

As the plane thrusts further into the heavens, I surprise myself when a sudden wave of emotions bubbles up to the surface. An uninhibited flood of tears runs down my face as I stare down at the land of my mother, father, and ancestors.

I close my eyes and think how much I love my country and appreciate everything I am today. In the depth of my heart, though, I know that when or if I return to my country, I will be a changed man. The boy of my youth will be long gone.

I weep for Dailess. For the first time, I regret the abrupt abortion of our relationship. I have been too engrossed in self-preservation to think about what brought us together in the first place. I cared about her and believed our relationship had a chance. But Dailess hastily introduced deceit and confusion before we knew what we would become.

Unlike this plane I am sitting on, Dailess rushed the relationship on the *runway* and forced it onto a premature and very rough *take-off*. Her motives, heavily laced with fear and underhanded motives, forced us to a cruising altitude of thirty-five thousand feet in one swift move—all at once. It's the surest way for a crash landing in any romantic relationship. And so, we crashed.

I reflect sadly on the circumstances surrounding our unborn child, which may or may not be mine. I have not run away from my responsibilities as a father-to-be. I'm simply trying to keep the fire of my life burning. Something Dailess appears not to want for herself. Is it just a girl thing? Why do women easily give up their future over men? For us dudes, we soldier on and aren't apologetic about it.

Dailess' approach to this whole crisis has me anxious. In the absence of marriage, I wonder if I'll have a say over this baby's life if it's mine. I don't want to be an absentee dad—a transactional figure in my child's life. I want to emulate my relationship with my mother and dedicate my life to my child. But how will I ever get round Dailess' mother?

Mrs Quietness Banda is a force of nature, and I don't mean that as a compliment. It will take divine intervention equivalent to the *parting of the Red Sea* to get her to see things without vengeance. How did I find myself in the middle of such a hot mess?

The flight's ascent appears to be easing into the cruising part, and the cabin lights are back on. I furtively wipe my tears and try to conjure happy and positive thoughts. My neighbour, a young lady of about mid-twenties, looks at me sympathetically.

"Are you afraid of flying," she asks, offering me a lollipop.

I smile at her. "No, I was just having a moment."

"Aww, it happens," she responds.

"Thank you for the sweet; it's kind of you," I respond, pulling my blanket around me.

I close my eyes and try to visualise my future in England. I wonder what life has in store for me, given how unpredictable I now know it is. At the same time, my spirit rejoices as the silver lining in my woes presents countless opportunities. Intuitively, I know I'll be alright.

Chapter Twenty-two

HELLO HEATHROW

The sudden burst of bright lights shock me out of my slumber. It irritates me as my eyelids open to a slit and I slowly take in my surroundings. Momentarily disoriented, I push myself upright to stand up. Ouch! The tight grip of my seat belt across my middle reminds me that I'm on an aeroplane. I must have crashed into oblivion after the Dubai transit.

Phew! A wave of relief washes over me as the captain's reassuring voice comes over the speakers. *Good afternoon; this is your Captain; we will land at London Heathrow Airport in the next 30 minutes. Cabin crew, please prepare for landing.* The announcement sends the passenger cabin into a frantic hive of activity. A jolt of electricity runs through my system as a flight attendant approaches me.

"Sir, please fasten your seat belt and put your seat in an upright position."

"Yes, ma'am, I will; let me find my shoes," I respond and spring into action.

I try to wiggle down to the floor to look for my trainers. But I'm trapped and can't reach the bottom of the cabin. There's nowhere to go between the reclined backrest of the seat in front of me and the *Auntie* to my right. Auntie has invaded my personal space, and she feels entitled for a reason I can't understand.

"Young man, don't crawl under my legs!"

"Oh, I mean no disrespect, ma'am. But I must retrieve my shoes."

The woman sucks her teeth, releasing a long hissing sound. "What nonsense! Wait until we land!"

The auntie haughtily ends the conversation, and simultaneously, my mission is to find my trainers. Unbelievable! How dare she use that tone of voice with me? The woman spent the last eight hours freeloading on half of my seat. Yet, I haven't complained about the discomfort or my stiff arm. I spent the whole time on one side of my body, trapped in half of my seat and unable to move.

Annoyed, I turn away from her and press my face against the window. I must maintain peace with *Her Royal Highness* before she steals my joy.

As our descent brings us closer to the ground, I marvel at the sprawling city beneath the soft, fluffy clouds. Wow, it's London, at long last! I rub my hands together, eager to experience the crisp air and vibrant autumn colours I've heard about. It's magical! Uncle Michael often says.

A thunderous round of applause erupts throughout the cabin amidst high fives, back-patting and nervous laughter.

"Hats off to the captain!" Someone shouts.

I rush to look through the window. A broad smile spreads across my face. I can hardly believe it—we've touched down! My heart leaps with excitement.

"Hello, Heathrow!" I say to myself, my *beef* with Auntie long forgotten.

***

Out of the plane, I soon arrive at the massive Terminal building. The sheer magnitude and the organised chaos in every direction are staggering. Little beads of sweat populate my forehead as a wave of trepidation washes over me. I quickly sidle to the side and reach for my mother's list of instructions—a lifesaver. I'm already disoriented, but the last thing I want is to appear shady—an illegal immigrant sneaking into the country from the belly of the *Boeing 777*.

Read the signs in the airport and ask if you are unsure. Instruction number one on my mother's list might seem obvious, but not when in my shoes. I look up, and much to my delight, I spot the *sea o*f people in the *ALL-OTHER PASSPORTS* section.

Anxious Foreigners from all over the world wait their turn to explain what brings them to London. Some will make it across the border, but others, for one reason or another, will not make it. Everyone's fate lies in the hands of the uniformed man or woman behind the glass pane.

I check that I am where I am supposed to be and join the queue. The uncertainty and waiting is like being in Purgatory. I scratch my head with an unsteady hand. Even though I have nothing to hide, I'm a nervous wreck. It scares me to think there's a fifty per cent chance things could go wrong for me. What if the Border Staff sends me back? I keep asking myself.

Deportation to Zambia would kill my mother. But it would make Mrs Banda the happiest woman in the country. She would pounce on me and tie me to a tree until I married her daughter. The thought of it all sends shivers down my spine. I glance through my list again—I can't afford to miss any critical information. There's no way I'll return to Mrs Banda's *voodoo trap*.

The queue moves slowly while the atmosphere remains tense, and everyone looks serious. Luckily, I spot a friendly-looking young lady a few heads before me. I watch her closely as she glances in my direction. Is she looking at me or someone else? I pluck up the courage and stroll over to her, which causes a stir.

"You can't jump the queue, just like that. You're not in Lagos!" The man in front of me, with a thick Eastern European accent, raises his voice and tries to stop me.

I frown at him. "Sorry, I want to say hello to the young lady there. What's Lagos got to do with anything?"

The man ignores me and does not let me get past him. But nothing can stand in the way of life's mysterious events, big or small. To my absolute delight, the young lady who has overheard the hostile exchange approaches me.

"Hello, my name's Muriel," she giggles.

"Hi, I'm Andrew. Great to meet you."

I can't stop smiling. A warm fuzzy feeling envelopes me—in an instant, my immigration woes are a thing of the past.

"It's my first time in the UK. How about you?"

Muriel's face lights up. "Great! I'm not the only newbie! I'm from Mumbai, India."

Her smile and dimples are so captivating that I could watch her talk all day.

"What?" Muriel asks as she catches me in a trance-like state.

"I didn't say anything—I'm listening to you talk," I give her a bashful smile.

"Okay, tell me where you're from?"

"Yes, of course! I'm from Lusaka, Zambia."

The ease and comfort of being in Muriel's company is enchanting. For a fleeting moment, everything disappears into oblivion. I feel like I have known Muriel my entire life. As I chat and laugh with her, the weight of the last three weeks lifts. It's like magic, the promise of a brand-new chapter waiting to unfold, filled with a million possibilities.

"Hey, we're both new to London; why don't we discover the city together?" Muriel suggests, daring me to say yes.

My heart flutters. "How am I to reach you though?" I ask as I hold my breath for her answer. Muriel takes my phone and punches her *digits* into the contacts list.

"There, you have no excuse. I'll wait for your call," she says with a playful smile.

Shortly after, we approach the top of the queue. My encounter with Muriel feels like wearing a good luck charm. Filled with a renewed sense of invincibility, I stand before the Immigration Officer with confidence.

"Passport," the Immigration Officer growls. He doesn't greet me, smile, or show any emotion. I guess it comes with the territory. But thanks to Muriel, I'm on such a positive vibe that the man's poker face can't intimidate me. Besides, my mother's words are like my armour. *Be polite at all times, no matter what happens. Don't let them send you back.*

I smile. "Good afternoon, sir. Here's my passport."

The Officer takes his time. He deliberately flips through my passport and glances back at his computer screen. My travel document isn't that interesting. I've only used it to visit South Africa and Zimbabwe a few times. But judging by the man's intense focus, you'd think I were *Christopher Columbus*.

"Is this your first time coming to the United Kingdom?" The Officer finally speaks.

"Yes sir, it is," I respond. I keep my answers short per my mother's notes—*do not volunteer unnecessary information. Please keep it simple.*

The man looks me in my eyes but says nothing for a second. "What's the purpose of your visit?" He demands.

"Sir, I do not seek to enter the country as a visitor. I'm here on a scholarship to study Climate Change at a master's degree level."

There's another pause—as if to rattle me. Without warning, the Officer gives me a big, toothy smile, stamps my passport and hands it back to me.

"Good job. We all must do our bit to save the planet. Welcome to London."

I clear my throat. "Thank you very much, sir. Have a good day," I reply. But the Officer's attention has already shifted to the next person in line.

Hurrah! I can barely contain my excitement. My knees tremble as I walk past the Immigration desk to cross the UK border. Where's Muriel? I frantically look around me. I must tell her I made it. But I can't find her—she could now be in the Baggage Claim section. I quickly descend on the escalator, which brings me into the Baggage Claim Hall.

The carousels are working at total capacity, surrounded by anxious travellers with trolleys awaiting their luggage. My flight had a lot of passengers; it might be a while before I could get my suitcases. I call my mother to help pass the time. She answers on two rings.

"Andrew! Thank God. I haven't slept the whole night," she exclaims.

I chuckle. "Mummy, I've arrived. Can you believe it?"

"You'd better have arrived. If only there were a direct flight from Lusaka to London. I almost lost my mind while I waited to hear from you," she complains.

My mother's *full-time job* is to fuss about me. Regardless of the flight time, she would have pulled out her hair for as long as I was in the skies. Going this far away from home is a new experience for both of us; it will take getting used to. Let's not forget that my mother planned to travel with me before the Bandas and Grandma Selina *threw a wrench in the works.*

From the corner of my eye, I glimpse Muriel on the phone. She looks up and waves at me. I try to hold her gaze, but she returns to her call. For a moment, I lose track of my conversation with my mother.

"Andrew, are you there? Did you hear what I said?"

I stutter. "Ye, ye, yes, I'm here, mummy. It's a bit noisy here, that's all."

"Where are you, anyway? My mother's voice sounds shrill with worry.

"Mummy, calm down. I've cleared Immigration; all is well."

"Thank you, Lord. But where are you now?" She asks again.

"I'm in the baggage claim section waiting for my suitcases. But it's so crowded I am nowhere close. Otherwise, everything is fine, Mummy," I comfort her.

My mother doesn't respond. For a moment there, I think the line has cut off when I hear her voice again. She is saying her favourite prayer, the *Hail Mary*. It's sacred to her. She believes *Mother Mary* helped her bring me into this world. So I don't interrupt her. We both say *Amen* as my mother wraps up.

"I packed your rosary in your suitcase together with your bible. Don't forget to pray, my son. The evil forces are still with us."

I shudder to think Mrs Banda, the *voodoo queen*, is going to be my baby's maternal grandmother. It's a reality that will cause me nightmares for the rest of my life. But for now, I press my *mental delete button* and turn my thoughts to my father.

"Mummy, what about Dad? Does he know I've left the country?"

"No, and neither does your Grandma Selina. I want you settled and secure before I can say anything to them. I'll let you know when I have handled them.

"Okay, Mummy, I'll call you later this evening. I've got to watch for my luggage before someone knicks it."

My mother giggles. "I'll call Francine to let her know you've arrived. In the meantime, call your Uncle Michael. I believe he's already waiting for you outside."

I hang up the phone and squeeze through the crowd for my bags. The jostling mob, young and old, each one with a trolley in every direction, presents a challenge. I'm stuck and starting to panic. What if I lose my suitcases? Eish!

I jump as I respond to a light tap on my shoulder.

"Hi, Andrew!"

It's Muriel—my face softens. "You got your bags already, lucky you."

"Yes, I know. Sorry, you don't have yours yet."

As Muriel turns to leave, I stall her and ask the obvious. "Are you leaving now?"

"Yes, my Auntie and Uncle are outside. I just wanted to say bye to you."

Our eyes lock. Muriel blushes and looks away. My face feels hot—I'm not sure what's happening here. We only met less than two hours ago. What should I do? Hug her? No, that might be too familiar and possibly offensive. I don't want to come onto her too strong. But a handshake might be too collegial and old-fashioned—I'm not her *sugar daddy*.

I take my cue from Muriel. She pulls the trolley handle close to her midsection. Her body language tells me she is not ready for any rushed familiarity. So, I thrust my hands into my pockets lest they do something I might regret.

"I'll call you at the weekend to see how you are getting on."

Muriel flashes her million-dollar smile and disappears through the Customs area without another word.

My heart soars. *Oh, Mummy, I think I have just met my soul mate!* I wish I could tell my mother and Auntie Francine about Muriel. But I know what they'd say—perhaps it's too soon.

And what does this mean anyway? Did I not love Maria and Dailess? If I did, it's nothing like the way I feel now. It's uncanny; I've never felt this connected with a girl. I'm super curious to see what happens next.

***

Finally, after thirty minutes of waiting, the mouth of the carousel spits out my two suitcases. I abandon my trolley and rush to grab them. I'm aware I should not leave my hand luggage unattended. But if I don't act swiftly, my suitcases will slip past me to the other side and get swallowed back inside. I use all my might to remove both off the conveyor belt and onto my trolley. I remember where Muriel exited. I cleverly follow the same trail through the *NOTHING TO DECLARE* section.

Phew! I emerge on the other side. OMG! I have never seen such a large, diverse group of people. Men, women and children of all races and ages stand behind the barrier in the arrival hall. They are all united by a common factor—a prayer for the safe arrival of a loved one or colleague.

I hadn't thought about it or knew what to expect. But I'm impressed with the number of black faces dotted across the barrier. I feel at ease knowing I'm not the odd one out.

Should I go to the left or right? I quickly scour the faces before me. Uncle Michael must be somewhere here waiting for me. And just then, two little excited voices catch my attention.

"Cousin Andrew! Over here!"

I turn to my right, and there they are. My adorable cousins wave at me and hop like bunnies. They fly into my arms as I approach them and almost knock me over. Their voices are high-pitched, and both compete to speak; keeping up with them is hard.

"We're so happy you're here!" Ryan exclaims.

"We've been waiting for you for ages," little Molly pipes.

"Welcome to London, my darling nephew!" Uncle Michael slaps my back and gives me a big hug. "My suit looks good on you."

I burst out laughing. "Blame your wife. She's the mastermind in all this."

"We promise London is going to love you," my little cousins chorus.

"Oh, I should hope so with you two as my guides," I delight them.

Walking through the Heathrow arrival hall to the car park, I reflect on the past three weeks. I am neither sad nor happy. Instead, I'm grateful, and I have decided to relax into my reality and be patient with life.

In three weeks, I have learnt first-hand how unpredictable life can be. There are no exceptions—no one is immune to life's changes. You can't tell what lies around the corner, no matter how hard you prepare not to fall. Unfortunately, you will wobble or fall; we are human, and that's how life goes.

Three weeks ago, I wouldn't have imagined I would be an expectant father at my age. Not in a million years. I keep going over everything in my head. Is there anything I could have done differently?

But things are what they are now. My goal is to make better and more conscious choices in the future regarding women and life in general. I plan to build a strong mind and spirit to help me when life catches me off guard. My life's journey must continue, and I owe it to myself to stay on my trail towards my purpose in life.

Most of all, I want to be a great father to my child, as long as it carries my DNA, regardless of birth circumstances. It's at this point where the cycle my father began ends. I won't inherit his *sins* and become *Roger Michelo 2.0*.

I know that not marrying Dailess is an obstacle, and Mrs Banda won't be easy to deal with. But like my mother said, every child is a gift from God. And I will fight for it.

I think of my beloved mother and her countless sacrifices in the name of love—her great love for me, her *Ibeli and Kasuli*. Her dedication to being the best mother a son can wish for inspires me to do better and make her proud. Oh Lord, how I thank you for the privilege of being my mother's son.